AFTER SHOCK

Also by Judy Melinek and T.J. Mitchell

First Cut

*Working Stiff: Two Years, 262 Bodies, and
the Making of a Medical Examiner*

AFTER SHOCK

A DR. JESSIE TESKA MYSTERY

JUDY MELINEK
AND T.J. MITCHELL

HANOVER
SQUARE
PRESS

HANOVER
SQUARE
PRESS™

ISBN-13: 978-1-335-14729-5

Aftershock

This edition published by arrangement with Harlequin Books S.A.

Hanover Square Press
22 Adelaide St. West, 40th Floor
Toronto, Ontario M5H 4E3, Canada
HanoverSqPress.com
BookClubbish.com

Printed in U.S.A.

For Jack Briley.

AFTER SHOCK

CHAPTER 1

A steel band cover of "Don't Fear the Reaper" makes for a lousy way to lurch awake. Couple of months back, some clown of a coworker got ahold of my cell phone while I was busy in the autopsy suite, and reprogrammed the ringtone for incoming calls from the Medical Examiner Operations and Investigation Dispatch Communications Center. I keep forgetting to fix it.

I reached across my bedmate to the only table in the tiny room and managed to squelch it before the plinking got past five or six bars, but that was more than enough to wake him.

"Time is it?" Anup slurred.

"Four thirty."

"God, Jessie," he said, and pulled a pillow over his head. I planted a nice warm kiss on the back of his neck.

Donna Griello from the night shift was on the phone. "Good morning, Dr. Teska," she said.

"Okay, Donna," I whispered. "What do we got and where are we going?"

I didn't need the GPS navigation from my one extravagance in this world, the BMW 235i that I had brought along when I moved from Los Angeles to San Francisco, because muscle memory took me there. The death scene was right on my old commute—a straight shot from the Outer Richmond District, along the edge of Golden Gate Park, then the wiggle down to SoMa, the broad, flat neighborhood south of Market Street. The blue lights were flashing on the corner of Sixth Street and Folsom, just a couple of blocks shy of the Hall of Justice. I used to perform autopsies in the bowels of the Hall, before the boss, Chief Medical Examiner Dr. James Howe, moved the whole operation to his purpose-built dream morgue, way out in Hunters Point. Along the way, Howe made me his deputy chief. The promotion came with a raise, an office, and a ficus, but I hadn't sought it and it wasn't welcome—I was only a year and change on the job and didn't have the experience to be deputy chief in a big city. Howe needed someone to do it, though. So the gold badge and all its headaches went to me.

The death scene address Donna had given me over the phone was a construction site. From the outside, I couldn't tell how big. They'd built a temporary sidewalk covered in plywood, and posted an artist's rendition of a gleaming glass tower, crusted in niches and crenellations and funky angles, dubbed *SoMa Centre.*

I double-parked behind a police car and walked the plankway between a blind fence and a line of pickup trucks with union bumper stickers. The men in them eyed me with either suspicion or practiced blankness while they waited for their job site to reopen. A beat cop kept vigil at the head of the line. He took my name and badge number, logged me in, and lifted the yellow tape. He pointed to a wooden crate. It was full of construction hard hats.

"Mandatory," he said.

"You aren't wearing one," I griped.

"I'm not going in there, either."

"Good for you. Give me a light over here."

I sorted through the helmets under the cop's flashlight beam. Sizes large, extra large, medium. I am a woman, five feet five inches, a hundred thirty-four pounds, and not especially husky of skull. I certainly wasn't husky enough to fill out a helmet spec'd for your average male ironworker, which seemed to be all that was on offer.

I tried out a medium. Even when I cinched the plastic headband all the way, the hard hat swallowed my sorry little blond noggin.

"Yeah, laugh it up, Officer," I said, while he did.

"Sorry, Doc. You look like a kid playing soldier!"

"Laugh it up," I said again, because I wasn't equipped, at that hour, to be clever.

Not all the workers were stuck outside in their pickups. A few men in hard hats stood around, waiting for work to get going. They shied away from me, in my MEDICAL EXAMINER windbreaker, polyester slacks, and sensible shoes, like I was the angel of death collecting on a debt.

I found Donna. She's hard to miss: more than six feet tall, eyes and beak like a hawk. Her hard hat fit just fine. She was leaning against the medical examiner removals van with Cameron Blake, her partner 2578—our bureaucratic shorthand for death scene investigators—on the night shift. Cam is round-faced and ruddy, half a foot shorter than Donna but just as brawny. He greeted me.

"Any coffee?" I said.

"The site superintendent says it's brewing. First shift is just getting here. That's how come they found the body. You want to talk to him?"

"The body?"

"The superintendent."

"Let's find out what the dead guy has to say first."

Donna chuckled in a dark way. "Just you wait and see, Doc."

The pair of 2578s led me across the construction site by flash-light. Work lights were coming on, but they left big dark gaps.

"Who found the body?"

Donna consulted her clipboard. "Dispatch says a worker named Samuel Urias, opening up after the night shift."

The construction site by flashlight was a spooky place, even by my standards. Dirty yellow machines loomed in the beams, and plastic sheeting fluttered from the shadows. Our feet crunched on gravel, then whispered over packed dirt. The only thing that was well lit was a mobile office trailer, on a rise to our left, sur-rounded by silhouettes in hard hats.

Donna led us toward a detached flatbed trailer, parked with its landing-gear feet pressing into the dirt. It was loaded with long metal pipes, six or eight inches in diameter, in bundles of twenty or so. The bundles were bound together with tight black bands at either end and had been stacked four high on the flat-bed. One of the bands securing the top bundle had snapped. It waved drunkenly in the air—and half a dozen pipes lay tum-bled in the dirt.

Underneath them was a body.

It was a man. He was on his back. His head and shoulders were crushed under the pipes. He wore a business suit and black wingtip shoes, the left one coming off at the heel. His arms were flung out. I determined his race to be white from his hands, which offered the only visible skin. They were clean and un-calloused, fingernails manicured, wedding band on the left ring finger, a college ring on the right.

I shined my flashlight at the pipes. They had done a job on him. We walked around the body, looking for a pool of blood. There wasn't one.

When I pointed this out, Donna elbowed Cameron and smirked. He scowled back.

"What?" I said.

"I noticed that too," Donna said. "Cam thinks it's no big deal."

"Can we just get this guy out of here?" Cameron said. "The superintendent is antsy. He's worried about press, and I don't blame him."

I crouched to take a closer look at that left shoe. The leather above the heel was badly scuffed. Same for the right one. The dead man's pricey wool dress pants were torn at the hems. My flashlight picked up a faint trail in the dirt running away from his feet. I warned the 2578s to watch their step until the police crime scene unit had photographed the area.

"What—?" said Cam. "CSI isn't here. This is an accident scene."

"Get them. This is a suspicious death."

"Oh, come on…"

"It's fishy." I pointed my flashlight around. "Where's all the blood from that crush injury? There's drag marks and damage to the clothing to match. Soft hands, expensive suit. Where's his hard hat?"

"Maybe it's under the pipes."

"Maybe. But does this guy look like he belongs on a construction site, after hours? No way I'm assuming this was an accident."

"Told you it was staged," Donna said to Cam.

"Whatever," he muttered back. He pulled out his phone, said good morning to the police dispatcher, and asked for the crime scene unit.

The sky was lightening behind the downtown towers a few blocks away, and more construction workers were starting to trickle in. "We need a perimeter," I said. "And I want to talk to the man who found the body. Do we have a presumptive ID?"

"We found this just like you see it, and didn't run his pockets yet," Donna said.

"Let's wait till crime scene documents everything before we touch him."

Donna smiled. "Because this is fishy, right?"

I couldn't help smiling back. "You won the bet. Leave Cam alone." I started toward the lit-up office trailer.

"Where you going?" Donna said.

"Coffee."

A figure in the small crowd huddling at the trailer saw me coming and met me halfway. He was a late-middle-aged white man with a gray mustache, dressed like a soccer dad in blue jeans and a collared shirt. No tie, no jacket, heavy work boots. He had a fancy hard hat. It said SITE SUPER.

"Where's the hearse?" the construction superintendent demanded.

I introduced myself and told him we were waiting for the police crime scene unit to arrive and document the scene.

"How long will that take?"

Fuck if I know, I thought. "It could be a while," I said.

"What's a while? We have work to do here."

Bałwan. I grew up outside of Boston, but Polish is my first language. Sort of. My mother is from Poland and my father is a son of a bitch. *Mamusia* taught me and my brother Tomasz the mother tongue—which Dad doesn't speak—and the three of us stuck with it inside the four walls of our three-decker flat on Pinkham Street in East Lynn. *Mamusia* said it was to preserve our heritage. It was also useful for hiding things from the old man.

Polish has a lot of terms for a son of a bitch. *Bałwan* was *Mamusia's* word for her husband Arthur Teska on a good day. If he had been drinking, he was a *sukinsyn.* So far, the site superintendent was turning out to be a *bałwan,* but the day was young.

"First the police will do their job, then my colleagues and I will do our job, and then you can get back to yours."

"But the police are already here, and they aren't doing anything!"

"We're waiting for the homicide division."

The superintendent went pale and stammery. "Homicide—? But this isn't... This is..."

"This is a death scene. It might be a crime scene. That's for the police to determine before I can continue my investigation as the medical examiner, and certainly before we can remove or even touch that body."

The superintendent said nothing. He dug into his pocket for a phone and walked away, dialing. Not an unusual reaction. People freak out when they hear homicide is coming.

I dug a hand under the wobbly hard hat to scratch my scalp. It was Anup's damn shampoo. I had been dating Anup Banerjee for seven, almost eight months. I live in a rental, a tiny back-garden cottage in the Richmond District, half a mile from the continent's Pacific edge. *Cottage* does the place too much justice—it's a converted San Francisco cable car called Mahoney Brothers #45. It was abandoned in the sand dunes at the end of the line after it had outlived its usefulness, until someone jacked the thing up, built a foundation under it, and added box wings for a bedroom and a kitchen and a water closet. Mahoney Brothers #45 covers 372 square feet of the most expensive real estate in the country. Back when I had lived in it alone with my beagle, Bea, it was my very own cozy paradise.

Anup and I were not quite living together, but he had started spending most nights in Mahoney Brothers #45, and the place is no cozy paradise for two grown adults and a demanding dog. It's more like sharing a Winnebago. I am not a domestic goddess. Anup is a lawyer by training and a fastidious, detail-oriented person by inclination. I ran out of shampoo; he got more. But it had turned out to be some awful stuff that only a man would buy, and it made my scalp itch.

I scratched at it. Then I headed up to the over-lit trailer to scare up some coffee.

I couldn't juggle three cups, so I roped one of the beat cops into helping. He told me that press and camera trucks were already arriving at the gate.

"And our LT wants us to wrap things up here. The captain's already riding his ass. That means someone with pull called the captain."

I didn't have the heart to tell him it was a complicated and hazardous crime scene, and we'd likely be holding vigil over that body for hours to come. Cam and Donna and I sipped our coffees and waited for the crime scene unit. They didn't take long. They rearranged our perimeter. They took pictures. We stayed out of the way.

I was about to mosey up to the trailer for a refill when Cam nudged me and pointed his chin toward the entry gate. A Black man in a blue suit was swapping a fedora for a hard hat. Even at a distance in the dismal predawn light, I could pick out that mustache of his. It scowled.

"*Zasrane to życie*," I muttered. My shit luck. It would appear that the homicide detective assigned to this case was going to be Keith Jones.

Inspector Jones and I had a history, and not a happy one. The year before, we'd done a case together, a drug overdose that he and his partner wanted to call an accident. I disagreed and tried to certify it as a homicide—but I was overruled by Dr. Howe, my boss. Jones had never forgiven me for putting them through a pile of work over a stupid OD just because I had decided it had to be a murder.

"Dr. Jessie Teska," he said. "On a construction site. So I'm gonna guess I'm out here wasting my time with another accident."

The crime scene photographer's camera flashed, illuminating the dead man and the pile of pipes across his head and shoulders. Jones nodded thoughtfully. "Will you look at that," he said.

I bit my tongue. "Hello, Keith."

"Why are we here?"

"It's a suspicious death."

"What's suspicious about a load of pipe falling off a truck?"

I ran through my initial findings for him: the decedent's inappropriate attire, damage to the heels of his shoes and pant hems, drag marks in the dirt, the lack of evident bleeding.

"So what? Maybe he got drunk and tripped and tore his pants. Maybe the blood's under those pipes."

"Maybe the scene's been tampered with. Maybe it's a homicide dressed like an accident."

"Who is he, anyhow?"

"We'll try to get a presumptive ID when crime scene clears us to handle the body."

"So you don't know. Witnesses?"

"No. One of the workers found him when they opened up the site this morning."

"You spoke to this worker?"

"I figured you'd want to."

"That's what you figured, huh, Doctor. Did you figure maybe he could give you a presumptive ID on this dead person? Get us started, at least?"

Again I bit my tongue. I didn't like being dressed down by Jones, especially in front of the 2578s and the precinct cops, but nothing good would come from calling him out. By luck of the draw, it was a case we had to investigate together.

Jones sighed and massaged his boxy eyebrows. "Okay, then, Deputy Chief Teska. You've got the whole circus rolling in, and it's going to be here for hours. Let's see what's what." He headed off toward the lit-up office trailer.

I rejoined Cameron and Donna, who were studiously pretending to ignore us by watching the crime scene unit photograph the death scene.

"How are we going to get those pipes off the body?" I wondered.

"Can't be that hard," Cam said. "I'll go talk to the superintendent."

The pallid sky brightened a little, and I could hear the growl of rush hour rising on all sides of the future home of SoMa Centre. I checked my phone. It was 7:05. Anup would be getting up soon. He'd take Bea out. He had no problem with the dog. I'm her alpha for sure, but Anup is a runner and Bea enjoys chasing him around Golden Gate Park. I thought about calling him, but decided it was better to let him enjoy his last few minutes of sleep. Anup had a nice desk job at the First District Court of Appeal. Never did he have to roll out of bed at 4:30 to sit around a construction site and watch cops take pictures of a mangled corpse.

Lucky him.

Cam returned. Behind him, the site superintendent had picked two men out of the crowd by the trailer and marched them over to a giant front loader.

"We have an issue," Cam said. Apparently, those two were the only workers on hand qualified to operate the equipment that would safely lift the metal pipes off our dead guy—and they refused to do it. They wanted nothing at all to do with dead bodies, especially if the police were involved. The superintendent was threatening to fire them both if one of them didn't shift those damn pipes.

A ripple went through the crowd of hardhats watching the confrontation, and they turned in unison toward a wiry, sharp-angled man approaching from the entrance gate. The way he stalked across the construction site told everyone he was not playing games. He went straight up to the superintendent, and the two of them got to shouting, nose to nose, like they'd had practice at it.

Homicide Inspector Jones intervened. He brandished his pad and pen, introduced himself, and asked the men to give him their names, addresses, and phone numbers.

"How come?" said the wiry man. "We didn't do nothing."

"I'm not saying you did, okay?" Jones assured him in a soft-glove way. "It's just that this is a crime scene here, and we need to document everyone who has been on it."

"You can't detain nobody that's not under arrest!" the man shouted, and repeated the message in Spanish to the crowd of hardhats.

"Hold on, now," said Jones, still softly. "We can't allow any of you people to leave this crime scene until we document who you are and how to reach you. All of you." He gestured to one of the precinct cops, who said something into his shoulder mic. Uniforms materialized from all around, and surrounded the crowd of hardhats.

The wiry man said, "Is anyone here under arrest?"

"Nobody's under arrest. There's been a death at your workplace, and there will be an investigation. We just need to see your IDs, and then anyone who wants to leave can go."

"These men were not even here last night."

"Until we get everyone's information, no one is leaving."

I felt Cam, next to me, tense up. He's a crime scene veteran. His instincts are worth paying attention to.

The wiry man tried to stare down Keith Jones. Jones didn't blink. Nobody in the crowd moved a muscle.

Then the wiry man nodded and pulled out his wallet, and we all unclenched. "I would like your business card, please, Detective," he said. "My name is Samuel Urias, and I am the union steward on this job."

I cast an eye to Donna and she nodded. Samuel Urias was the man who had called 911 to report the dead body.

Urias said something to the two men behind him, and without a word they produced their IDs, too. Jones handed out his card. "Mr. Urias," he said, "we can't determine what happened here to cause this death until we get those pipes lifted. Will one of these machine operators be willing to help?"

21

"No," Urias said, without bothering to ask the workers. "They're not doing it. But I am certified on this equipment. I will move the pipes."

Urias started off toward the giant front loader, and over his shoulder he said, "Clear the area."

Jones let a narrow smile slip past his mustache. Then he said to the nearest uniform cop, "You heard the man. Safety first."

———

Samuel Urias took his sweet time moving those pipes off our corpse. He did a thorough walkaround inspection of the front loader. Then he powered it up, fiddled with the coupling on its talon-like grabber arm, and did another walkaround. Donna yawned. Cam worried out loud about press helicopters being bound to appear, now that there was daylight. One of the beat cops reported to Jones that a clot of trucks trying to get onto the site had gummed up the intersections across Sixth Street for blocks in all directions. That gridlock was spreading to the Central Freeway off-ramp, which was, in turn, backing up the Bay Bridge.

"You know who lives in these condos?" Cam murmured. "Tech bros. The Google bus can't get down Eighth Street, that's a class-A clusterfuck."

"DEFCON 1," Donna agreed.

I scoffed at the pair of them. "Come on. It's traffic. There's traffic every day. Big deal."

"Just you wait and see," Donna said for the second time that morning. Her boardwalk soothsayer routine was starting to grate on me.

The site superintendent complained that the duty contractor should be here managing this emergency, but that he wasn't answering his phone.

"Maybe that's him under the pipes," Donna said to Cam.

"Not in that suit. Or those shoes."

It was getting near 8:30 by the time Urias finally swung the arm of the heavy machine up in the air, opened the grabber, and lowered it slowly onto our death scene. The grabber's tines closed around the pipes and they clattered. The truck roared. It heaved the pipes, pivoted them well away from the body, and dropped them in the dust beyond the flatbed trailer.

Jones lifted the police tape to approach the body, then jumped clear out of his shoes at a deafening blast from the front loader's air horn. Up in its cab Urias was wagging his finger wildly. He swung the grabber arm away to the far side of the machine, lowered it to the ground, and killed the engine.

"Okay," Urias hollered. "Clear!"

It's not easy to rile a big-city police detective, but at that moment Homicide Inspector Keith Jones looked like he had developed a burning desire to clean Samuel Urias's clock for him.

We followed Jones under the tape to get a clear look at the body. The head, neck, and upper rib cage had been obliterated. I'd never seen a worse case of disfigurement, except maybe in one or two bodies that had been left to decompose in the open, where animals had gotten to them. A case from the year before, involving a coyote in the woods near the Lincoln Park Golf Course, came vividly to mind. This pulpy slew leaking into a business suit was even less recognizable as a human body. Brain matter was smeared into the dirt, and hairy chunks of skull had been scattered like pottery shards. The crushed area was pink in places, red in places, but mostly just kind of tan colored.

Donna was seeing what I was seeing, and shaking her head. "That ain't right."

"Well," I replied, "it's interesting."

"What about it?" said Inspector Jones.

"I'm concerned that we're not seeing a giant puddle of blood here. I would expect much more bleeding from such a violent crush injury. Practically all the man's pressurized blood should have gushed out of those ruptured neck vessels."

"So where is it?"

"I can't tell you that until I perform the full autopsy. But just on first impression, this looks like postmortem injury to me."

I didn't have to explain to the homicide detective what that meant. "You think this is a homicide staged to look like an accident."

"I think the visible evidence indicates that this man was already dead when those pipes came down on him. Let's see what else we can determine right now."

"Uh-huh," said Jones with zero percent conviction.

The beat cops tried to keep the construction workers from crowding the tape cordon, but it was no use. We had an audience. The crew from CSI moved back in to take more pictures, then gave us the go-ahead to handle the body.

"'Bout time," Cam grumbled.

"Chill, big guy," one of the crime scene cops snapped back. Cam didn't like that.

Identification is our first job and top priority. We went straight for the dead man's pockets and found a wallet. It had a California driver's license under the name Leopold Haring, address in San Francisco on Castenada Avenue.

"Forest Hill," Cam said. "Money."

Jones peered at the picture on the driver's license, then at the pulp piled on the end of the man's shoulders, and grunted. I manipulated an arm. The body was in full rigor mortis. That meant, I told Jones, he'd been dead at least six hours. Three a.m., maybe two a.m. at the earliest for a ballpark time of death.

"But," I reminded him, "that's the outside window. It could be a lot earlier."

"Can't you narrow that down?"

"Let's do a body temperature," I said to Cam.

We put the wallet back in Leopold Haring's pocket where

we'd found it, and Cameron yanked down the trousers. It required some effort thanks to the rigor mortis. He inserted a thermometer into the cadaver's rectum and told Donna it came to 80 Fahrenheit. She wrote that down, consulted an outdoor thermometer she kept in her death scene kit, and told me the ambient temperature was 54. I looked at the time and did the math.

"He probably died between six and ten last night."

"That's the best you can tell?"

"Yes. And I might be wrong."

"You guys always say that."

"We mean it. Time of death estimation is unreliable. It depends on too many variables…"

"Okay," the detective said. I recalled from working with him before that he said okay a lot, but usually didn't mean it.

"Detective!" someone yelled from behind the cordon line. It was the superintendent, cell phone still on his ear. "Do we know who it is?"

Jones wasn't about to shout the dead man's name into the crowd, so he gestured the superintendent over. I watched Jones read the name off his notebook. The superintendent's jaw fell open. He bobbled the cell phone, dropped it in the dirt, and scrambled to pick it up. He stared at the shattered corpse in disbelief. Then he dusted off the phone and walked away, dialing frantically.

"Hey!" the detective called out, irked. "You know this guy?"

"Google it," the superintendent said, and disappeared into the crowd of hardhats.

"Goddamn people," said Jones, and stalked after him.

Donna already had her smartphone in hand and was typing. Cam and I huddled with her.

Leopold Andreas Haring, 52, born in Austria, immigrated in 1989 as a graduate student in architecture at the University of Pennsylvania.

"Oh, man," said Cameron.

Leopold Haring was one of the most famous and acclaimed architects in the world, known for a boldness of vision coupled with a towering intellect, said the one article. "'Haring's work unites a classical rigor of form with a disciplined attention to, and intention of, function as the *sine qua non* of a building,'" Donna read. "'His use of materials has proven famously visionary, yet has always been coupled with a miraculous lack of pretension…'"

"Enough," said Cam.

"Wait, you gotta hear this one. 'He is our great cityscape cubist, the Picasso of the building arts.'"

"Donna," said Cam, "our shift ended half an hour ago. Can we get the pouch and gurney, please, before we end up on the news? I don't like being on the news."

"Fine, fine." She produced a white sheet, which she draped carefully over the acclaimed architect's mortal remains, and the two of them trekked back to the van.

I scanned the crowd of hardhats for Jones, but didn't see him. My cell phone rang. It was the boss, Chief Medical Examiner Dr. James Howe.

"Jessie…?" He sounded faint and far away.

"Dr. Howe," I hollered, and stuck a finger in my left ear. The morning shift had been standing around with nothing to do for more than three hours, and had apparently decided to fire up every heavy vehicle on the lot in preparation for the moment we allowed them to start work. I started walking and talking, searching for a quiet spot.

"What the hell is going on up there?" Dr. Howe said. "I've got everyone from the highway patrol to the mayor on my ass about your death scene. They're saying you've locked it all down…?"

"Yeah, it's not looking like an accident over here…"

"What do you mean? It's a construction site with a fatal crush injury, right?"

"Not exactly. The injuries all look postmortem. It turned into a suspicious death pretty quick, so I had to call in CSI…"

I finally found a sheltered spot, a section of unfussy concrete foundation behind a chain-link gate. It was below grade and dark, but good and quiet.

"We just got access to the body a minute ago," I told Dr. Howe. "We also just got a presumptive ID, but that's another complication."

"Why?"

"Now it's suspicious *and* high profile. The driver's license in his pocket belongs to a Leopold Haring. Apparently he's a famous—"

"Oh sweet Jesus."

"You've heard of him."

"Get that body into the truck and out of there before the press shows up, Dr. Teska! What happened to him?"

I described the circumstances as we had found them, and what we had gone through to extricate the body. Dr. Howe didn't like the story—especially once he reckoned how many scene spectators there were among the hardhats, and how many of them might have been sneaking cell phone pictures. I issued the soothing assurances I'd perfected in my short career under short-tempered boss men. I was good at it, and it worked. Dr. Howe let me go.

I climbed back up to the cordon line. Donna and Cam had staged their gurney and were laying out a body pouch next to Mr. Haring.

"Hang on," I said. "Let's get some pictures of the damage to the trouser hems and the shoes, while we still have them in situ with the drag marks in the dirt."

"*If* those are drag marks," Cam groused.

"That's why I want to document them, Cam. If."

Donna lifted the sheet off the body and set it aside, and Cam summoned the CSI photographer to take some close-ups of the ripped fabric and scuffed leather, the socks balled down, and pale pink abrasions on both Achilles' heels.

27

"Those look postmortem, too," I started to say—but was cut off by an anguished cry from behind us.

"Oh my God! Oh my God! What…"

It was a lanky man, well dressed, with silver hair. His face had gone as white as the morgue sheet.

"Is that…is that Leo?"

"That's what we need you to tell us, Mr. Symond." That was Jones. He was standing on one side of the pale man. The site superintendent stood on the other.

"Do you recognize him?" Jones said. "I mean, anything among his effects, maybe?"

"His head…what happened to his head? Oh God… Leo…"

Jones put a hand on the man's shoulder. "Take all the time you need."

The superintendent cleared his throat and turned away. "I'll be in my office, Jeff," he said, and strode briskly toward the trailer.

"Oh God…" the pale man—a Mr. Jeff Symond, evidently—said again. "That's his suit. It looks like his shoes. Is he wearing a U-Penn ring?"

Jones turned his flat gaze to me. I lifted the dead man's hand and examined the college ring.

"Yes."

"What year, Mr. Symond?" asked Jones gently.

"Nineteen ninety-one."

They both looked to me. I nodded.

Jeff Symond's mouth hung open. His breathing was shallow, eyes glassy. He swiveled suddenly, stumbled, and vomited into the dirt under the police cordon tape.

Cameron muttered, "That's another DNA profile to rule out," and Donna stifled a snicker. I glared daggers and ordered them to get going with collecting the remains.

Symond wiped his mouth with a handkerchief, his back still turned. I went to him, asked if he was dizzy. He shook his head. I waved over a patrol cop.

"Take Mr. Symond up to the trailer and get him a chair and a glass of water, okay?"

They started off, carefully. Symond did not look back.

"Can I talk to you, Keith," I said to Jones, and walked away from the cordon. He followed.

"What the hell is wrong with you?" I spat, too loud, and turned the heads on a couple of nearby beat cops. I tamped down my temper and dropped into a church whisper. "You don't bring a civilian to a crime scene! What were you thinking—?"

"What's wrong with *me*? You're forgetting this is my scene." He kept his body language lax for the benefit of the uniforms and hardhats craning to eavesdrop, but the anger in his voice matched mine. "This guy shows up at the gate, says he's the decedent's business partner. Apparently the superintendent called him, asked him to get down here. He demands—*demands*—to see the scene of the accident. He wants to see how it happened."

"Accident—?"

"Yeah, accident. To me this looks like an industrial accident. You say different, based, as far as I can tell, on intuition about the blood spatter. Okay. Maybe you're right—we'll all find out sooner or later. But you've been *way* wrong, calling accidents homicides before, and I'm not taking any chances with your work, Doctor."

"That is not fair."

"Maybe not. Like I said, we'll all find out sooner or later. This Mr. Jeffrey Symond is the partner of the man who holds the presumptive ID for our corpse over there. I figured he could tell us something about the pipes and how they fell, maybe. Or at least he could confirm the ID—"

"On a guy with no fucking face? Give me a break, Keith. You and I both know we're going to get fingerprints off that body as soon as we get it back to the morgue, and those prints will match the DMV database for our presumptive. The ID will be solid. You didn't have to drag that poor man over here. It's un-professional and sadistic."

"Sadistic—?" Keith Jones was losing his struggle to keep his body language from matching his words, and the hardhats were starting to notice. "*Sadistic* is leaving that dead man out there for, what…? Four hours now? Why don't you do your job and get the body out of here."

"Your crime scene, Inspector, but my body. You know that. The body and everything on it is my jurisdiction."

"So why don't you go look after it."

"So why don't *you* go—"

I stopped myself, which was just as well. We turned our backs on one another and walked away.

Donna and Cam had slid the body onto the white sheet, scooping up the mess that remained of the man's head and shoulders, along with some bloody dirt and rubble. They tied the ends of the sheet into knots like a shroud, then lifted it up and placed it in the body pouch, which in turn went onto the gurney.

I told them to take it back to the morgue without me. "It's too late to start the autopsy today. Print and weigh him and hold him over for tomorrow in the cooler."

The 2578s calculated overtime while they pushed the gurney across the dirt lot to their truck. I covered a yawn and rubbed my face. If Mr. Jeffrey Symond was still recuperating in the office trailer, I figured I might as well go talk to him and see what he could tell me about the late Leopold Haring.

I opened the flimsy door to find Mr. Symond propped on a folding chair in a corner, drinking water from a paper cup. He looked badly shaken, but not on the verge of puking again. I got him a refill of water. He thanked me, absently.

I introduced myself. Jeffrey Symond did the same. I asked him how he knew the decedent.

"I'm his business partner," he said. "Twenty years. More than that. This project is one of ours—his design, his blueprints. I do operations and permits, pitching new clients, the business end. Leo is the creative one."

He sighed in the desperate way some men do to keep from crying.

"Mr. Symond," I said, "I'm very sorry you went through that. No one should have to see a friend in that state."

His eyes had a plea in them. I knew what was coming next. It was the vanguard of the denial phase.

"Are you sure that's him?"

"The driver's license he was carrying says it is, and the college ring you asked about substantiates that. We'll know for sure when we compare his fingerprints to the database at the Department of Motor Vehicles."

"Oh," he said, despondent again. "Right."

"He wears a wedding ring. Is he married?"

"Yes. Natalie. Natalie Haring." I wrote it down, and asked him for Mrs. Haring's phone number and address. He knew both from memory. "We all work together," he said. "We have a company. Natalie and Leo and myself."

"Does Mrs. Haring know yet?"

"I haven't spoken to her…"

"I'm going to ask you not to, then. Our office will provide notification once the fingerprints come back and it's official, which should be in the next couple of hours. Okay?"

"Okay."

I gave Jeffrey Symond a moment to fiddle with his paper cup, then I continued.

"Did Leo use drugs or alcohol?"

"He drank. Not a lot."

"No history of substance abuse that you know of?"

"No drugs, and I can't remember the last time I saw him drunk, or even tipsy."

"Was he on any medications? And do you know if he has any medical history?"

"I don't know. You'd have to ask Natalie."

"Okay. When did you last see Mr. Haring?"

"Yesterday around six."

"In the evening, you mean?"

"Yes."

"Where?"

"At our office. Natalie and I were both there, expecting him to be working with us. When he finally showed up, he was agitated—he'd been in a fight with his son."

"What's his name and age, the son?"

"Oskar. He's twenty-three."

"Natalie is his mother?" I asked.

"Yes."

"But Oskar wasn't there, at the office."

"No."

"Did Mr. Haring say what the fight was about?"

"No," Symond said. "But he did say he was planning on coming down here, to the SoMa Centre site."

"What for?"

"I don't know exactly. He had a lot of complaints about the way they were doing this job."

"What was going on?"

"Leo kept telling me the contractors were cutting corners. Materials, even methods. He was worried about it. You heard of the Leaning Tower of Pine Street?"

I nodded. The Leaning Tower was infamous. One of the city's tallest new skyscrapers, right downtown, had been built with the wrong sort of foundation or something, and had started listing to one side. Pipes ruptured, electrical wires snapped, and windows were cracking—one had even popped out and crashed to the street below. No one knew what was going to happen to that building. Hundreds of people—very rich people—had already invested in luxury condos there. They were bleeding untold millions of dollars in lost real estate value. Demolishing the building was out of the question and repairing it was impossible. Years in the planning and construction, and it had yielded nothing but finger-pointing and lawsuits for everyone involved.

"The Leaning Tower is every architect's worst nightmare," Symond said. "Something like that happens, it ruins your life. So Leo was worried about the foundation work on this place, on SoMa Centre."

"Is that why he came down here last night?"

"He didn't say as much, so I don't know."

Jeffrey Symond looked around the superintendent's trailer, as if noticing for the first time where he was. There was a poster of the artist's rendering. He rose and went over, contemplated it.

"They're trying to keep too fast a pace on this thing," he said. "I'm not surprised there was a fatal accident. I'm just surprised it was Leo."

He moved to look out the trailer's little window. Jones must've allowed the site opened up for work, because there was a lot more action—voices shouting commands, workers hustling around, machinery belching smoke and hauling off. The death scene cordon was still in place, but someone had shifted the fallen pipes farther off. A man in a hard hat stood over them with a hose, rinsing them down. He was washing bloody bits of Leopold Haring into the dirt.

CHAPTER 2

The conference room at the San Francisco Office of Chief Medical Examiner has a table and some chairs, a fancy electronic whiteboard for presentations, four walls, and a door. It has no windows. When I arrived for work on Thursday morning, I found that it had no forced air ventilation, either. Worse, the seasonal Diablo winds had started blowing during the night, bringing hot air and frayed nerves. The OCME conference room felt like a furnace and smelled like a gym.

My colleague, Assistant Medical Examiner Dr. Theodore Nguyen, was running the morning meeting.

"What is it this time?" Sunshine Ted (as I referred to him, in secret, to Anup) wanted to know. He wanted me, as deputy chief, to tell him.

"I don't know what it is this time, Ted. I've called facilities maintenance. Let's make this meeting quick and get out of here, okay?"

"Out of here, and then where? There's no A/C in my office. Is it working in the autopsy suite?"

"No."

Groans around the room, even from the half-dozen medical students on rotation from UCSF.

The break-in period for our shiny new morgue had been hard going. This facility, after a decade in the planning and millions of taxpayer dollars in the building, turned out to have doors that got jammed in their frames and double-glazed windows that cultivated black mold. The lighting fixtures lit things we didn't want lit and left the things we needed to see in shadow. The wiring couldn't handle the load from our collection of high-wattage diagnostic equipment, especially the shockingly expensive full-body X-ray machine. That thing filled half a room, and included a conveyor belt that fed the body through the sensor array. One of the students had observed that it looked just like a quick-bake machine from the fast food joint where he worked; and so it was dubbed the Quiznos 5000. The Quiznos 5000 sucked so much current that it would routinely trip the circuit breaker for the entire facility. So we had mostly stopped using the Quiznos 5000.

The newest crisis in our physical plant involved the sudden and complete loss of all climate control systems for an hour or two at a time, or sometimes more. The last guy from facilities maintenance had referred to it as "HVAC gremlins," and said he'd get right on it. It seemed he had made it worse.

"Three hours!" Sunshine Ted said. "Right, Cam?"

Cameron nodded. "It went down in the Operations Center a little before five this morning."

"Did you try to get it back on?" I asked.

Cam looked at me like I had sprouted a new head. "How? Do you know where the HVAC lives? 'Cause I don't. Air comes through the vents in the Ops Shop, or it doesn't. Believe me, Doc, if there was a box to kick-start somewhere, I'd give it a try."

Donna giggled. Cam nudged her and grinned.

"Okay, okay," I said, and wiped sweat from my brow. "I'll get on the building people again."

"Dr. Howe has already ripped them a new one," Donna said.

"Good. So what do we got on the case list today?"

Morning meeting is the only time during the day when all the morgue principals—doctors, investigators, and autopsy technicians—get together. We discuss and assign the day's new death investigations. For more than a year we had been running a shorthanded shop with only two forensic pathologists instead of three. Hell, optimally we'd have four. But we had two: me and Ted Nguyen.

Cameron made short work of rattling off the details about the Leopold Haring scene, and just as quickly presented the day's four other new cases. An elderly woman had suffered a fatal fall in a nursing home. An inpatient with schizophrenia died in the General Hospital's psych ward. A sixty-seven-year-old man with a history of heart disease collapsed while waiting for a seat at a popular restaurant in Hayes Valley. And, finally, a twentysomething woman was found cold and stiff on a girl-friend's couch after partying all night.

Donna sighed. "Wild Wednesday nights. I remember those."

"All right," said Ted Nguyen, "Jessie, you've already got yesterday's holdover from the construction site, so you take the geriatric fall and the OD on the couch, and I'll handle the other two." He shuffled the folders and slid mine over the tabletop.

"Let's get to work."

The autopsy suite was even more oppressive than the conference room. We perform our work under surgical lights. They're hot. Worse, before we start cutting into dead bodies, we first have to suit up in several layers of personal protective equipment, including a Tyvek gown, an N95 respirator mask, a bouffant cap, and three layers of gloves. I felt the sweat trickling down my backbone before I'd left the women's locker room.

Someone with no sense of irony had put up a bunch of Halloween decorations in the morgue. They were childishly incongruous ones, to boot: smiling Frankensteins and goofy Draculas, waltzing ghosts with Day-Glo imprecations like *Beware of Zombies*, and *Life's a Witch*. The medical students were clustered around my autopsy table, which didn't make the airflow problem any better. Yarina Marchenko barked at them to clear a path, then elbowed her way through before they had a chance to.

"*Dzień dobry, proszę Pani*," I said.

"*Dobroho ranku, Likarya*," Yarina replied. It was our good morning ritual. Yarina was our one and only morgue technician. We really should have had three, at a minimum two, but we had one. Yarina was a diminutive woman of late middle age, trained as a physician in her native Ukraine. We'd worked together for nearly a year and a half, and had learned to accommodate one another. Mostly.

Yarina and I made quick work of the first two cases. The nursing home death was a simple external examination with chart review of a seventy-three-year-old had who fallen and broken a hip, dying of pneumonia and heart failure a week later. Cause: complications of hip fracture. Manner: accident. Next was the midweek party guest who woke up dead on her friend's couch. I shined a flashlight up her nose and spotted a hole eroded in the nasal septum. You get that from snorting coke. When I opened her up, I found an alcoholic fatty liver. Drug overdose, probably combined cocaine and alcohol. Toxicology results would tell us for sure, though they would take weeks to come back. In the meantime, cause and manner pending.

We were done with those two cases in less than an hour— though it felt like three. I had to change my bouffant cap after brow sweat leached into the thing and soaked it to dripping.

The air in the morgue was getting swampy, and it was a labor to breathe through the N95 mask. Yarina wheeled in the dusty nylon pouch that contained Leopold Haring's remains. I warned the students that this was a pretty gnarly one, then unzipped it. There were some gasps, but no one fainted.

I went through the external examination carefully. The decedent was wearing a dark blue business suit and white shirt, all of fine manufacture. His wallet was in the left hip pocket where we'd replaced it after checking ID at the scene. The other held the keys to a Lexus and a vial of eye drops. His suit jacket's flap pockets had a small notebook full of scribbled figures and a handheld laser ruler similar to the ones the CSI crew uses to measure distance. An inside breast pocket was zippered closed. It held something bulky. I pulled it out.

"Rocks," one of the students observed.

"Rocks," I agreed, but then examined more closely. It was a lump of aggregate, pebbles held together in a dull yellow matrix that looked and felt like a cross between cement and dried glue. There seemed to be tiny silvery hairs mixed in there, too. The lump was lighter than its size suggested it should be.

"What is this?" I asked.

"It's a rock, Dr. Teska," a student said. "Construction sites have lots of them."

"Yeah, but this one is weird looking. And how come it was zipped up inside his jacket?"

The medical students stared back at me like a small herd of sweaty cattle.

"It didn't land there by accident," I said, and logged it as *rocky aggregate building material* in the man's personal property, along with his wedding band and class ring, and the other things that had come out of his pockets.

Now that I had the body under the hot lights of the autopsy suite, I could see that his pants were torn from the butt all the way down both legs, with the hems really ripped up. All the damage was to the rear; the front was pristine. The skin of the lower calves and Achilles' heels on both legs showed significant abrasions, tan in color and nonhemorrhagic.

I asked the students what that meant. Two answered in unison: "Postmortem injury."

"That's right. Now look at the damage to his clothes. What does it tell you?"

Nervous silence.

"What's the direction of force appear to be?"

"Um," a student said, "down?"

"Exactly! Along the length of the limbs. Look closely. There's more tissue damage at the bottom of each wound than at the top. These defects were caused by friction force applied in a superior to inferior direction, without lateral vector, while clothed, on a man who was already dead. Hand me the camera."

I took the pictures myself, since Yarina had fired up the bone saw and was busy cutting a halo around the skull on Ted's psych ward case. Leopold Haring's limbs were limp, past rigor mortis, which meant decomposition was advancing. It was going to happen fast in the jungle heat of the autopsy suite. It worried me.

"Let's get this evisceration going, people," I said to the students, and collected my lucky pink #22 scalpel from among my tools.

"Hello…?" said an unfamiliar voice. It belonged to a man. He was standing inside the secure door from reception. He was dressed in street clothes. He wasn't wearing a mask or gloves, or any other PPEs.

"Stop right there," I ordered. "How did you get in here?"

"I have a key card," the barefaced man said, brandishing it.

The sweltering autopsy suite stank of cadavers. Yarina was sawing into a human head, making a hellish din and throwing up flecks of skull. Ted Nguyen used a long knife to take a slice out of a fresh human heart. I was standing over a man in a sharp suit who had a grimy pile of hamburg in place of his head. It was clear from his expression that this wasn't at all a place the man in the doorway had been expecting to end up.

I shouted over the bone saw. "Where'd you get a key card?"

"Facilities maintenance. I've been sent to help with the HVAC system…"

Yarina finished, and the saw racket wound down. "Good!" she said. "You must wear mask. Gloves, paper booties. Go back now. Hurry fast, we need air!"

She pointed the bone saw toward the door. The bone saw is a 250-watt tool that calls to mind a mammoth hand blender. The serrated blade sticking off its business end was dripping blood. The man swiveled and went through the door, fast.

"Hope he comes back," Sunshine Ted said.

I asked one of the male medical students to chase after the guy and get him into minimum PPEs from the locker room. The two of them came back, suited up, inside five minutes— and the man was carrying a stepladder and toolbox. The other medical students broke into a spontaneous, sweaty cheer. The man's eyes crinkled into a smile over the N95 mask.

"I'll hand it to you, Mr. HVAC," I said, "you're dedicated."

"Denis. Denis Monaghan," he said automatically. He had an Irish brogue.

"I'm Deputy Chief Jessie Teska. What are you doing in our autopsy suite, Denis?"

"I've isolated the problem with the climate control system. It's a unit in the ceiling here."

"Is there another way to get at it?"

"The only access panel is in here, Deputy Chief Teska."

"Call me Jessie. That strikes me as an unfortunate design choice, if you'll forgive my saying so, Denis."

"I couldn't agree more, Jessie. I'm only here to fix someone else's mistakes, and I'm afraid there's no other way to do it."

"And I'm afraid I can't let you stay in here while we're doing autopsies. Occupational Safety and Health would have a conniption and levy a nasty fine."

"Fair enough," Denis Monaghan said. "But this is a negative-pressure space. With the system down, no air can get in at all. It's brutal hot in here now, and if I don't get that unit in your ceiling working, it'll be desperate."

"It's desperate already," Ted muttered. He and Yarina were pulling out the schizophrenic's brain.

"No," I said. "I can't let you do it."

"Right," said Monaghan. "Well, then." He waved the key card he'd used to get into the autopsy suite. "I've been sent here to do an urgent job, and I intend to do it. May I ask to speak to your supervisor, please?"

I was just about to tell Denis Monaghan that I, as deputy chief, was the final authority in this matter, when another man's voice boomed across the autopsy suite.

"Good God…! This is horrible!"

Chief Medical Examiner Dr. James Howe had arrived for morning rounds.

"This is insane!" he hollered. Howe wore, as he wore every morning, a surgical apron over his staid business suit. Sweat beaded on his bald head. He had young eyes that belied his age, and knotted hands that exaggerated it.

Howe locked on to Denis Monaghan. "Who is this?"

Monaghan introduced himself and, before I could beat him to it, told Dr. Howe about the broken HVAC unit.

"Well, what are you waiting for?" Howe said. "Fix it!"

"I'd like to," Monaghan said, and tipped his head sidelong toward me. "But I'm being told I'm not allowed to work in here so long as your crew are using the place…"

"Why the hell not?"

I cut in. "OSHA rules, Dr. Howe."

"OSHA?" Howe said. "To hell with OSHA! We can't work like this."

"But we can't—"

"We can if it's an emergency," Howe said. "And it's an emergency if I declare it is. This goddamn well fits the bill!"

He pointed a bony finger at Monaghan. "You. Get to work."

"Yes, sir," said Monaghan. He lifted his stepladder and carried it across the autopsy suite. He had to skirt my table. As I made room for him to pass, he thanked me, and—I shit you not—he winked.

Monaghan set the ladder and climbed it, and pushed a panel in the drop ceiling. His top half disappeared, and shortly there came a sound of discouragement and the clank of tools.

"The show must go on!" Howe declared. Then he told Yarina to come get him in his office once the air-conditioning was turned back on. He'd delay morning rounds until then.

And he left.

"Okay then," I said. "Let's keep at it."

I turned my attention back to Leopold Haring. He was definitely starting to stink. The students looked miserable, though one, a woman with gorgeous, curly black hair leaking out of her bouffant cap, seemed eager and engaged. I asked her to help me peel the clothing off the corpse, stopping to take photos when I came across anything interesting. The pattern of bleeding, for one thing. That was very interesting.

"There's a lot of hemorrhage here on the posterior side," I pointed out to the students. We peeled off the dead man's jacket, dress shirt, T-shirt. All three layers were soaked through with a round bloodstain, about six inches in diameter. I took pictures, then washed the blood off the skin of his upper back. Sure enough, left behind when the blood drained away, I saw a hole.

"How do you like that," I said.

"It's a gunshot wound!" the student with the great hair said.

The hole was oblong, with ratty edges. I pressed them together with my gloved fingers, and showed the students that I was not able to reapproximate the wound margins. "Punched-in hole characteristic of a bullet entrance wound."

"Where's the exit?"

"When I cut into him, I'm going to trace the wound track underneath that hole. Then we'll find out."

"This is great!"

I asked her name.

"Patty Alvarez."

"Take a close look at the clothing, will you, Miss Alvarez? Anything we ought to document?"

She fingered the bloody cloth. "There's a hole here, too. Right in the middle of the bloodstain, in all three layers."

"Let's get pictures."

"Hold on..." said another student, one who had impressed me as slow on the uptake. "This is a shooting?"

"This is a wound with vital reaction hemorrhage that might be from a bullet."

"I thought you said somebody dropped pipes on his head."

"There was a load of pipe lying on his head when we arrived at the scene. What that means, I don't know yet."

"It means somebody was trying to make a shooting look like an accident," the thick student said.

"We don't draw conclusions until we've gathered all the data. For starters, now that we have the body stripped and photographed, let's hose it off and do an inventory of injuries. Maybe we'll find another wound that corresponds with this one."

We started with the head and neck. Once I had rinsed away the dirt and arranged the pieces of scalp in approximately the right places...it was still a grotesque mess, even by my standards. Most of the face was a tan-colored pulp—postmortem injury, just like the abrasions on the legs and heels. The nose, though, was different. It was swollen and pinkish, like a recent injury had been starting to heal.

I palpated it. Could be broken, a little hard to tell with all the other damage to the facial bones. "Dried blood in the nostrils, and inside the lips," I noted aloud, then sliced down with my scalpel and cut off a chunk of the nose. This horrified several of my students. I explained that I don't like to deface bodies, but that I needed to get a tissue sample and examine it under a microscope.

I looked over the whole body again. The injury to the back had definitely happened while Leopold Haring's heart was still beating. Between the lack of blood at the scene and the drag marks and damage to his legs, it was possible he died from that wound somewhere else, and was then staged under the pipes to make the death look like a work accident.

"Time to get cutting," I announced.

I made the Y-incision from the shoulders to the sternum, then straight down to the pubis, opening the torso. His clavicles were shattered, the sternum snapped in half, and his uppermost ribs were in pieces. All these bony injuries were dry of blood.

I heaved the tree lopper tool I use for snapping ribs and went to work on the ones below the area of injury. It's hard under normal conditions to cut open a full-grown man's rib cage, and it became an athletic feat in the sweltering heat of the unventilated morgue. Yarina came over to assist, and I was grateful to set her to the painstaking task of peeling the scalp off the smashed skull bones. Those, too, were minimally hemorrhagic.

"Well, this is for sure," I told the students. "He was already dead when his head got smished."

"Smished?" said Patty Alvarez.

"Write that down."

I lifted out the front of the rib cage. Immediately underneath it was a lot of blood.

"Hand me that ladle and a measuring cup." Someone did, and I scooped it out. It measured a liter and a half, all from the left side of the chest cavity. The left lung had a big honking hole in it. I cut into it with my scalpel and found a hemorrhagic track going clear through the lower left lobe, and then into the muscles between the fifth and sixth ribs. The wounds all lined up with the hole on Leopold Haring's back, and his bloody clothing.

"Pictures, Yarina," I said.

"What's with the heart?" said the dense student.

The pericardial sac was distended and rigid. I cut it open and collected 300 ml of bright blood. I removed the heart, turned it around in my hand, and immediately found the source: a ragged defect in the thick muscle of the posterior left ventricular wall.

"Well, we've found the end of that wound track," I said. "Let's see what's inside."

I brought the heart to the foot of the autopsy table and the students crowded around. I dissected it.

No bullet.

"Ted!" I crowed, genuinely excited, "I think I've got a bullet embolus here!"

"Good for you," Nguyen muttered.

"Anyone know what that is?" I asked the students. They didn't. "If this is a gunshot wound, and if the bullet stopped here in the left ventricle without getting lodged in the muscle tissue, then it's possible that with the next heartbeat it got pumped into the aorta." I pushed a finger into the aortic valve to show them how easy that would be. "From there the slug might have surfed the pressurized blood stream through smaller and smaller arteries until it got stuck. That's a bullet embolus. They're exceptionally rare!"

"How are you going to find it?" a student asked.

"Good question! By X-ray for sure, after we finish cutting, but that might not be necessary. I might come across the darned thing in gross anatomy. Sometimes they end up lodged in the liver. What a great case!"

I plugged up the scupper pipe in the autopsy table so that no slugs or fragments could disappear down the drain, and filtered the blood I had collected. No bullet. I continued the autopsy, cutting into each of Haring's other internal organs. In the end, the only place I found any bleeding was from the wound that had skewered his left lung and punctured his heart. That was the cause of death.

Given the effort someone had apparently put into covering up that event, the manner of death was definitely not accident. Haring was a homicide.

After spending nearly an hour taking the man's entire body apart, I had failed to find a bullet to match the penetrating wound. That meant I had to X-ray the body. Leopold Haring's lungs, heart, liver, intestines, and the rest of his eviscerated organs lay in a glistening heap at the foot of the autopsy table. I scooped them into a biohazard bag. Then Yarina and I shifted the corpse and the bag back onto a gurney and rolled it—with great care—across the morgue. There was a man perched on a stepladder between my autopsy table and the radiology room, and I didn't want to sideswipe him. I shuddered to imagine the OSHA report on that.

"Hey, Mr. HVAC!" I yelled. I'd forgotten his name.

"Denis. Call me Denis." His legs were on the ladder, the rest of him still in the ceiling.

"Yeah, Denis. How's it going up there?"

"Just brilliant." He made some clanking noises, presumably to demonstrate the work in progress.

"We can't take much more of this, Denis. If you can't get it fixed soon, I'm going to have to shut this place down."

"Doing me best up here," he said from the ceiling as I eased the gurney past his ladder.

Yarina and I sweated through the job of feeding the body through the Quiznos 5000 X-ray rig, then I scanned and zoomed around the image on the computer monitor, looking for foreign objects.

Still no bullet. Nothing metal in the radiograms at all.

"It's not a bullet embolism?" said the dense student.

"No."

"So where'd the bullet go?"

"Maybe it was never there."

"Huh...?"

Before I could explain, there was a whooshing sound and a breeze came through the vents.

"Hallelujah!" somebody yelped, and the whole morgue, except for Sunshine Ted, broke into muffled, nitrile-gloved applause.

Denis Monaghan descended from his stepladder. He'd let the mask fall off his face while he worked up there. It was a happy face, and a sweaty one.

"I'm not quite done, but it should stay on for now, so you don't have to quit." His smile was replaced by a pious earnestness. "I admire the work you're doing here, all of ye."

Ye? I wondered if Denis Monaghan was putting us on. *The map of Ireland on his face*, as I'd heard said of some of the guys I grew up with in Boston. Monaghan fit the bill, with a short nose and bulb chin, dimples, small gray eyes. He was handsome, in an elfin sort of way.

"Put that mask back on, Denis," I said. "And, thanks."

Yarina phoned Dr. Howe to give him the good news, and the chief arrived right away. He joined us in the radiology room and stood over the naked shreds of Leopold Haring while I presented my autopsy findings.

"So," he said, after I'd finished, "if there's no bullet and no exit, what do we conclude?"

"This isn't a gunshot wound," I said.

The thick student muttered something in surprise. The student with the enviable hair, Alvarez, was nodding along like she was already one step ahead of Dr. Howe.

Howe palpated the hole in Haring's back and pressed its edges together. "What is it, then?"

"A knife wound?" another student guessed.

"Not with these margins. It may be a stab wound, but not a knife wound."

"Then what?" said the thick kid.

Howe said, "A round, slender weapon. An ice pick, maybe."

"Or a crossbow bolt," I added. "Remember that case out by the Beach Chalet…?"

The chief's eyes were sparkling again. "You see a lot of crossbow injuries on construction sites, Dr. Teska?"

Patty Alvarez beat me to it.

"A screwdriver!"

Howe smiled tightly and nodded. "I've seen screwdriver wounds just like this."

I winked at Alvarez. She beamed. It was adorable.

"Take histology sections of the entry and the wound track," Howe said. "Maybe it'll tell us something. Follow up with Homicide before the end of business today. Call CSI, too, and have them look out for screwdrivers."

The boss stretched his neck up and closed his eyes. The air-conditioning tossed his thin handful of hairs around. "The press will be coming after you. You will have no comment. I'd advise you to put a hold on the body for now, make sure you cover your bases. This is high profile."

I caught Yarina's attention. "You got that?"

"In cooler he goes."

I cast my voice across the room again, toward the workman's trousers perched on the stepladder. "Hey, Denis—how's things in the cold storage room? Did climate control fail in there, too?"

Monaghan descended, peered over at me. "Sorry, didn't catch that. What'd you need?"

I repeated the question about the cooler.

"Which one's that?" he said.

I pointed to it.

"Oh, that area's not affected," Monaghan said. "Completely separate controls, it's been working fine all along."

I cast my eyes skyward and pressed my gloved hands together.

"*Dzięki Ci, Boże.* Thank You for small favors."

CHAPTER 3

Once we got finished in the autopsy suite, I cleaned up and drove over to the Hall of Justice to meet with Inspector Jones. I wanted to show him the rocky aggregate material I'd pulled out of Leopold Haring's zippered jacket pocket. I brought along a morgue photo of the penetrating wound's entrance in his back, too.

Keith Jones met me at the Investigations Division window and led me back to the Homicide bullpen, a mahogany-dark repurposed courtroom. His partner, Daniel Ramirez, sat at their shared desk. Ramirez didn't offer his hand, and didn't mitigate his steely cop scowl. I was getting a little tired of this stone-cold act he and Jones were putting on, all because they disagreed with my findings on a case we'd worked together more than a year before.

"You said you had something to show us," Jones said.

"Chief Medical Examiner Howe sent me." That made the pair of them sit up and take notice. "He agrees that Leopold Haring's death was not due to a workplace accident. The injuries from the pipes were all postmortem. That, combined with the drag marks, points to a staging of the scene. Here."

I spread out the pictures from the morgue. "This is the cause of death—a stab wound, made with a round, penetrating weapon approximately a quarter inch in diameter and at least five inches long. Like an ice pick, or a screwdriver."

Jones looked over the photos. "Chief Howe saw these?"

"Yes," I said, flat as I could manage, and produced an evidence bag with the yellowish aggregate stuff that I'd pulled out of the dead man's pocket. "I was hoping you might be able to tell me what this is."

Jones scrutinized the evidence bag, then handed it to his partner. Ramirez held it up, rotated it, and nodded knowingly to Jones. Both men turned to me.

"Rocks," Ramirez said. "These are rocks."

"You're hilarious. So you don't know?"

They just smirked back, in that way some men do when they're saving a private joke for later. A joke about dumb blondes.

"Thank you for your time," I said, and gathered the evidence off the desk. Just as I was putting the last of it into my bag, Inspector Jones had a thought.

"Dr. Howe said this is a homicide, right?"

"That's my determination. He agrees."

"Okay, but you're saying the scene was staged, and the body was moved. If you're right, then it's possible only the killer knows about that. All the rest of those workers who saw the body under the pipes still think it was an accident."

"That's possible, yes."

"Then we want the case restricted."

"Sure. I'll pend the death certificate for further investigation, cause and manner under wraps, no public disclosure."

That response surprised them. Medical examiners usually hate the cloak-and-dagger nonsense of police-restricted cases. For this investigation, though, it sounded like a fine idea to me.

"The family's going to be pissed that we're holding on to it," I added. "It's high profile, all over the press already. They're going to apply pressure on me, on you, on everyone."

"No problem," said Ramirez.

"You got anything else for us, Doc?" said Jones.

"Yeah." I told them about my interview with Jeffrey Symond, Haring's business partner. "He said Haring had been in a fight with a son, named Oskar. On autopsy I found Haring had a recent injury to his nose. It didn't match the postmortem injury from the pipes, and it could fit the time frame if he was involved in a physical altercation within a couple of hours of his death."

"Can you narrow it down more than that?"

"I might be able to age the injury with more precision once I look at the tissue under a microscope. It'll be a couple of weeks before I get the slides, though."

"Okay," said Jones.

"Okay," I said back.

Ramirez said nothing.

Here's your hat, what's your hurry, I thought. Something my dad used to say. I turned my back on the detectives and saw myself out.

The Crime Scene Investigation Unit's office was just downstairs from Homicide, so I figured I'd stop by to tell them to be on the lookout for screwdrivers. Or ice picks. Crossbow bolts.

The drab olive floor and gray marble walls sucked the life out of everything that moved through the Hall of Justice. Old furniture and burned-out fluorescent tubes cluttered an alcove where a row of public phone booths retained only a dangle of wires and the half-hinges of missing accordion doors. One entire section of wall had been ripped away and replaced with an enormous X of steel beams. A sign said it was part of an "interim/conditional" earthquake retrofit. I wondered what exactly that meant.

The door to room 419, Crime Scene Investigation, was locked. On the milky chicken-wire glass someone had posted one of those cardboard clocks with movable hands. They were gone until 2:00, either out to lunch or at a scene. If they were at a scene, it could be my scene, the SoMa Centre construction site. I remembered with longing a place around the corner from there that did pressed Cuban sandwiches. I could grab a *pan con lechon* and return to the scene of the crime to talk to the CSI guys, or to poke around myself and see what I could find in the light of day, now that I had a better idea how Leopold Haring had died. For one thing, I wanted to look for more of the rocky aggregate building material that the architect had thought so important that he had made a point of collecting a sample.

I could walk to the Cuban sandwich place. Hell, I could walk to a dozen restaurants within ten minutes of the Hall. Our new workplace stood on a spit of poisoned land across from a power grid substation and down the road from a sewage treatment plant and the city dump. So I enjoyed hoofing to the sandwich shop for my roast pork panino. I missed walking during lunch. Then again, having no eating options anywhere near our new office had made me more frugal, brown bagging most days rather than getting into the car to drive somewhere. And the more frugal I could be, the better: I was carrying two hundred thousand dollars in student debt. The BMW was an extravagance, but it was my only one.

No problem. My brother Tomasz and I had grown up way worse off. Our father was an abusive lowlife, our mother a depressive shut-in, and we never had enough money. I had always worried that my brother was likely to burn out young. He had a wild streak, a propensity for rule-breaking. Instead, God love him, Tommy had channeled those traits into success in Silicon Valley.

The panino place had the local news going. I picked up the

words "prominent architect," and scooted into the corner under the TV.

They had started with a wide shot of SoMa Centre and the morgue van leaving it, while the newscaster talked about the death of Leopold Haring. It was nothing I didn't expect to hear. What came next, though, was. They cut to Jeffrey Symond, Haring's business partner, looking rumpled and shell-shocked, facing a blob of reporters with microphones.

"...saddened by this shocking event, but we are going to continue to pursue Leo's artistic vision, and we're going to ensure that SoMa Centre takes its place in the Haring legacy."

"Were you there when he died?" a reporter shouted. Symond shook his head and looked down in sorrow.

"Do you know how it happened?" another asked.

"Yes," Symond replied, his head still down. My blood pressure went up. "It was a workplace accident. A tragedy." He raised his eyes. They were clear, his expression grim but determined. "We're working with the investigating authorities, of course."

The newscast cut back to the anchor, who delivered a few more platitudes about Leopold Haring's genius while the picture switched to a stock shot of a corporate sign reading *Haring & Symond*. Then it cut to a black car outside a nondescript glassy building, while a woman in a business outfit and giant sunglasses hurried from the one to the other.

"Leopold Haring is survived by a wife and son. Mrs. Haring was not available for comment," said the newscaster.

So that's Natalie Haring. I watched her disappear into the building and hoped that she was sticking to her no-comment policy, because Jeff Symond had just complicated my life. Why would he tell the reporters that Haring had died in a workplace accident? I mean, as far as he knew, it was one, sure—but why tell them anything at all?

"No way to run a railroad," I muttered at the TV's talking heads.

The sandwich was ready, with a big smile from the old man behind the counter. He remembered me, and asked why he didn't see me so much anymore.

"They moved us down by the dump," I said.

The panino man thought that was terrible. I agreed it was.

The *pan con lechon* was as good as I remembered; maybe better. I was still chewing the last bits when I signed in with the muscly kid standing watch at the SoMa Centre gate, his back to the scorching devil wind. I picked out another wobbly hard hat and made my way across the roaring and clanking work site to the crime scene. The pipes were still in the same place they had been moved to, but I was surprised to find that the spot where Leopold Haring's body had been lying was trampled over with countless boot prints and a Caterpillar machine track. No yellow tape, nothing to keep the area secure. I was annoyed with Inspector Jones. At a scene like this, with a restricted homicide investigation, he should have maintained the perimeter for at least forty-eight hours.

It seemed kind of silly to search for screwdrivers in the trampled dirt. But, what the hell, I did anyway. I also pulled out the bag with the weird yellow rocks, and looked around to see if anything in the vicinity matched them. Nothing did.

"Hey…!"

Samuel Urias, the union steward, was coming through the windblown dust toward me.

"Who are you?" he demanded. "What are you doing here? This is a work site—it's dangerous."

"I was here the other night, Mr. Urias." I pulled out my badge.

He had a knee-jerk reaction to it. "You with DBI?"

"No," I said, trying to be soothing as I assured him that I was not from the Department of Building Inspection. "I'm here from the medical examiner's office, investigating the death of Leopold Haring. I need to reexamine the scene."

"What for?"

I held up the evidence bag with the yellow cement. "Can you tell me what this material is, and where it might be used on this site?"

Urias took one quick look but didn't touch the bag. "Lady, I don't care what you think you doing. I'm the steward here. Safety is my job. You're leaving. Now."

"Well, no," I said. "I'm not. I am here investigating a death. That's my job."

"What for?" Urias said again. "He was bound to get hurt down here."

"How do you mean?"

"Like I said, this is a busy site on a tight schedule. Dangerous if you don't know what you doing. That stupid man, marching round here in a suit, with no hard hat, no gear."

"Is that unusual? For the architect to be so hands-on, I mean?"

"Hands-on!" He loosed a sour little laugh. "Yeah, hands-on. He think he knows everybody's job. Think he's better than everybody, getting on my crew and yelling at them they're doing it too fast, too sloppy, whatever. He treated my men like dirt."

Urias kicked some up. "Like *dirt*! I've seen men die on the job. It happens. Sometimes it's their fault, sometimes not. This time? No question. He was a…a accident waiting to happen, like they say. I'm only glad he didn't take none of my men with him."

Urias spotted something behind me and whistled for attention. It was the site superintendent. Urias marched over to him, and the pair of them kept their eyes on me while they traded words. The superintendent nodded. He put on a hostile smile.

"Dr.…Tesla?"

"Teska."

"Sorry. I'm going to escort you off the job site now."

"No, you aren't. I'm conducting a death investigation." I waved my shiny gold Deputy Medical Examiner badge. His smile only hardened.

"Sam here is right. We are in violation of union rules. And OSHA regulations."

"I work for the city and I'm on official business."

"No one from the city gets in here unless they're from the police department or the Department of Building Inspection. And if they're police, they need to produce a warrant."

"I don't think you understand the seriousness of my task here. The death of—"

"PD or DBI, and PD only if they have a warrant in hand. That's it."

Samuel Urias had made his way to the entry gate and was yelling something to the muscly young watchman. I glared at the superintendent but said nothing—because I knew he was right. When Dr. Howe had promoted me to deputy chief, I had sat through twenty tedious hours of training for the job. A couple of those hours were devoted to a lecture about the legal powers vested in the medical examiner's office. Once the body is no longer at a scene, the scene becomes private property again, inviolable without a warrant if the property holder is unwilling to allow us in.

That was all I needed—Dr. Howe getting a call from the chief of police, yelling about me being arrested for trespass. I agreed to leave voluntarily.

The watchman was abashed about escorting me out, and kept his distance. I said something about not holding it against him, he's only doing his job, chain of command. He graced me with a smile when I handed off the hard hat and signed out.

The Department of Building Inspection can waltz onto a job site anytime, eh? Okay boys. DBI you want, DBI you'll get.

The receptionist at the Department of Building Inspection sent me down the hall to the permits counter and told me to ask for Peter. Peter was ruddy and round, clean-shaven but for his sideburns, which were tapered to a sharp point. It was a terrible look for a man closing in fast on forty. I couldn't stop staring at them.

Peter asked what he could do for me. I told him I was investigating a death on a construction site, and that I had some questions.

"Like what?"

I handed the bag of yellow rocks over the counter. "What's this stuff?"

Peter examined it. "Polypropylene fibrillated high–alumina cement. Is your site underwater?"

"No."

He looked puzzled. "A furnace or something? High heat environment?"

Again I said no. "It's part of an ongoing medical examiner investigation. I'm told that for safety reasons I need to arrange for a DBI escort to inspect the site."

Peter perked up. "Who died?"

"I can't discuss it. Who do I talk to about having one of your inspectors visit the site with me? This is an urgent matter."

"What's the site?"

"It's called SoMa Centre. Corner of Sixth Street and Folsom."

Peter blanched. "Hang on a minute," he said. He went away from the counter to a desk, opened a drawer, fingered some files. He came back with a sheet of paper. "Fill out this form. We'll start our own investigation and get back to you."

"What? No—this is urgent, I said. Somebody died down there."

Peter shrugged apologetically. "I understand, but we have our own procedures to follow. I need to get some information before I can direct your request to the right inspector. Just fill that out and send it back to us, by fax is best. The information is at the top of the sheet…"

Peter assumed a quizzical look and made a point of digging into his pocket. His hand came out with a phone. He glanced at it.

"Sorry, I have to take this." He turned away, stuck the phone to his ear, and hurried through a back doorway and out of sight.

I hadn't heard that phone ring. Maybe it was on vibrate. Or maybe Peter really, really did not want to talk to me about SoMa Centre.

"He shut down as soon as I named the building site," I said. I was in the DBI garage, on the phone to my friend Sparkle from the privacy of my car. Sparkle is a bounty hunter. Her business, Baby Mike Bail Bonds—named after her gargantuan and reliably imposing cousin—sits across Bryant Street from my old office at the Hall of Justice.

"I know fishy when I see it, Sparkle. There's something fishy about these rocks."

"Maybe. I know someone you can talk to about it."

"Baby Mike?"

"No, Cousin Michael is your man if you need to move a fridge or three. This is an old client of mine. He does exactly what you're talking about—concrete pours and general masonry. Or he used to, at least, before some life challenges. He's getting back on track, working a side job for now."

Sparkle gave me the man's name and told me where to look for him. Then we spent some time catching up. The bail bonds business had gone into a slump, so she had been expanding her range of services.

"Fingerprinting, background checks, due diligence screening. There's tons of demand for private-sector security services. All the tech companies are getting deeper into them. Trouble is, demand has gone up but so has supply. And, well… Jessie, are you sitting down?"

"I am."

"Some of these tech companies—? They aren't eager to hire a Black woman and give her password access."

"Goodness! I am shocked, *shocked*, to hear that."

"Honey, it surprised the heck out of me, I will just tell you."

"But you're managing?"

"I'm managing."

"I should hook you up with Tommy."

"Do *not* hook me up with your brother."

"I meant business-wise—"

"Yeah, that's what I meant, too. I need to keep my nose clean, thank you very much." Sparkle and Tommy had helped me out with some computer sleuthing the year before, and Tommy had spooked Sparkle with his willingness—eagerness, even—to hack into places he didn't belong.

"Which recipes did you decide you wanted?" Sparkle asked. We were swapping, three each, for Thanksgiving, and had given one another a bunch of choices. I told her I wanted the candied yams, the collard greens, and the scalloped potatoes.

"Classics. Are you sure you don't want the garlic crabs? That's my favorite."

"I don't want to experiment. This is a big deal." I had learned when I'd first moved to San Francisco about my new city's passion for local Dungeness crab as a Thanksgiving dish. Sparkle, a native, was performing her due diligence in pushing it on me. But I was making a Thanksgiving dinner for Anup and his parents, and the stakes were too high.

"Anything new with the parents?" Sparkle asked, reading my mind.

"Radio silence."

"How long you been dating that man?"

"Coming up on eight months."

Sparkle tsked. "Long time without meeting the parents."

"It is. That's why I'm sticking with the Thanksgiving staples."

"I hear you. They aren't vegetarians?"

She had a point. Anup's parents were immigrants from India. "They've lived in Cupertino for thirty years. They enjoy the occasional pot roast—and an annual turkey."

"So Anup tells you."

"Why would he lie?"

"I'm not saying he's lying. I'm just saying you should've met them your own self by now, that's all."

Damn it, Sparkle. Nothing gets by that woman.

"Well, we're all getting together to break bread over Thanksgiving, and I'm confident they'll find me lovely and charming."

"No doubt, no doubt. How the heck are you going to do all the cooking in that silly little cable-car kitchen of yours, though?"

"I'm not. We're presenting the meal at Anup's place. I'm doing all the cooking, but in his kitchen."

"He gonna help?"

"So he says. Which of my recipes did you choose?"

"The sauerkraut thing, the corn pudding, and the dried-fruit poultry stuffing."

"Bold. Bold choices."

"I'm bringing it over to my mom's, bunch of cousins coming. No one to impress and nothing to prove."

That cracked me up. She joined in. I told Sparkle again how much I missed our semiregular lunches, back when I was working at the Hall of Justice. Now that I was deputy chief, though, and with our office still shorthanded, I just didn't have the time to go out. We made a date to meet up for dinner instead, over the weekend.

The address where Sparkle sent me to talk to her old client the cement man was near the Hyde Street Pier. I parked in Ghirardelli Square and dove into the sidewalk crowd, surfing the stream of tourists sweating in the unseasonable heat, past the quick-sketch artists and amateur jewelry makers, until I found the right spot. It was a tour company that rented out those horrible little three-wheeled, canary-yellow tourist buggies.

I shouted at the guy working the counter, asking for Sparkle's old client. He pointed to a mechanic who was bent over one of the machines. He was a dark-skinned Black man with short gray hair, wearing a jumpsuit the same ridiculous color as the buggy. He killed its engine and apologized for the noise.

I dropped Sparkle's name, and the man lit up, asked how she was doing, how was her mom. I said Sparkle was fine, and her mom was in good health and looking forward to having everybody around for Thanksgiving. Then I said I was looking for advice on concrete masonry, and heard he was an expert. He worked some degreaser into his hands, told the guy at the counter he was going on break, and agreed to a cup of coffee.

I suggested a famous tourist trap on the corner, but the cement mason didn't want to be indoors. We grabbed coffees from a cart instead, and sat on a shaded park bench, watching the snaking line of people at the cable-car turnaround. The mason asked me how I knew Sparkle and I told him. He reacted with the look some people take on when they find out I'm a medical examiner—the look of someone who has had to deal with our office. In the mason's case, he'd been arrested at a death scene.

"Painkiller addiction," he said. "It started with a work accident. Nothing serious, just everyday back pain that kept getting worse no matter what kind of brace I wore or how much lifting from the knees I did. So I went to the doctor and he gave me these pills, and…" The mason turned away from me. "Well, you must know the story. I'm lucky to still be breathing. Pills ran out, and I figured out how to buy them on the street. That got too expensive."

"So you started using heroin."

The mason turned away, put his eyes on the ferries and sail-boats playing tag in the bay, and said nothing.

I apologized. *Strzelić gafę*, my mother used to call it, my talent for putting my foot in my mouth.

"I lost my job, went way down in a hole. Had a couple of arrests. That's how I met Sparkle." He swirled his coffee. "Anyhow. I'm trying to get my union card back. This—" he pointed his chin back to the garage "—is temporary."

The mason asked why Sparkle was sending me to him. I showed him the bag of rocks.

"High-alumina cement," he said right away. "HAC for short. This mix is a structural concrete reinforced with polypropylene fibers. I'll bet it came out of a marine job, or someplace that has to handle high heating loads, right?"

"Well—no," I said, and kept to myself that Peter at the DBI had made the exact same assumption. "It has to do with one of the new high-rises going up South of Market."

"Which one?" the mason asked.

I balked. The case was restricted. That meant that I couldn't discuss anything about the cause and manner of death. It didn't mean I couldn't talk about things that were known to the public, and Haring's death had been all over the news.

"Before I tell you anything about this, I'm going to ask you to keep it confidential. Okay?"

"I'm no gossip," the mason said.

"Thanks. The death I'm investigating happened at a job site on the corner of Sixth and Folsom. It's supposed to be a building called SoMa Centre."

"That place," said the mason. "Oh, yes. That place is bent."

"Bent...?"

"Oh, yes," he said again, and nodded like he meant it. "Word gets around. I know people working that job."

The cement mason, who was no gossip, lowered his voice and held his coffee cup close to his lips. "The whole thing is rushed.

They've got deliveries down to the minute, tasks overlapping, heavy equipment always on the move. Everybody's racking up overtime, but they're still getting yelled at to pour on the speed. In my line of work, that's how people get hurt. Or dead. Wait— is this that big architect, the one all over the news?"

I told him I couldn't answer that question. Then I asked where on that site I might find the HAC aggregate being used—and what for.

"Well now, that's something *I* can't answer. Like I said, I would expect to find this in a wet job or a hot job, but SoMa Centre hasn't got anything like that going on. HAC is a specialist's material. The standard product you'll find for all kinds of masonry applications is good old Portland cement. Reliable stuff. I love working with it. But a concrete put together this way…well, it's different. Less forgiving. It cures three times faster than Portland cement. It's resistant to high heat, which is why you find it in industrial applications like furnaces and such. Where did you find it?"

Zipped inside a dead man's pocket? I couldn't tell him that, either, and said so. The mason bristled and reminded me that I had come to him seeking free advice. He turned the HAC over in his hand for a minute, then went on.

"It also makes a decent emergency patch—and in my line of work, if there's an emergency, it likely has to do with the foundation. My guess? Something's gone bad in the foundation work, and someone is trying to fix it quick or retrofit it."

"Is that a problem?"

"It can be. High-alumina cement is no substitute for properly poured, steel-reinforced Portland cement concrete. If you don't mix HAC just right, it gets compromised when it sets. If you pour it next to Portland concrete that hasn't fully cured, it can crack. It's a great material for certain jobs, but it's finicky."

He handed the evidence baggie back to me. "My opinion? Something ain't right. You use this stuff when you're in a hurry.

And if you're in a hurry, at the stage of construction where they're at now—? Something ain't right."

I thought about Peter at the DBI, and his tight-lipped reaction when I'd told him where the rocky stuff had come from.

Something ain't right.

"What do you know about the Department of Building Inspection?" I asked Anup, right when the soup dumplings arrived.

We were out to dinner at one of our favorite local joints, House of Shanghai Taste—eight tables in a narrow glass storefront looking onto Balboa Street, with its dozen other restaurants, a yoga studio, a bakery, a florist, the two banks and the corner store and the bait-and-tackle shop. Directly across the street was the neighborhood's anchoring landmark, a marquee cinema with a towering, blinking-neon sign. It had taken some getting used to after the move from Los Angeles, but I had grown to love the windswept, fog-bitten Outer Richmond District.

The lady at House of Shanghai Taste serves the soup dumplings, ten to an order, in a bamboo steamer, with a soy-ginger sauce on the side. The challenge with soup dumplings is the patience required to allow them to cool to a nonscalding temperature.

"Why you want to know about DBI?" Anup said. Lawyers. They always answer a question with a question. Prosecutors—or former prosecutors, like Anup—never fail to pull this stunt. Putting you off guard is a reflex.

"I dunno," I said. "I mean, I'm sure there's graft there, right?"

"Hard to imagine there isn't some."

"So...how much? What kind?"

Anup dug into a plate of cold jellyfish salad. The man would eat anything. He claimed to enjoy cold jellyfish. I grew up stepping on dead jellyfish on the beach at Lynn Shore Drive. I stared down the soup dumplings and willed them to cool.

"Not really my area," Anup mumbled through his chopsticks.

"Did you ever charge anyone from DBI?"

"That's the City Attorney's Office. Civil litigation."

"You don't remember *any* criminal cases having to do with construction? You were at the DA's office for five years, Anup."

"It's hard to prosecute cases like that unless there's real, de-monstrable, one-sided negligence. What you'll typically find instead is a jumble of bad actors and incompetence. Everybody points fingers at everybody else, and they all end up getting off. Until it goes to civil litigation, and then they all get screwed."

He picked up the special spoon, oblong and flat-bottomed like a miniature dinghy, and coaxed one of the soup dumplings onto it.

"Too soon," I warned.

"The major players in the construction industry are all big donors—to the mayor's campaign, the Board of Supervisors. The district attorney." He shrugged cynically, blew on his dinghy spoon. "Let's put it this way—there might be an investigation, but no one's ever going to see an indictment."

Anup dribbled a little of the ginger sauce onto his soup dump-ling and tipped it into his mouth. Then he did that thing you do, opening your mouth and flapping your hands and whistling out steam, when you're impatient with soup dumplings.

"Told you so," I said.

Anup had left the DA's office because he'd seen too many rich and powerful white-collar miscreants skate, and too many poor people, too many emotionally disturbed people, too many newcomers who didn't speak the language and couldn't work the system, too many drug addicts and sex workers and home-less and hopeless San Franciscans ending up with prison time instead. He used to believe it was a long game—that he or one of his colleagues would be able to build cases that would punish the powerful scofflaws one way or another, if they just had enough time and patience. He had run out of one and got tired of wasting the other. When he made the move out of the DA's office, he was able to pursue the area of the law he really loved: appeals of factual innocence. Exoneration.

I gazed at Anup, gulping down his hot dumpling. Even grimacing, he was a handsome man—huge eyes, long lashes, deep brown skin. Soft cheekbones spaced wide beside a slender nose. I had fallen for Anup more than a year before, when we were working a case together, and found myself falling more passionately as time went on. Under his sharp, quick-witted facade was a soulful, caring, righteous person.

"I love you, Anup," I said. "You silly creature."

Anup dabbed his brow with his napkin and scooped another soup dumpling. "Why, how nice of you to say, Doctor." He looked right at me with those big brown eyes, and I melted. "I love you too."

The realization came suddenly: we weren't spending enough time together, enough time like this, happy and relaxed, over a meal. The added responsibility of carrying the Deputy Chief Medical Examiner badge meant that the task of running the shorthanded morgue fell mostly on me. Anup sometimes accused me of caring about the job more than I cared about him. That was unfair, and would start us fighting. It was like blaming me for bad weather, I would tell him. Like blaming me for the summer fog.

I scooped a dumpling of my own, and sauced it, and waited. "I talked to Sparkle today," I said. "She gave me a couple more recipes."

Anup's smile dropped off, and his gaze retreated.

"What's wrong?"

"Nothing," he said.

"It's not nothing. This happens every time I mention Thanksgiving. What is it?"

"Nothing. I just don't want to talk about it."

"It's exciting!"

"If you say so."

"I do say so! We're going to have candied yams and collard greens and scalloped spuds… Do you think your parents will like that?"

Anup took another soup dumpling. "I'm sure it'll be fine."

"Well, good. Because if it isn't, you just have to tell me, and I'll—"

"It'll be fine."

"Okay. I'm going to go to that fancy meat market in Laurel Village and get a natural bird. I'll aim for one on the small side, maybe twelve to fifteen pounds, if they can—"

I was stopped by a thud and a jolt. Anup bobbled his dumpling and it splashed open on his plate.

"What…" he said.

That's when the real shock, the one the news people would talk about later as the shear wave front, hit. Something tossed me straight up in the air and I landed on the floor, my chair on top of me. The chair was jumping around. The floor was lurching. It sounded like a freight train was running across the restaurant's roof.

"Earthquake!" somebody yelled.

I flipped onto my belly, saw that our table was still standing, and crawled toward it. Anup was already under there. He grabbed me and pulled me in.

The shaking got worse. People were screaming. Glass shattered somewhere close. The freight train roar was all around us, deafening, dizzying.

"This is bad!" Anup was yelling, right in my ear. "This is real bad!" He kept hollering that over and over. The earthquake was somehow jerking us up and down and back and forth all at once. It felt as if a giant had grabbed House of Shanghai Taste and was shaking it to see what would fall out. Plates and cutlery tumbled around us. Tepid tea was dribbling off the table into my hair. I brushed it back and turned to look outside, through the restaurant's glass door that now had a huge diagonal crack. The apartment building across the street had scaffolding, for a paint job. It was swaying crazily. While I watched, it came crashing down. I tried to see if anyone was under it, but the room was still shaking so much that I couldn't focus.

The lights went out—in the restaurant, on the street, over the marquee cinema, everywhere. The screaming around us got louder and more hysterical. A blue-white flash lit the darkness and hung there, trembling atop a telephone pole, till it flared out in a blossom of sparks and a sharp boom. There was another flash and boom, and then another, and another, marching east up Balboa Street. I remembered learning about that from my disaster training as deputy chief medical examiner: overloaded electrical transformers, exploding in a chain reaction.

I clung to Anup. I couldn't see him, even skin to skin, in the total darkness. Under the earthquake's rumble I could hear the building's timbers groaning like a ship in a gale. I tried to yell that we had to get out before the roof came down on us, but I could hardly hear myself, much less if he was responding.

And then, just like that, it stopped.

CHAPTER 4

It seemed like everyone in the restaurant got their phones out and the tiny flashlights on all at once. Anup was already on his feet and had gone to help a woman pinned under a toppled table.

I didn't help. My head was still swaying. I didn't get up, didn't move. I just sat there on the floor of House of Shanghai Taste. I wasn't sure the floor was staying put the way it ought to. I looked out the restaurant's full-length windows and saw nothing. Half a dozen car alarms chimed over one another from the blackness. I felt somehow like I was out on the street, watching myself in the restaurant.

"I'm in shock," I said—and, saying it, came out of it.

Was I injured? I did a quick check of myself. It seemed I was okay. My right elbow ached, but I could move it just fine. I might've landed on it when I went flying out of my chair. I pulled out my own phone and shined it around. People around me were hurt. Some were bleeding. I got to my feet.

I went first to an older man whose head was smeared with

fresh blood. It was in his eyes and he was blinded by it. Turned out to be a cut to his brow. Those bleed like stink, and look worse than they are. I got him to apply direct pressure to the wound with a napkin.

"Jessie…" It was Anup's voice, calling from the back of the restaurant. I shined my feeble light and caught him. He was standing in the pass-through behind the counter. "We need you back here. Now."

I pushed through the broken plates and scattered food, the upturned tables and the chairs that had bounced across the restaurant. When I got to the counter, I heard screaming from the room beyond.

It was the kitchen. A clutch of figures huddled around a cook who was lying on the wet floor, writhing in pain, shrieking in Chinese. Next to him was a cauldron, upended, steam still rising around it.

I took a quick assessment. The cook's legs and feet were the affected area. His head and upper torso seemed uninjured. I pointed to the closest guy in an apron and demanded, "Was that oil or water in that pot?"

The poor guy didn't speak English, and just looked back at me in a panic. But another kitchen worker, a teenager, said, "It was boiling water. Landed right on his legs…"

I marched straight over to the dishwashing station and turned on the tap. Water flowed. I squeezed the spray hose. It worked, and the water was good and cool. I turned down the volume till it was a gentle rain, then turned the hose on the cook.

"What's your name?" I asked the teenager.

"Terrence."

"What's his name, Terrence?" I said, sprinkling water over the man's legs. He was howling in pain and gasping for breath.

"Wen."

"Okay. You can talk to him?"

"Yes."

"Then tell Wen that we're going to take off his shoes and socks and pants, and then I'm going to treat his burns. I'm a doctor. Ask Wen if this is okay by him."

Terrence translated. The cook nodded. He couldn't speak for screaming, but he nodded.

"Get somebody to find the first aid kit. There must be one somewhere. And get somebody to find me a big pile of clean dish towels."

Terrence, God bless the kid, started barking orders in Chinese and strong-arming his coworkers. Wen had bitten through his lower lip, and it was bleeding. He might be going into shock. That would be a bad complication. I mimed for one of the workers to take the spray from me and keep it on him.

Somebody came running back with the first aid kit. It was a good one. I donned the gloves that I found in there and prepped the burn cream and gauze. I got Terrence to hand me a scissors, and cut the cook's trousers off him. The guy with the spray asked Terrence something in Chinese.

"Should he stop?"

"No—tell him to keep it up till I tell him to quit."

Terrence did. Then I got him to help me remove Wen's shoes and socks. Wen's agonized howls got louder. One of his buddies cradled his head and said something soothing. I signaled to the guy with the hose to shut it off.

"Get a couple of these guys to shine their phones on his legs," I said. I took one of the dish towels off the worker who'd come back with them and started patting down the affected areas, gently. The burns stretched from the middle of his thighs all the way to his toes. I applied a little bit of the burn cream to them, then wrapped both his legs loosely in gauze.

I asked Terrence if anyone had called 911. He said they'd tried, but their cells weren't working.

"You have a car?" I said.

Terrence pointed to the guy holding the towels. "He does."

"All right. Listen. Your friend here is going to be okay for now, but you need to carry him carefully out to the car, then drive him to the St. Francis Hospital emergency room. St. Francis Hospital, corner of Bush and Hyde. They're the best burn ward. Bush and Hyde—you got it?"

"I got it," said Terrence. Then he said something in Chinese to the guy with the dish towels, who said something to the guy cradling Wen's head. The three of them lifted him gently and started for the back door.

I slumped onto the floor and peeled off the gloves slicked with burn cream and Wen's dead skin. I was soaked through from the dishwashing spray. As I pulled myself to my feet, it occurred to me that the only available light in the restaurant kitchen came from the cell phones shuffling out the door with the workers. I felt my way gingerly through the pots and pans littering the wet floor, back to the dining room of the House of Shanghai Taste. Anup was still doing triage on some people.

"Is he okay?" he asked. I told him yes. He brought me to the couple of more serious casualties among the customers. One was a kid, maybe ten, with a broken arm. I sent Anup to the kitchen for a wooden spoon, and splinted it with that and a couple of cloth napkins I secured with oversize surgeon's knots. Three other people had cuts. The first aid kit contained everything I needed to bandage or patch them up.

One customer, a white woman with piles of beautiful gray hair, was beyond our help. She seemed to be fine, physically— but she was freaking out.

"Earthquake weather! I've been saying it since the winds came... Hot and dry, eighty degrees, and it's nearly Halloween? Earthquake weather!"

Everyone else ignored her.

Balboa Street outside House of Shanghai Taste was transformed and terrifying. First there was the darkness. It was total.

I'd never experienced anything like it with pavement under-foot and buildings around me. A car came creeping down the road, its headlights cutting into everything and throwing out shifting shadows, and I could see downed power lines, draped like snakes over parked cars and buildings, lying in ambush on the sidewalk. The car had its windows open and the radio on. A DJ babbled in panic.

"I don't know if anyone out there can hear me... The lights are out but my board is still lit up here, so, maybe... Um, any-way, I can't say how bad the damage is, but it must be pretty se-vere, so everybody out there, um, please stay safe and..."

The car was gone, and we were in the dark again, but Anup had spotted a police car parked outside the block's biggest cof-fee house. We made our way to it, holding hands and stepping with care—the bricks from a nearby building had tumbled off their facade and were piled in the street.

The barista had lit up a battery lantern on the counter. I told her I was a doctor and a first responder, and needed their land-line if it was working. It wasn't.

"None of them will be," said Anup.

I peered into the recesses of the ruined café. "Do you see that cop? Maybe I can use his radio."

"What for?"

"I need to reach Dr. Howe."

"*That's* what you're worried about? I figured you were trying to reach Tommy or something! Jessie, this was a goddamn big quake. I'll bet there's buildings down, fires breaking out every-where. And what if that was only the foreshock?"

"I still have to check in with the chief. The OCME has its own emergency generator, and whoever is working the Ops Shop will know what's going on."

"Please, Jessie—"

Someone with a bright flashlight was coming through the café. It was the patrol cop, leading a couple of customers out. I joined them and told him who I was, and that I needed to use his radio.

He was skeptical. "Where's your badge?"

"At my house."

"You got any official ID?"

"Officer, what do you think I'm trying to pull, here? Will you just take a moment to call dispatch, please, and let me talk to them?"

He thought about it, and decided that he'd better trust me. So he keyed up the dispatcher from his car's radio and said he had a medical examiner who needed to talk to them.

He handed me the mic. "This is Dr. Jessie Teska, Deputy Chief Medical Examiner, star one-zero-two, call number zero-echo-three."

"Copy," said the dispatcher. I heard the clatter of fast fingers on a keyboard, then, "Go ahead, Dr. Teska."

"I need to know if you've logged any activity involving the medical examiner since the earthquake hit."

The fingers danced on keys again, and the voice came back. "The ME reported at 2115 hours out to a scene after Fire Eight radioed in one known fatality, unknown possible others."

"What's the scene?"

"Collapsed road structure." She told me where.

Boże mój.

I handed the mic back to the cop, shook off the dread, and started down the avenue toward Mahoney Brothers #45, my silly little cable-car house. I hoped to hell it was still standing. I hoped too that nothing had fallen onto my BMW. I was going to need it.

"Jessie—!"

Anup hustled to catch up. We walked right down the middle of the street, staying clear of downed wires and line after line of terracotta roof tiles that had slid off the houses and shattered. I had my sad little cell phone light, but soon found I didn't need it—the sky was clear, and my eyes adjusted to the light of the crescent moon. The stars overhead looked like the high desert way outside Los Angeles. I could see the Milky Way. I'd never seen the Milky Way under city skies before, not that much of it, anyhow.

"We'll never forget this," I said over my shoulder. "Do you realize that? This is an event we will never forget."

"We're going home, right? To your house, I mean?"

"No, Anup. I'm going to get my badge and my car keys. Then I have to go to work."

"What do you mean?"

"Mission Bay. The 280 off-ramp to King Street."

"I don't understand."

"It's collapsed."

Anup made his way in front of me, held out a hand to stop me. "And you want to go there…? A freeway collapse? What could you possibly do to help?"

I sidestepped him. "I don't know what. That's exactly why I have to go. They dispatched the van twenty minutes ago, because the fire department confirmed one person dead. There might be more. I have to evaluate the scene so we can marshal resources if this earthquake turns out to be a mass-casualty event…"

"That's not your job—it's Dr. Howe's, he's the chief. It's the other end of the city… There are no streetlights, no stoplights— and, apparently, roads are collapsing? It'll be like *Mad Max* out there! Please, don't do this."

"I have to." I kept marching down the middle of the avenue. "Without phones, I can't call Dr. Howe for instructions. I don't know who is at our office, or if I can even get in there if the power's down—everything operates on electronic locks in the new building…"

We reached the corner of Cabrillo Street and a sound stopped me. It was a single car, hauling ass down the road. I grabbed

Anup's arm and stepped back. The car blew right through two stop signs and just kept going.

Bad omen. Anup sure thought so.

"Look. Everyone's in a panic," he said, putting on the good-cop prosecutor's voice he seldom attempted with me. "I know you have responsibilities as an emergency worker. I understand, believe me. But let's stay together and hunker down until it's safe for you to go to work, okay? At least until the power comes back on…"

"I don't know when that will be, and already there's a con-firmed death resulting from this event. My crew is down there right now, or heading there—"

"That's exactly my point! Let them work the scene—that's their job—and you do your job in the morgue, in the morning."

We made it to 41st Avenue and turned the corner. Down the end of the block, the tree line of Golden Gate Park swal-lowed the thin moonlight and loomed like a black wall. Some of my neighbors were out on their stoops, trading rumors. I didn't want to get pulled into all that, so I made a beeline for my Beemer—which, thank Christ, was parked, intact, outside the gate to number 892, my cable-car cottage.

Something occurred to me when I pulled out the gate key.

"Anup… I'm going down there. I know you don't want me to. But I have to ask you to do something for me. Will you take care of Bea?"

"All this going on—what we just did in that restaurant—and you're worried about the *dog*?"

"I can't leave her alone—and I… I don't know for sure when I'll be able to get back."

Anup didn't say anything. He was looking at me in a way I hadn't seen from him before. I didn't like it. It was like the time Father Kabaty figured out I'd been skipping Mass at St. Michael's and lying to my *mamusia* about it. That was the look. Grave disappointment.

"I'll do it for Bea's sake," Anup said.

Anup wasn't wrong about the *Mad Max* chaos on the night-time streets of San Francisco, with no light and no laws, in the wake of the earthquake. The traffic signals were mostly dead. Some cars were creeping along, others were flying by, weaving all over the road. Complicating this anarchy was the amount of debris in the way. Downed wires were the scariest—I passed a toppled stanchion for an electric Muni bus that was sparking wildly. Hauling ass along the edge of Golden Gate Park, I spotted three or four small fires and one big one glowing in the distance. Red lights and sirens sped toward it. There were plenty of flashing lights, red and blue, here, there, and everywhere.

A couple of radio stations had their own emergency power and were still transmitting. Official estimates put the magnitude at 6.5, the epicenter on the Hayward fault in the Berkeley Hills. They were reporting sizable aftershocks but no tsunami danger, which was a relief. I had to shut off the news updates, though, because it suddenly occurred to me, sometime after I'd passed the edge of the Panhandle, that I wasn't certain where I was. I'd worked in San Francisco for nearly a year and a half, and had driven to death scenes in most every corner of the city—but without light there seemed to be no landmarks, and I couldn't read the road signs until I was right on top of them. Every block looked the same, and the last thing I wanted to do was to end up lost.

I started to hit police roadblocks. Red flares, white smoke, nervous cops. One checkpoint on Market Street had a SWAT team in full tactical gear, assault rifles at the ready, backed by an armored personnel carrier. My badge got me through—though the SWAT guys glared like I had no business crossing their lines.

As I got closer to the scene, more and brighter emergency lights flashed up and down the canyons of spanking new housing blocks in Mission Bay. They lit up the condos and the cars parked along Berry Street, and blinked off windows and windshields. I had to stop my Beemer before they blinded me. Countless police vehicles, a couple of ambulances, and half a dozen fire trucks—maybe more—were jumbled at an alley beside the soaring 280 freeway overpass. Two trucks had their ladders extended. I could make out geared-up and helmeted silhouettes clambering the ladders onto the ramp that climbed away from King Street to the freeway.

Used to climb from King Street. I sat in the Beemer and let it sink in that the ramp no longer did. A piece of the viaduct between the surface road and the ladder trucks was missing.

I left the car and jogged across the scene, scanning for the OCME van. Down on the pavement, a pair of paramedics were working on a man covered head to toe in gray dust, one putting an IV line into him, the other ventilating with a bag valve mask. A line of firefighters with pry bars and a hydraulic spreader ran past me and disappeared behind a truck. When I rounded it, I saw where they were going. A section of the viaduct had collapsed into rubble. The broken roadway loomed above, rebar sticking out, pebbles of concrete still falling. The stretch below it was fifty or sixty yards of pancaked pavement crawling with rescue workers.

I found the medical examiner removal van, and, with it, Cameron and Donna. They had one body loaded in the van already, they told me.

"The medics called it—crush injuries with evisceration of major organs," Cam said.

Donna added, "They think it was someone sleeping on the street—" But my screech cut her off. I'd screeched because there was another earthquake—another rattle, another rumble, and the alleyway under my feet jumped around. It lasted only a second.

"Aftershock," said Cam. "We've had a bunch."

"That was a pretty good one," said Donna.

I stared at the pair of them. They were leaning against their van, which was still bouncing on its springs in the middle of an ongoing disaster scene, and they were shooting the shit about earthquakes like earthquakes were the fucking weather.

"Hey," hollered one of the paramedics who had been trying to revive the downed man. "We're calling it."

"That's our cue," said Donna, and grabbed a gurney.

Cam pulled out his camera and started taking pictures, documenting what had just become our second case at that death scene. The paramedics peeled off their gloves and packed their gear, preparing for whatever else might come out of the rubble. Police dogs scrambled over it, followed by their handlers. The rescue dogs were working hard, sticking their heads into crevasses, staying focused, moving quickly. One was a beagle and I thought of my own Bea, back at home in Mahoney Brothers #45, worrying by candlelight with Anup.

I made my way to the fire department command vehicle. The captain was there, and filled me in.

"First casualty was DOA, and we've got three others, two with multiple blunt trauma and one with minor injuries—"

"The medics just called time of death on one."

"Okay," the captain said, and seemed to check off a box in his head. "The other trauma's on his way to the General Hospital, but the guy with minor injuries won't leave. He says this was a homeless camp, a big one. He's got friends under there."

"The camp was under the viaduct?"

"That's what he says. PD confirms."

"The guy on his way to the General—what were the extent of his injuries?"

The fire captain stopped scanning the rescue operation and looked at me. "Multiple blunt trauma, like I said."

"Yeah, but—are they likely to be fatal?"

"I can't say, Doctor. I have *living* people to worry about here."

"Sorry—I'm just trying to get a handle on what our operation is going to entail…"

A voice on the pile yelled something, and the fire captain turned. The voice yelled again, louder.

"Foot!"

The captain ran, and I followed. The rescue beagle was sitting at attention on the pile. Firefighters and cops started working a bucket brigade, carrying out whatever pieces of concrete they could. Three others got pry bars under a slab and lifted it. Someone shined a light.

In the space under the slab was a human figure crushed to pieces.

The fire captain stood with his crew, opposite. I met his eyes. I steeled myself to face his anger, but it wasn't there. The fire captain was scared.

I climbed off the pile and made my way to the 2578s, to tell them we had another one. Donna pointed out they only had room for two bodies per removal van, and they only had one of the two vans there.

"We're allowed to commandeer ambulances in multiple-fatality incidents," she suggested.

"No way," I said. "This city is going to need all the ambulances it can get for the living casualties." I grabbed a pair of work gloves from the van. "I'm staying here to help recover number three. You guys drop numbers one and two in the cooler, then turn around with both vans and come straight back. Okay?"

The 2578s started up the van and flipped on its flashing yellow lights. As I made my way back to the pile, I took in the jarringly beautiful view of downtown San Francisco. A handful of the skyscrapers must've managed some kind of backup power, because they had some windows lit. The rest were flickering in reflected emergency lights from the street, the reds and blues melding to purple across the mile or so of darkness that separated us from them.

I pulled on the gloves and joined the bucket brigade hauling chunks of concrete off the spot where the King Street viaduct's third victim lay buried. We had almost succeeded in clearing access to the body when a commotion rose from another crew near us. Voices called for medics. The two paramedics scrambled over to a scrum of firefighters, and I followed. They were shining their lights into the rubble, shouting, asking if anyone down there could hear them.

In the hole they'd uncovered I could see a pile of at least five people, maybe more. They weren't moving. They didn't respond to the shouts.

I stuck by the medics. If there was anything I could do with my medical training to help the living, I would. If they were dead, I would follow my disaster protocol to do what I needed to do with the bodies until I could get them back to the morgue.

The medics climbed into the hole and tried to evaluate the nearest patient. I followed. It was all right. It was going to be okay. My training had prepared me for this and worse. I wasn't scared. I wasn't nervous. I was ready to do my job.

The rescue dogs started barking, all at once. Then there was a deep thump and a jolt. Another aftershock hit—I braced my arms against the rubble as dust and pebbles fell on my shoulders and a ripple of force went through my legs.

From above I heard something slide. Then I saw shooting stars and my skull exploded in pain and…

CHAPTER 5

I was in bed. It wasn't my bed. It smelled funny. Like plastic.

I opened my eyes. A fluorescent room. Sterile. I tried to turn my head, but a blast of pain stopped me and I gasped.

"Why, hello there, you. Take it easy, okay? Good to see your eyes open. Just take it easy."

A vampire. It was a vampire woman talking to me. That's what I saw. My head throbbed and my vision went blurry for a moment, but I definitely wasn't imagining the vampire. Unless she wasn't there. Maybe I was dreaming? If I was dreaming, why did my head hurt so bad?

"Hurts wicked bad," I said.

"Okay, honey, just take it easy," the vampire woman said.

The fluorescent lights flickered and went out. The vampire looked up anxiously. The lights came right back on. She turned and walked away.

From behind she looked like a nurse.

I craned my neck and looked around. I was in a hospital bed, in a room with a bunch of other beds, all of them occupied. I was in a paper gown. The nurse was in a vampire costume.

"Halloween," I said.

"Tomorrow, honey," the nurse said over her shoulder. "You won't be going trick-or-treating this year." She laughed. She thought that was hysterical, the vampire nurse did.

There was an IV in my left arm and monitor leads on my chest. Something covered the top of my head. I lifted my right arm, felt it. Bandages. A big wad of ACE bandages, like a character in a Saturday morning cartoon who'd got clocked on the noggin.

"Wicked bad," I said again.

"That's the spirit, honey," said the nurse.

I tried to sit up. Jesus, but it was hard. "Where am I?"

"Still in the emergency room."

San Francisco General Hospital. I recognized the grimy windows, the rickety old operable beds. The walls were absolutely crawling with Halloween decorations. It was… What was it?

"Unseemly," I said.

"Just take it easy, honey."

"Wha happen?"

"You took a blow to the head."

Man, did it hurt. And I was so woozy. I wondered if they'd given me a sedative or something. I tried to ask, but it came out gibberish, and the nurse just said again, in that deathly patronizing way they have, that I should take it easy.

I took a moment and concentrated. I looked the nurse in the eye, and spoke slowly. "How long was I out?"

"Please, honey, you don't need to worry about—"

"I'm an MD. What's my Glasgow Coma Scale?"

The vampire nurse sighed and trundled over to a computer. "Well, *Doctor*. You were unresponsive to stimuli for an hour, and the paramedics scored you a GCS of three. When you came to, you were in a minimally conscious state at a GCS of ten, and graduated up to eleven—but then you became combative right after the CT scan, and had to be restrained and sedated."

So I *was* gorked out on sedatives. I could shake that off. A head injury was a different story.

The nurse clicked another page in my electronic medical chart. "Says here that you were responding to verbal stimuli sporadically, mostly in Russian."

"Polish. What'd the CT show?"

"I don't know. You can ask the radiologist later, if you'd like."

"What time is it?"

"Four."

"In the morning?"

"Yes, honey, in the morning."

"How long have I been here?"

The nurse checked the chart.

"Four and a half hours. Now, will you please take it easy? Don't tax yourself…"

"How come you have lights? Is the power back up? What's going on with the quake…?"

The lights flickered again—then went out. The darkness was total for a few seconds, long enough for somebody at the far end of the crowded ward to start screaming about another earthquake, and then the power came back on.

"Darn generator," the vampire nurse muttered.

A generator. I remembered another detail from my disaster protocol training: San Francisco General Hospital has its own emergency power plant.

The Office of Chief Medical Examiner does, too.

"I have to get out of here," I announced. I forced myself up. The pain got worse, but it was only pain. The room wasn't spinning. I wasn't nauseated. My ears weren't ringing.

"Whoa, hold it, there."

"Take out this IV. I have to go."

"No way. You have a head injury—"

"I'm a first responder. And I'm fine to ambulate out of here, so pull this IV line right now."

"Need help?" a man's voice said from somewhere.

"No, Doctor, I've got it," said the vampire nurse.

"Doctor—!" I yelled. "Are you the attending?"

A man appeared from around the flimsy privacy curtain between my bed and the next one. He wasn't in costume—not unless ugly-ass glasses and a blond weasel of a haircut counts as a costume.

"I'm the chief resident."

"Good enough. I'm Dr. Teska, Deputy Chief Medical Examiner, and I need to get out of here. I have mandated disaster duties at the morgue, and we're short-staffed on a good day. Get this IV out of my arm."

"You don't remember me?" the resident said.

"No."

"I stitched up your head."

"Oh…! Oh, right. That was you." I put my hand up to my bandage, palpated it. "I couldn't see you all that well."

That was a lie. The resident wasn't fooled, but didn't want to call me on it.

"You've sustained a traumatic brain injury, Dr. Teska. We've had a busy night and we're short on trauma beds, but we've got you on the list. You need to remain under observation for at least the rest of today and maybe one more overnight."

"No way. Nope. What kind of TBI? Show me the scans."

"The scans?"

"You did CT imaging. Show it to me."

"You're a pathologist, right?"

"I interpret radiology every single day, Doctor, just like you do. You want me to believe I've got a brain injury? Prove it."

The young doctor with the weasel hair tried to stare me down. I outlasted him. He shrugged, went to the computer, and conjured a bunch of black-and-white blobs onto the monitor.

"Okay. Come on over and we'll take a look."

I swung my legs over the side of the bed. The pain in my head came back, but I ignored it. I couldn't get my feet on the floor, though—the IV line in my arm and the monitor leads on my chest got all tangled up.

"Elissa," the doctor said to the nurse, "would you help her, please."

Oh, you crafty bastard, I thought. It was a trap. He was assessing my neurological status.

"No, thank you," I said to Elissa the vampire nurse. "I'm fine on my own." I calmly arranged the tubes and wires, and grabbed hold of the IV stand to roll it with me.

I hobbled four steps. My head threatened to explode. I pretended not to feel it. I wasn't dizzy or weak in the knees. The trouble was only in my head. There was a whole crew of little tiny construction workers crammed in there. They were all built like the muscly young man at the SoMa Centre gate, and they were all swinging sledgehammers against the inside of the left side of my skull, except for the pair with the jackhammers and the one little fucker who I swear to God was wiring up a dynamite charge.

I made it to the computer scanner and studied it with what I hoped was a suitably thoughtful and professional mien. I clicked over the CT images of my very own skull and brain.

"This all looks normal," I said, and pointed with the computer mouse to one spot with a thick gray band over the thin white bone. "A little soft tissue swelling on the scalp here." I reached up and touched the spot under the bandage. "So it's a scalp laceration with sub-Q edema. No big deal."

"Oh, come on." The chief resident was losing patience. "Not all TBIs present with intracerebral hemorrhage. You walk out of here, you could develop a brain bleed. They never taught you that in autopsy school?" He stuck his ugly glasses closer to my face and spoke very slowly. "Brain bleed bad. Right?"

I had several violently unkind thoughts. I buried them, and

smiled as sweetly as the pain in my head allowed. "Watch," I said. I walked toe-to-heel, balancing in a steady line, back to the bed. I sat on it and turned to nurse Elissa. I held out both my hands, fingers stretched wide. "Test my motor strength," I told her. "I dare you."

The nurse balked and looked to the doctor.

"Hey, lookit this…!" I stuck my tongue way out. "Intact cranial nerves!"

The ER doctor scowled.

"What's the story with the two other casualties that came in just before me?" I said.

"What do you mean?"

"Are they expected to survive."

The ER resident was taken aback. "Yes."

"Good—that's two fewer cases for us to handle at the morgue. We already have plenty. Am I getting through to you, Doctor? I need to get over to the OCME and get to work, and I'll sign out against medical advice if I have to. I don't give a damn."

The doctor came to the bed and pointed a penlight in my eyes, told me to squeeze his fingers with both hands, and all that. Garden-variety neurological assessment. Apparently I passed. He returned to the computer, typed something, and said, "Elissa, we need this bed. Would you please get this woman out of my emergency room?" Across the room, I heard a printer whine.

The nurse gave me one last look up and down, more in sorrow than in anger, and went off in the direction of the printer.

I looked around for my personal belongings. The little men in my skull were still hammering away, but I was getting used to them.

***

I needed my cell phone flashlight to make it safely across the carriageway circle in the hospital courtyard. I thought sunrise should be due around 7:30, but there was no hint of it. The city felt like it was hunkering down, waiting out the stifling Diablo winds that still hadn't let up.

The cab stand was empty. I pulled out my phone to get an Uber. It took a few seconds of puzzled peering at the thing before I remembered it was good for nothing without signal or Wi-Fi or some other tether to the vast ocean of data that the world outside the disaster area floated across.

A man in a rent-a-cop jacket stood next to a dinky white car with a security logo. His hands were buried in his pockets and he wore a black watch cap. I hobbled over to him. We were the only souls around.

I showed him my badge, gave him my spiel about being a first responder. "We're in a state of emergency. I need you to drive me to the medical examiner's office down at One Newhall."

The security guard thought about it. On the one hand, we both knew he didn't *need* to do one damn thing for me, badge or no. On the other hand, it was cold out and he was bored as shit.

"Okay," he said, finally, and climbed into the dinky car.

It was a scary drive. The roads were still ink black and the security guard took it slow. I spotted the OCME from a mile away, lit up like a ship in a dark sea. It was only when we'd pulled right up in front that it occurred to me I had another problem to solve.

"Hey," I said to the security guard. "I'll give you ten bucks for that hat."

He put the car in park and looked at me, amused. His eyes went to the bandages on my head. No fool, this guy.

"Let me see that badge of yours again," he said. I held it out. He admired it. "Gold shield. That means you're brass, huh? Management?"

"I'm the deputy chief."

"Okay, then," he said. "Twenty bucks."

Bałwan. I pocketed the badge and opened my wallet. The security guard smiled.

I went straight to Dr. Howe's office and was relieved to find him there, presiding over the usual clutter of paperwork and stray bits of old evidence spread across his huge oak desk.

"Where have you been?" he barked.

I didn't even need to lie. "I was at the General."

He grunted. "What's going on over there?"

"Two guys they pulled out of the rubble of the King Street viaduct collapse are doing okay, expected to live."

"That's good. We've got ten other bodies out of there to deal with, right now—but there are multiple eight-oh-one calls all across the city, and we're going to have a lot more coming. We've got radio comms back, at least. Dr. Nguyen is here, but Yarina can't…"

Howe's eyes drifted north of mine. "Why are you wearing that hat?"

"It's cold in here," I said.

Again Howe grunted. "The damn HVAC. It's still wonky, running hot and cold, never quite right."

"It's probably the generator power supply. Messes with the computer controls."

"I don't care what the reason is. This is not a good time for a climate-control malfunction in the morgue!"

Dr. Howe debriefed me on the logistical nightmares that had followed the earthquake. Most of the OCME's staff lived outside San Francisco and couldn't get into the city. The Bay Bridge was shut down for evaluation. The BART subway, too. The freeways had jammed up and road rage had devolved into gunplay so fast that CHP had decided to close most on-ramps. Some drivers had tried to run around the roadblocks and nearly got themselves shot.

"The 2578s are reporting that it's not quite martial law yet, but it's close," the chief said. "Phones are still mostly down, but texting is starting to work. I got word to UCSF that they should send us some medical students to work as emergency morgue techs. A couple are gowning up now."

Howe looked tired and anxious. I didn't like it. Lord knows I have issues with that man. He's a managerial bully and a Machiavellian political operative. But he's also a fine doctor and a personally decent human being; most of the time, at least.

I crossed the room to his desk and surprised the hell out of the old goat by chucking him on the shoulder.

"Then what are we waiting for, Chief?" I said.

Luckily I had the women's locker room to myself when I doffed my twenty dollar hat and pulled a surgical cap over the bandages. The headache was still there, and still bad. I kept worrying whether that ER resident was right. The pain could be a sign of a delayed subdural hemorrhage growing slowly into a hematoma. If that's what was going on, the blood could keep pressing my brain against my skull until I blacked out and died. I pictured myself falling over, right on top of whatever corpse I was cutting into.

Saves on transport, anyhow.

Ted Nguyen and I had to do five fatalities each from the viaduct collapse. Two others were ordinary cases, a suicide and a maybe-overdose, left over from the regular prequake caseload. Dr. Howe himself suited up in PPEs to cut those cases, clearing the way for me and Ted to do the more important quake-related ones—the ones the media and the politicians would be asking about. I felt for the poor med student Dr. Howe picked to assist him, but was delighted to find that the other student was Patty Alvarez, the quick-witted one with the excellent hair.

Howe finished fast and headed out to visit the viaduct disaster area, which he hadn't yet seen. Alvarez and I started on the disaster victims. Our first two were men who had died of over-whelming blunt trauma, with evisceration of brain material and disarticulation of limbs. The third, a woman, was less horrible, but no less dead. There was concrete dust in her hair, and bits of it embedded in her scalp. She'd suffered a single blow to the head. It had cracked her skull and caused a giant subdural hem-orrhage. Pulling off that woman's sawn-off skullcap and seeing the fatal pool of blood inside her head made my headache much worse, and I had to take a break. I lied to Alvarez and said I was probably just dehydrated. I lied and said I'd be fine in a minute.

We decided to conjure up a lunch break around noon. In the locker room, I managed to slip the watch cap back over my bandages without Alvarez noticing. Howe returned from his visit to the disaster scene and found the four of us, doctors and students, in the Ops Shop, ravenously snarfing old pizza out of the communal fridge. The chief was glad that we'd decided to take a break. Glad, he told us, because we were going to have to pace ourselves. More corpses were coming.

"The viaduct collapsed onto a homeless encampment," he said, waving off the offer of a cold slice. "PD thinks there were between thirty and fifty people under there last night. They're shoring up the structure so they can continue working, but for now it's still being designated a rescue, not a recovery."

"What's that mean?" Patty Alvarez asked.

"Rescue is when the fire department has made the determi-nation there may still be living people trapped under there. Re-covery phase is when everybody's dead."

"Oh," said Alvarez, and looked despondent.

Dr. Howe smiled gently. "That's a valid question, and it relates to our role going forward. The viaduct collapse—the homeless camp—seems to be the only multiple-fatality scene. This was a serious quake, but it's not the Big One."

"The Big One," the other medical student repeated, mostly

to himself. I remembered his saying he was from the Carolinas somewhere.

"How about the power grid and stuff?" Ted wanted to know.

"Retail electrical and gas service are still down, but traffic signals are back, so getting around by car is…well, less-impossible. Still no BART trains. Freeway access is limited, especially now that they've got crews out there assessing the safety of…"

"Hello…?" said someone from the hallway behind the Ops Shop.

"In here!" shouted Howe.

Denis Monaghan appeared. Howe glared his most ferocious glare.

"Right, so," said Monaghan, and started rocking back and forth on his feet. He was dressed in overalls and carried a bright orange toolbox. I offered him a slice of pizza. He demurred.

"Your damned HVAC is fubar again," said Dr. Howe, quietly.

"Ah," said Monaghan. "And ye must be very busy today?"

"You could say that."

"I'll get right on it, then."

"You do that."

"Right. I'll…just get me things, and start with the main unit…"

He looked from one to the other of us, for further instructions, or encouragement, or something. Howe wasn't offering any, that was for sure.

"Thank you for coming out here, under the circumstances, Denis," I offered. "It can't have been easy driving in."

Monaghan smiled gratefully and said, "Oh, it wasn't so bad. I was on a job nearby, and I don't fancy going home until they've got the lights sorted."

He nodded a nervous goodbye to Dr. Howe, and left. Howe went back to looking exhausted and worried. I realized his bad attitude had been an act to drive the contractor out of the room as quick as he could. "A lot more cases are coming in," he said, looking at each of us to assess how we would handle that news.

"From the viaduct?" I said.

He nodded. "When I left, they were pulling bodies out one after another. They haven't even managed to get tents down there, so they're laying them out in the sun till they can get them transported. It's going to be all hands on deck around here. We'll be working through the weekend, and I want you to be prepared for what you're going to see—blunt trauma, evisceration, disarticulation, and accelerated decomposition from the environmental exposure."

Ted Nguyen stretched his arms and cracked his knuckles. "Okay. We'd better get back to it, then."

I tried again to text Anup and give him that news. I'd made a bunch of attempts, but they all bounced back. This time, though, it went through. I learned that he'd gone home to his own place and was bunkering there. His mother, God bless her, had driven all the way up from Cupertino to bring him food.

Yr folks ok? I texted.

Yes no damage

Thx 4 watching Bea last night, I'll be back b4 her walk 2nite

I brought her 2 my place, she here now

Oh gr8 thx!!

You come here get dog after work pls

Will do. Luv u

Luv u 2

Getting through to Anup made it easier for me to gown up again and go back into the autopsy suite. That was another item I recalled from my emergency protocol training as deputy chief: a supportive home environment contributes mightily to a first responder's resilience in a disaster's aftermath.

Two more medical students had arrived to help out as technicians, so the afternoon autopsies went faster than the morning ones. Howe wasn't exaggerating—the bodies were mutilated and decomposing, and got more so as the day wore on. To make matters worse, the air-conditioning had gone off again.

Denis Monaghan let himself into the morgue, toolbox and stepladder at the ready. "Sorry for the interruption, there," he said. "I had to shut down the main unit before I can diagnose this bloody beast again." He erected the ladder and reached up to pop open the same ceiling panel where he'd been working the day before.

"Don't say 'bloody' in a morgue, Denis," I said. "It's bad luck."

He blanched, frozen, with his arm in the air. "Christ... I didn't—"

"She's pulling your leg," Ted said.

"Oh, Christ," Monaghan said again. I felt kind of bad. Then he stepped down off the ladder with one leg to steady himself, and he laughed until he turned pink.

"*Fierce* funny, that is," he said.

"Don't encourage her," Sunshine Ted snapped right back at him, which only made Monaghan laugh harder. The four medical students did, too—one after another, like they were wired in series. Then I started up myself. Soon everybody but Nguyen was laughing.

It felt good.

But it didn't last long. We got back to work, documenting as best we could the result of unmeasured tons of elevated roadway crashing down on unsheltered human beings. Monaghan got the

HVAC working again. Nguyen finished an autopsy and struggled to fit the body on its gurney into the cold storage room.

"Almost full in there," he said, wheeling out his last case of the day.

Monaghan popped his head back down when he heard that. "You ever have that many, ah, deceased in there all at once?" he asked. I told him no, we definitely had not. "We'd better make sure the system can handle the load, then. No fooling with the temperature in that space, right?"

"No fooling," I agreed.

Monaghan came down off the ladder, grabbed his toolbox, and stopped in front of the cooler's stainless-steel door. He paused nervously, then grabbed the heavy handle, pulled it, and went in. After five minutes the door reopened and he came back out, wearing an expression of relief and waving an electronic instrument.

"Operating within expected parameters."

"Good," I said. I had just finished a case, and pushed the loaded gurney toward the cooler. The gurney didn't want to cooperate—they're damned heavy, and this one had developed a wonky wheel, like a beat-up shopping cart.

"Hang on, now," said Monaghan, and bent to look at the wheel. He opened his toolbox, pulled out a couple of things, tinkered with the gurney, and, presto, fixed it. I thanked him.

"Dr. Teska," he said, "I meant what I said the other day. I admire what you are doing here. It's a hard task, and I imagine a thankless one—except to the families. To the families, what you're doing must mean everything."

I didn't have the heart to break it to him that, so far, several of our disaster victims had turned out to be John Does and Jane Does. People who are reduced by circumstance to living under a bridge sometimes have family who are worried about them—but often, in my experience, they do not.

I told Denis I appreciated the sentiment. And I meant it, too.

Ted finished his last autopsy at five thirty. I finished mine at six—a twelve-hour day on the heels of a night in the hospital, unconscious and head-injured, fueled only by stale cold pizza. Plus I had a transportation problem—my BMW was still over by the viaduct collapse site, where I'd parked it before getting clonked on the head. I asked one of the day-shift 2578s if he would give me a lift to retrieve it. It was about time for the shift change, so I figured he'd be on his way home, too.

"Home?" he scoffed. "I'm not going home. We're implementing a two-hour shift overlap, subject to extension."

I'm not a taxi service, and you should be staying here till we've cleared all the quake cases, Doctor, his body language and tone chided. Denis Monaghan witnessed the exchange.

"Where d'you need to go, Jessie?" he asked. I told him. "Ah, that's no problem at all. I'd be happy to take you."

I told him I was grateful, and followed him out to the parking lot. Our building was still the only one in the immediate vicinity that seemed to have power. Monaghan put his toolbox and ladder in the bed of a shiny new pickup truck, opened the passenger door, and closed it behind me after I stepped up. Old World chivalry.

"Thanks again," I said, when he climbed in.

"Don't mention it a bit." He put the truck carefully onto the street. "It's a pleasure to have your company." He looked over at me and smiled in a suitably charming way.

Monaghan wore a Claddagh ring. It was an unusual one, bigger than most, the hands and heart and crown more expressive than the cheap, two-dimensional silver Claddaghs that every Irish kid in my hometown seemed to get around their fourteenth birthday. I commented on it. Monaghan was surprised that I knew what it was.

"I'm from Boston," I said.

"That explains it," he replied.

Yes, I know what the Claddagh ring is, and what it signifies. A pair of hands holding a heart, the heart wearing a crown—friendship, love, and loyalty. If the heart faces inward, then your heart is taken. If the heart faces out, then your heart is open. The heart on Monaghan's Claddagh ring faced out. That made me feel better about his flirting with me. He wasn't married, not a creep. He seemed, in fact, a perfectly decent man. He was handsome, fit, charming, and funny in a bone-dry way. His accent was sexy as hell. His offer to chauffeur me to my Beemer was generous, and he wasn't giving me any bad vibes while I was alone with him, in close quarters, in his vehicle. He was a careful driver. Doing what I do for a living, I appreciate careful drivers.

Monaghan's Claddagh ring made me think about my own fingers. No rings at all, what with gloves always going on and off and on again. Besides, I had no need of rings. I wasn't married, and Anup hadn't offered me a diamond.

Denis Monaghan seemed to read my mind. "Are you hungry?" he said. "I know a good place near here. My treat."

"They'll be closed."

"Never know until you try."

I declined, and he shrugged affably.

Maybe some other time, I didn't say. But I nearly did.

Monaghan gave me a sly side-eye while the truck glided along, up through Dogpatch and into the Mission Bay condo zone. "You'll want to take good care of that noggin, Jessie."

"What—?" And my hand shot up to the wound under the watch cap, without my meaning it to. Monaghan chuckled. I said, "How'd you know...?"

"Plenty of head injuries in my line of work. I've caught people trying to cover up bandages before. I send them home when I do."

"Good thing home's where I'm going, then."

"Amen. You know what to watch for? Warning signs that you need to go straight to the hospital…?"

"Denis," I said, "I'm a doctor."

"You are, you are…but I'd have to point out to you, Doctor, that all your head-injured patients are dead." The truck stopped at one of the functional red lights across Third Street. Monaghan turned to me. His gray-sky eyes were kind, and delved into mine with true concern.

"Take care of yourself. Promise?"

"I can only promise I'll try," I said.

The light went green, and he turned back to the road. "I supposed that'll have to do."

As we got closer to the collapsed roadway, we started to see flashing emergency lights. It wasn't the blinding riot it had been when I'd first come to the scene, fresh after the disaster, but, still, Denis knew well enough to keep away. I directed him around the back way, down Berry Street. I was relieved to see my BMW 235i was right where I'd left it.

It had a parking ticket on the windshield.

"You have got to be kidding me!" I hollered, and leaped out of the truck. Red zone. One hundred ten dollars.

I let loose a string of Polish curses that would've given my *mamusia*, were she nearby, a coronary and a half. Monaghan found all of this extremely amusing.

"Get out of here, you," I said.

"Not till I see you started," he said.

"Huh?"

He pointed to the Beemer. "I'm not going anywhere until I see that your engine turns over."

I grumbled about the line between Old World chivalry and male chauvinism, and got in the Beemer. It started.

"Happy?"

Denis Monaghan smiled and saluted, and turned back to his pickup truck. Before he got in, he said, "I hope your HVAC system holds up for good, now—but I do hope too that we meet again, Jessie."

I couldn't help smiling back at him. "Yeah. I wouldn't mind."

———

I drove, carefully, crosstown to Anup's apartment in the Outer Sunset. I had to take surface roads; the freeway entrances were still blockaded by police. Streetlights had come on in some places but were out in others. Under a pool of light somewhere in the Lower Haight, I saw a man heaving orange tiles out of his front yard. They'd come off his Spanish-style roof and his neighbor's and several more, in a line, like a barnstorming plane had taken them out. Across the road, all the houses looked fine. They seemed the same vintage as the ruined ones, but their roof tiles were still in place.

A local in my neighborhood dive bar had once told me that earthquakes can be like tornadoes, devastating one side of the street and sparing the other, depending on soil composition, buried creeks, minor fault lines. *The ground is not solid under your feet*, she said. I thought at the time she was drunk. She may have been—but, as I was seeing, she sure wasn't wrong.

I got to Anup's around seven o'clock. Pragmatic Anup had bought solar-powered lanterns for his stoop, and now they were paying dividends. All the other houses on the avenue were dark, but at least I could climb his stairs without cracking my skull any worse.

Bea the beagle greeted me at the door with even more hyperactive joy than she greeted me when I came home to my own place. Anup was on the couch in the living room. I said hello. He looked through me and didn't answer. He'd lit some candles, but the mood wasn't romantic.

He got up and moved to the dining room and I followed. If Anup was giving me the silent treatment, I knew something was seriously wrong. He didn't do it like most men do, out of petulance. He goes silent because he's thinking, processing, and not ready to talk about what he's come up with. The dining room had a lit candelabra, and a place setting for one.

"You're not eating?" I asked.

"I did already."

I sat down. Anup took my plate, disappeared into the kitchen, and came back with a heaping pile of curry over rice. The fragrance, before he'd even set the plate down in front of me, made my stomach growl.

I put my nose to it and let myself enjoy a couple of deep breaths. "Your mother's?"

"Yes." He sat down at the other end of the table.

"She's a saint, driving all the way up here with it. The freeways are closed, you know that? I can't imagine how long it took her—"

"They didn't get hit that hard down on the Peninsula."

"That's a relief."

"Yes."

I dug in, and asked Anup if he wouldn't like to have seconds or something. "I feel like I'm in a zoo, you watching me like that," I joked.

His expression didn't change. "I have to make sure you eat."

"Make sure I eat? What d'you mean?"

"You don't take care of yourself. I have to make sure you get food into you."

I laughed it off and shoveled some more curry.

Anup didn't laugh. He was monitoring me like a subject in a deposition. I didn't like it.

"That's not fair," I said.

He shrugged again. "I think it is."

"Oh really."

"Really. What do you have in your fridge, right now, over at your place?"

I thought back to Mahoney Brothers #45 and the ancient nickel-handled refrigerator that came with my cable-car cottage. He was right. It was probably pretty pathetic in there. I didn't press the point. I ate. Anup watched. When I was done, I told him I'd really like him to thank his mother profusely, on my behalf, for the excellent meal.

Still he said nothing.

My head was aching again. I hadn't really slept the night before (traumatic unconsciousness is not sleep), and I had worked more than thirteen hours doing autopsies on five mangled people, three of them as yet unidentified. On top of that, some zealot in the city's parking enforcement squad had continued, in the immediate wake of a motherfucking *earthquake*, to write tickets for red zone violations—even though I have a placard in my vehicle identifying it as belonging to the deputy chief medical examiner, on official business.

I do not have a long temper even in the best circumstances. I know this about myself. Anup knows it, too. I suspected he was picking a fight, itching for one. I could feel it coming off him, an electric current barely held in by his skin. I didn't want to close the circuit between us.

But, in the end, I didn't see any way to avoid it. When Anup Banerjee is determined to do something, he does it.

"Okay," I said. "Spill it."

"Spill it?"

"What are you so mad about?"

"You can't guess? I'm not a dog sitter, Doctor."

"That's what you're so pissed off about—? It's one night. You don't have to do it again."

"You think I wanted to sit around here in the dark, wondering when you'd come?"

"You didn't have to."

"I *did* have to. Like I said, I had to make sure you fed yourself. No joke."

"Jesus, Anup. I'm not a child!"

"You're doing one hell of a job adulting."

"Says the man who enjoys mommy's home cooking."

The stern lawyer face Anup had worn since I'd darkened his door dropped off, and he showed how much that jab stung. I shouldn't have thrown it. Well, too damn bad.

"You know how many people are *dead* out there, Anup? You know what I've been doing since you last saw me?"

"Your big important job."

"Damn right! You have no idea…and here you are, complaining that—"

"Why are you wearing that ridiculous hat?"

Kurwa. He had me there. I whipped off the watch cap. His eyes went wide. He rose and came over to me, hands out toward my head. I brushed him off.

"Let me see," he said.

"Why? You don't care."

Anup planted himself in the chair right next to me. "That's where you're wrong, Jessie." He pulled out his cell phone, turned on the light, and shined it up and down my neck, my arms. "You've got cuts and bruises and a bandaged head. What happened?"

I told him about the King Street off-ramp, the bodies, the aftershock. I told him about waking up in the ER. Then he began cross-examination.

"You were wearing the hat to hide your injury?"

"Anup…"

"From Dr. Howe? You were hiding a head injury from your boss? Holy shit." He looked away from me, off in the middle distance somewhere, gazing into the gloom like he'd just seen a ghost vanish into it.

What could I tell him? That I'd been afraid Howe would kick me out of the morgue and send me home if anybody at work knew about my visit to the ER? That I was willing to risk my health to get into work in the wake of the disaster, when I was most needed there—when I was irreplaceable? Should I tell him that I was willing to risk my *life* to do my job?

It was the truth. The ghost he was watching in the dark middle distance was the realization of it.

Finally he turned back to me. "Why?" he said.

I was suddenly bone tired. I pushed the chair back and slumped. "I couldn't let him send me home."

"I don't see why not. I really don't."

"You didn't see those bodies in the rubble, either."

"You could've ended up next to them in the morgue."

"They have families, Anup! Loved ones, waiting for them."

Anup shook his head but didn't take his eyes from mine. "So do you."

"Oh, very clever. Well played."

"I'm not playing," he shot right back. He wasn't, either. "I don't want to lose you. I didn't know if you were alive or dead, and now you're telling me I had damn good reason to worry...? I don't want to do that again."

Over by the door, Bea started whining. I swear, that damn dog has the worst bladder timing of anyone I've ever met.

"Try to imagine what I told my parents, when I finally got a phone line to them," Anup continued, his eyes still locked on mine. "I lied to them. I had to. I don't like lying to my parents." He waved around the room. "There's damage here, you know. Your place, too. I spent all day cleaning up both of them— picture frames off the walls, dishes and broken glass all over the kitchen. I found new cracks in the plaster that worry me. One of my neighbors, down on the corner, you know the one with all the garage doors? Their place has so much damage that they're afraid to go back inside. They grabbed birth certificates, bank records, some clothes, and that's it. It's *leaning*. Their house is leaning. It's probably going to be red-tagged and demolished, and they're homeless now." He pointed out the window. "Right there—three doors down the hill."

He stood and took my dirty plate off the table. "You aren't the only one hit by this disaster."

I went to Bea by the door and collected her leash. She started yelping.

"Thanks for cleaning up my house and walking Bea, and thanks for the meal."

I opened the door and went out.

Behind me, Anup said, "Jessie. Don't expect me to take care of you. I'm not here to take care of you."

I didn't answer that. I closed the door and followed the dog down the steps in the dim solar lights.

CHAPTER 6

I had never been so happy to see a garden-variety multiple gun-shot wound homicide as I was the next Wednesday.

We had operated the Office of Chief Medical Examiner on emergency protocol for four days. That meant twelve-hour shifts—me and Ted, side by side at our stations, performing one autopsy after another on the earthquake's victims, all day Friday, straight through the weekend, and into the next week. We did forty-eight disaster-related cases over those four long days. Twenty-six were victims of the viaduct collapse, more than half of them John or Jane Does. Among the other earthquake cases, I autopsied a woman who had been killed by a beam falling off the roof of her own porch, a man electrocuted by a downed power line, and another man who had a heart attack in his car while it jumped around on its springs.

There were no child deaths. That was a blessing.

At the end of our twelve hours on Tuesday evening, Dr. Howe came back from a meeting with the heads of the city's emergency response agencies and announced that he was returning us to regular work schedules. We had accumulated a huge back-log of ordinary cases while we cleared the earthquake autopsies, but the chief knew he couldn't keep pushing us so hard. Every-one in the office was exhausted and short-fused, especially the 2578s. On the evening of day three, Donna Griello bit off my head in the locker room, about the way I'd laid out my shoes.

"And what are you doing in that stupid hat all the time?" she snapped, to boot.

By Wednesday morning I was ready to hang up my twenty-dollar watch cap. The bandages had come off, leaving behind some bruises and transient headaches, plus a fat, itchy scar under my hair. I hadn't seen Anup since the week before, when he'd fed me his mom's curry. By the time I'd finished each of my twelve-hour shifts and showered and changed and driven home through the traffic snarled by earthquake damage and its cleanup, I'd had only enough time and energy left for Bea and my bed. Plus Anup hadn't so much as texted me—and I wasn't going to be the first to reach out.

Uparty jak osioł, my mother used to mutter after me, especially as I got into my teenage years. She was right. I was and remain stubborn as a mule.

I was relieved, then, to be standing over a young man with three bullet holes in his chest. That morning, that ordinary Wednesday morning, I performed his autopsy and two more—a pedestrian-versus-car fatality and a pulmonary embolism hos-pital case we'd held over. Then, as a reminder that the disaster work wasn't finished, I did an external on a delayed blunt trauma death from the viaduct collapse, bringing the total for that scene up to twenty-seven.

I had lunch at my desk. I didn't enjoy it. Anup is a creative and clever cook. I am not. I chewed on a sad cheese-and-butter sandwich and a couple of pickles, and decided that it was time to step off the stubborn-mule train. If Anup wouldn't do it first, it would have to be up to me. I texted him.

Before he could reply, my office phone rang. I didn't recognize the number, so I let it go to voice mail. When I checked the mailbox, I found a whole bunch of messages, and realized I probably hadn't checked them since the quake hit, so I dialed in. Two were from Natalie Haring, widow of the famous architect in the SoMa Centre case, looking for the death certificate. Another was Jeffrey Symond, Haring's business partner, seeking the same thing on behalf of the firm. Then came messages from first an insurance company with a claim by Natalie Haring, and then a lawyer representing her.

"Hot potato," I muttered to my empty office.

The last caller was a man who didn't identify himself. He spoke at a rapid clip.

"Hello, this is about Leopold Haring. I need you to call me back right away. He was murdered. I know who did it. They'll deny it, but I know it's true. I'm not going to the police because they won't believe me, they never have before. I mean, they… They won't take me seriously. You will—I know you will believe me—because you've seen what they did to my papa. I need to talk to you. Call me right back, this is Oskar Haring."

That was the end of the message. He'd hung up without leaving his number.

Psiakrew. Okay, I needed to triage the calls. Natalie was going last, that much was for sure, if she was already sending lawyers after me. I was dying to hear what Oskar Haring had to say, but had to check in with Inspectors Jones and Ramirez first.

I dialed them up and got Ramirez. "The family wants answers about the cause and manner of death. What can I tell them?"

"Nothing."

"Thanks a bunch."

"Tell them the case is still under investigation."

"Haring's son, Oskar, left me a message claiming Haring was murdered, and he knows who did it."

Ramirez grunted. "That guy. He's fucking nuts. Did he sound nuts?"

"That's not a term we like to use, Detective. I'll grant you that he did exhibit a markedly manic affect in his phone message."

"He's a frequent-flier at our switchboard over here, been leaving me and Keith nonstop nutso messages. Don't call him back, whatever you do. The case is still restricted."

"Any idea how long it's going to stay that way?"

"We're working some leads."

"What kind?"

"We been down the job site and done a bunch of interviews, picked up a few things. And a couple things off the hotline, too. We're getting some motion."

"I can't just ignore these people."

"Ignore Oskar Haring. Trust me on that."

"What about the wife and the business partner? There are insurance companies involved now, and the wife's sending lawyers after me."

"You'll think of something."

"That's your advice—?"

Ramirez laughed darkly. "Best of luck, Doc."

I hung up on Ramirez and decided to start with Jeffrey Symond, Leopold Haring's business partner, hoping he'd be the most levelheaded of the bunch. Right after the returning-your-call pleasantries, though, he put me on my back foot.

"What are the police doing about Leo's death? That was a homicide detective at the site."

"Inspector Keith Jones. Yes. But—"

"So they're investigating this as a homicide?"

"Mr. Symond, I'm afraid I can't talk about police procedure."

"They have to take a look at Oskar. He's certifiable—bipolar with paranoid features, and when he's off his meds, he's violent and dangerous. Have you talked to him?"

"I…uh, again, I can't discuss…"

"Of course. But don't believe a thing he tells you, Dr. Teska. Oskar comes up with all kinds of fantasies, believes they're real—and then he acts on them. Poor Natalie. He's given her nothing but grief since he was a teenager."

"When we first spoke, you told me that the day Leo died, he had been in a fight with Oskar."

"Oskar assaulted him. Bloodied his nose."

"How do you know that?"

"When Leo arrived at our office, late to meet me and Natalie, he had a bloody handkerchief still pressed to it. There was blood on his shirt, too—he asked Natalie for one of those laundry wet wipes."

That was interesting. It explained the recent trauma to the nose I'd found during the autopsy, and the dried blood in the dead man's nostrils.

"Was that the first time they'd come to blows, that you know of?"

"It's happened before."

"Were the police ever called out?"

"No."

"You sound sure about that."

He hedged, then said, "Natalie has spoken to me about it. She didn't want police involved. Leo certainly didn't, either. But now they'll have to be involved. They have to arrest Oskar. Right?"

"I don't know. That's a question for Inspectors Jones and Ramirez."

"They'll have to," Jeff Symond said again. "What about the death certificate?"

"It might be a while. The earthquake—"

"Of course. But we need it right away." Two things I didn't like about Jeff Symond: he liked to cut me off, and he liked to say *of course*. "The insurance company is telling us we need the death certificate."

"Who is *we*, Mr. Symond?"

"The company, of course. Apart from this being a personal disaster for me, and for poor Natalie, it's a professional disaster, too. Leopold was one of the two principals in our firm. I'm the other. He was the one with the international reputation. He didn't have much of a head for business, but he was a true creative genius, the soul of the firm. With Leo gone... Well, we're going to have to restructure, of course. In the meantime, we need the insurance settlement money. Immediately. It's a matter of dire urgency to the continuing survival of Haring & Symond. That's Leo's legacy, the business. I intend to preserve and protect it."

I gave him my boilerplate answer about getting the death certificate filed as soon as circumstances allowed. Then I tried to sign off—but Jeff Symond wouldn't let me.

"I'm begging you, Doctor," he said. "Get the detectives to bring Oskar in. I'm... I'm afraid of Oskar. I'm certain he must've been involved in Leo's death."

I said something noncommittal that definitely did not include the word *homicide*, and suggested that Symond should call Inspector Jones to share his concerns. "Be sure to tell him everything you know about the bloody nose and any other incidents of domestic violence, okay?"

He agreed he would. I repeated my promise about filing the death certificate as soon as possible, and managed to end the call.

Why would Jeff Symond suspect that Leo Haring had been killed by his son? Symond had seen Haring's body crushed by those pipes, to all appearances the grisly aftermath of a workplace accident. He didn't—or shouldn't—know about the bloody patch on Haring's back and the fatal wound under it.

I typed up some call notes and added them to the activities

section of my case file. Then I took a deep breath and called Natalie Haring.

Right off the bat, Natalie was talking about "closure." Considering the calls from her insurance company and her lawyer, I figured by closure she meant money. She wanted the death certificate, with cause and manner. Cause of death and manner of death. She was careful and insistent in the way she demanded this. She'd done her homework.

"I'm afraid that, at this time, I can't talk to you about the cause and manner of your husband's death."

"Of course you can, Doctor, that's why we're speaking."

"There's an ongoing police investigation, Mrs. Haring—"

"Wait. Why is that?"

"Because the death occurred at a workplace. Can you tell me why your husband went to the construction site that evening?"

"Leopold visited SoMa Centre nearly every day. He liked to go by at different times, so he wouldn't be expected. He was sure they were rushing the work. Time is money in our business. Leopold could see that the contractors on that job were cutting into one to save on the other, and he wouldn't stand for that. He wasn't going to end up like Carlo Farnell."

She didn't explain what that meant, so I had to ask.

"Carlo drew up 185 Pine Street."

Again—I had to ask.

"The Leaning Tower," Natalie said, like it was a curse. "Carlo drafted the plans, handed them off, and walked away. But I'll bet you can guess who is getting sued into bankruptcy now, after those plans were so badly executed. Leopold was *not* going to let that happen to him. He hasn't had a major lawsuit resulting from his commissions in thirty years as an architect, and he wasn't about to let this silly little job soil his reputation."

It seemed to me that there was nothing silly about a six-hundred-something foot skyscraper in the beating heart of the most expensive real estate market in the country, but I kept that opinion to myself and asked instead what exactly Leopold Haring had suspected was going on that was so shoddy it merited his personal supervision.

"I don't know," Natalie Haring said. "He would only say it was substandard work. My part in our business is PR and marketing—I'm not an architect. I tried to get Leopold to tell me more, but he found the whole subject of SoMa Centre unbearably stressful and wouldn't discuss it."

She stopped, and I said nothing. I'm good at letting people talk. Sometimes they need to if they've just lost a loved one. Sometimes they tell me things that the autopsy never would have revealed. So I waited for Natalie Haring to keep talking about her husband, and she did.

"There were complaints from other stakeholders in the project, complaints that Leopold's unbending quality control was slowing construction and costing everyone money and momentum."

Something occurred to me. "Was one of those stakeholders Jeffrey Symond?" I asked.

Natalie surprised me: she laughed. "God, no. Jeff and Leo were partners. They had worked together for a long time and been friends even longer. No, Jeff is one of the only men Leopold really trusted."

I wanted to ask her about Jeffrey Symond's accusation that her son and husband had been in a fight on the day he died, but couldn't be too blunt about it. I found a way in, as I always can, with the physical findings at autopsy.

"When I examined his body, I found your husband's nose to be bloody and swollen. The injury looked like it was several hours old when he died."

I paused to give Natalie a chance to volunteer what she knew. She didn't.

"Can you tell me anything about that injury?"

"Leopold and Oskar were in a tussle that evening. Leopold wasn't badly hurt. Neither was Oskar."

"Were you there when it happened?"

"No. They were at our home and I was at the office with Jeffrey, working."

"Waiting for Leopold to join you?"

"No."

That was interesting. Jeffrey Symond had said they were expecting Haring to come.

"Did that kind of conflict happen often between Leopold and Oskar?"

"They challenge each other. They are, both of them, strong-willed. They have their moments of tension, but it doesn't affect their love for one another. Oskar is very protective of both his father and me, you see. Sometimes overprotective—and it can cause him to fly off the handle a little. He's a passionate boy."

I scrolled through my notes. Oskar was twenty-three.

"Sometimes Oskar says things that are simply untrue, and this upsets Leopold."

Natalie Haring didn't sound defensive or even especially evasive. She sounded, if anything, a little rueful.

"What time did Leopold arrive at your office?"

"Six thirty or thereabouts."

"Did he stay long?"

"Oh, no. He was in a hurry to get to SoMa Centre. I asked him not to go, but he was in a state. About the job site, I mean. He was adamant."

So if Leopold Haring left his office a few minutes after 6:30, he was probably at SoMa Centre sometime around seven. That fit into the broad time-of-death estimate I had computed for Keith Jones. I would have to update it for him. That was a relief, at least: one solid piece of information pertaining to our investigation into the death of Leopold Haring. One piece of information, buried in a pile of blather. Natalie Haring and I went through our cordial goodbyes, and I hung up.

My perpetual stack of unfinished paperwork loomed over the phone. It was even taller than usual, thanks to the backlog of cases we'd deferred during the disaster. I rubbed the wound on my head with the heel of my hand, which eased its itching but sent a ricochet of pain across the inside of my skull.

"Hell with it," I said out loud to no one, and decided, then and there, to swallow my pride, bug out of the office, and go spend some time with Anup—even though he hadn't placed the first call. Before I could gather my things, though, Cameron Blake knocked at my door and stuck his head in. He informed me that someone named Oskar Haring was waiting for me.

"What...? Where?"

"He showed up at the public window, looking for you, and wouldn't take no for an answer. He seems kind of agitated."

"Great."

"Who is he?"

"Remember the dead architect, with the pipes? His son."

"Oh."

"Daniel Ramirez in Homicide says they interviewed this guy, and he's batshit crazy."

"Oh." Cameron was looking worried.

"Did you tell him I'm here, Cam?"

"No."

"Good. Where is he?"

"I stuck him in the chapel."

"Why would you do that?"

"It's dark and quiet. I figured it'd calm him down."

"Good thinking. Okay, here's what we're going to do. Donna's here?"

"She's covering for me at the public window."

"Perfect. Bring Oskar into the Ops Shop and sit him down.

Tell him I'll be right there. That way you can be handy while I talk to him."

"Hey, Jessie—we aren't muscle, you know."

"Oh, sorry. Then you go back to the window and send Donna to Ops. I'll bet she could take him."

Cameron Blake turned red. He resembled a fireplug whenever that happened. He got all stiff and formal, and said, "If you're concerned about your safety while conducting an interview in this office, Doctor, then you ought to call the PD and ask them to send an officer."

"We aren't in the Hall anymore, Cam. They can't just take an elevator down."

Cameron, by way of answer, glared and shrugged. I was going to have to play my ace.

"Cam, do you remember last year? When I was assaulted in the morgue—?"

Cameron went from red to white. "Now, hold on…"

"I don't want to repeat that experience."

"I wasn't even there!"

"Right."

Cam started to protest again, but then thought better of it.

"Okay," he said—and we proceeded with my plan.

Oskar had nervous eyes under bushy brows, small nostrils in a mousy nose, and bluish stubble against a complexion like an altar candle. He impressed me as a man who climbed out of bed every morning wound up three turns too tight.

"Are you the one investigating my father's death?"

"Yes."

"He was murdered."

Yikes. I was going to have to tread carefully around the police restriction on discussing cause and manner with this guy.

"So you said in your message. What makes you think that?"

"My mother and Jeff Symond did it. One of them, or both. Or they hired someone. I don't know the details."

I said nothing, folded my hands across the table, put on a psychotherapist's poker face.

"They're sleeping together," he added.

Over Oskar Haring's shoulder I could see Cam at his desk, going through the motions of making noises on his keyboard. He had one eye on us.

"They needed to get rid of him. They arranged my papa's death to get him out of the way, and to collect on insurance. They have a *lot* of insurance riding on him."

Cam's face came fully off his computer screen. I didn't waver from my kindly-listening stance.

"They might have hired a hit man. I know I'm being followed. If you get my body, you'll know, okay? You'll know that if I turn up dead, it's a hit."

Oskar Haring watched my lack of reaction to his opening pitch and started to get, as Cam had put it, agitated. His head jerked on his neck, first left, then right. Cam returned his attention to his computer monitor before the jittery young man's eyes could swing around and catch him eavesdropping.

"Tell me about the fight with your father," I said.

"What fight?"

"I saw the injury to his face. The bloody nose."

Oskar Haring looked down at his lap like a kid who'd been caught in a lie. "I didn't mean to."

"You hit him?"

"He hit me first."

"Can you tell me what you were fighting about?"

"Something…that belongs to me."

"What was that, Mr. Haring?"

He still had his head down, and mumbled the reply. "Opa's rastengasser."

"Sorry?"

Oskar Haring's eyes came back up to meet mine, and I almost flinched from the ferocity behind them.

"You tell *me* something, Doctor. Tell me what else you found when you did my father's autopsy. I'll bet it isn't what it looks like, is it? It wasn't an accident."

"I can't talk to you about our investigation."

"Oh, sure. Questions but no answers, like the cops." The spring inside Oskar Haring was getting tighter. "How did they kill him? My papa didn't lie down on the ground and let a pile of pipes get dropped on his head. So tell me how they did it."

"I'm sorry, but I've already said that I can't discuss the investigation with you. Now, if you—"

"How?" he barked. "I know you know! How'd they kill him?"

"Mr. Haring, I'm going to advise you to reach out to Inspector Jones. He's the one you ought to be talking to about your concerns."

That was the signal. Cam and I had agreed on the homicide detective's name as my safe word.

"Dr. Teska?" Cam said, holding up his phone. "Call for you."

I nodded to Cam and said, "Please excuse me for a moment," to Oskar Haring. The young man's lips flapped like a gaffed cod's, but he didn't object aloud. I crossed the room to Cam's desk, pretended to talk, and punched a button to put the fake call on hold.

"I'm sorry, Mr. Haring, but this is an urgent matter." I turned my back on him and faced Cam. "I'll take it in my office."

"Yes, Dr. Teska," Cam said, and gave me the evil eye for leaving him to do the dirty work.

I walked right out of the Ops Shop without another word to Oskar Haring. I stopped on the other side of the locked security door, to listen up and make sure Cam really could handle him. He did—calmly talking Oskar down from his frustration at the abrupt end to our meeting, and advising him that the next time he wanted to have a personal interview with a San Francisco medical examiner in the wake of a deadly earthquake, it would be best to call first and make an appointment.

We are, after all, busy people.

Anup wasn't waiting for me at Mahoney Brothers #45. Bea certainly was, of course, and came bolting through the tiny, overgrown yard to tackle me at the gate. I gathered her leash for our nightly walk and sent Anup one more text, telling him I'd made it home safe. That would be all the texting, though. I wasn't about to start spamming him like a worried wife.

Maybe we were a bad match, Anup and I. Thinking about it made the pain ricochet in my skull again. "Don't let a man be a headache to you, Bea," I counseled the dog. She paused her snuffling in the weedy underbrush of Golden Gate Park to glance up, but didn't offer any advice in return.

Bea the beagle seemed especially passionate about one particular patch of dirt in a meadow of shaggy dune grass, so I let her linger there while I gazed up to enjoy the sunset, a beauty—a handful of high pink clouds, the red glow settling over the Pacific Ocean just beyond the eucalyptus and cypress trees. I was happy to be at leisure for a change. I still had plenty of time to cook dinner, have a bath in my cable car's tiny tub—sunk into the floor under a trapdoor in the living room—and get to bed early. I could pay down some of my sleep deficit.

Assuming Anup didn't call. What was my time limit? I decided I ought to decide one. Then I further decided that, never really having practiced at battle-of-the-sexes head games, I wasn't about to start. Anup had better get his shit together.

Bea's barking broke my spell. She stood over the weedy patch—only now it was a hole in the ground. I hadn't even noticed her digging; she must've been fast. She barked one more time and then stood stock-still, nose out and tail rigid, one fore-leg off the ground in a pointing pose.

Something was in the hole. I couldn't see it, but it set off my alarms.

It smelled strongly of decomp.

I fished around in my pocket for my phone and got the light on.

It was a dead cat. Couple of weeks dead, in my professional opinion. Next to the cat was a dirty greeting card. Bea's digging had flipped it open. Under the printed condolence message someone had written in pen, *Rest in Peace, dear Rocky.* A small bouquet of faded wildflowers, tied with a ribbon, completed the morbid tableau.

Bea was still pointing. I opened my mouth to admonish her for digging up poor Rocky's grave—but then thought better. Instead, I gave her one of the training treats I kept in the pocket of my dog-walk jacket. I thought of the cadaver dogs at the King Street viaduct. I'd had Bea since she was a puppy, and hadn't trained her to go around exhuming cats. She was a natural.

Anup finally texted me back while I was reinterring Rocky. He'd had to work late—they had a deadline on a hearing, and the judge wasn't taking San Francisco's earthquake delay as an excuse against timely submission.

First I was overworked. Now I had a break—for an evening—and Anup was overworked. It couldn't be helped. But it was doing us no good, either.

I tamped down the dirt on the cat's grave.

CHAPTER 7

I only had two autopsies on Thursday morning—an overdose and a hanging—and was delighted to find that Sparkle was available to meet for an early lunch. I needed to go down to the Hall of Justice anyhow, to talk to Jones and Ramirez about all the finger-pointing from the Haring family. We wouldn't be able to keep both them and the press in the dark for much longer.

I stuck my Beemer in a loading zone right in front of Baby Mike Bail Bonds and popped my head in. Sparkle was at the small room's only desk. She is a petite, light-skinned Black woman with a dancer's delicate bearing and infallible fashion sense—that day, a pale blue blouse under a winter wool burgundy suit and matching cap. She had done her nails in French-tipped deep purple and wore just enough silver jewelry to impress without distracting. The effect was stunning. It made me grateful that I wore scrubs and personal protective equipment at my own workplace, because I would never have the style skills to pull off what my bondswoman friend Sparkle pulls off on the regular.

"I'll run down to the taco truck if you'll keep an eye out for anyone with a ticket book," I said. "Lunch is on me if you chase them off. Bribe if you must."

An eclipse fell across Sparkle, her desk, and most of the room as a figure slid into the back-office doorway, and filled it.

"You shouldn't joke like that," the figure said.

It was Baby Mike, Sparkle's cousin, and he was dead serious. I have professional practice in sizing up human bodies. Baby Mike is six foot four and has got to weigh two hundred eighty pounds. Muscles, yes—but not a steroidal two eighty. Baby Mike is just plain large. Large, bald-shaven, and Black—with a nose that's been bashed flat a couple of times, hands like iron fry pans, and no sense of humor.

I apologized to Baby Mike for my bad joke. "You want the Herrador regular, Sparkle?"

"Yes, please."

"And what can I get for you, Michael?"

"Oh no," Baby Mike—he preferred Michael—said. "I'm all right."

"My treat."

"You sure?" he said.

"Yeah, babe," added Sparkle, with a warning look. "Are you sure you want to offer to feed Michael?"

"Yes, I'm sure!"

"Okay then," said Baby Mike. "I'll have one carnitas burrito with everything on it, one chile verde burrito with everything on it, a quesadilla supreme, large nachos, and a Gatorade. Jalapeños and extra sour cream on the nachos."

I mimed peeping behind him. "You hiding a crew of guys back there, Michael?"

"No."

Sparkle grinned her *told you so* grin and I went off to El Herrador, our favorite taco truck, in the jury-duty parking lot half a block down Bryant Street. I managed to cart the order back without having to ask the cashier to help me, but just barely.

It was a damp and dreary day, so we stayed in Sparkle's office to eat. Baby Mike wasn't fooling around—he worked methodically and silently to demolish that meal. Then he thanked me and excused himself, saying he had fridges to move. He was out the door before I could ask him what in heaven's name he meant by that.

Sparkle explained. I already knew her cousin had little to do with Baby Mike Bail Bonds. She'd named the business after him and had hung his portrait behind her desk as a boogeyman, but Baby Mike's day job, she told me, was delivering refrigerators.

"My uncle, Michael's dad, is a contractor. He gets regular work doing Section 8 maintenance for the county. Lots of units, lots of refrigerators. Michael brings the old ones out and the new ones in. He can pick up a fridge and carry it right into the apartment, alone, no hand truck or nothing."

"Jesus."

"Jesus got nothing to do with it."

Sparkle and I hadn't seen each other since the earthquake, but before we'd even caught up on that news, she wanted to know how things were with Anup.

"How come you always know the number one thing that's bothering me, Sparkle?"

"Professional hazard, I guess."

I filled her in—his fears about my working conditions, my fears about his closing something off from me, hiding something, my working too hard, his working too hard. Sparkle shook her head, and her coiffed hair wobbled under the burgundy cap.

"Bad news. I'm telling you. You can't keep going like this— something's gotta give."

"Don't I know it. I'm having conversations with the dog."

Sparkle rolled her chair away from her desk, stood, and paced. She said, "Now, look—"

I stopped her. "Nope. You are not setting me up, I don't care how cute he is."

"But he's an *artist*! He builds things. With power tools! And he cooks, too."

"No, thank you."

"He plays guitar. Think how soothing that would be, after a long day cutting up the dead folks and all."

"I'm fine, thanks."

"Artists have plenty of time, and they're flexible with it. They're *generous* with it. That's what you need. Never mind these go-getter men. They're never around! You need a man to take care of you, that's all I'm saying."

That stung. She didn't mean it to—Sparkle didn't know that taking care of me was exactly what Anup had promised he would not do.

"Think the rain'll ruin the rhubarb?" I said.

Sparkle flopped back down in her chair. "Fine," she said. "Be miserable."

I looked around the office. "Looks like you weathered the quake just fine," I said. "Everything okay at home, too?"

"Some plates and stuff fell out of the cabinets and broke, but nothing major. How about you?"

"Same. A little breakage." I didn't tell her that Anup had spent hours cleaning up the cable-car cottage in my absence, or that some of the breakage had damn near included my skull.

"There is something, though," Sparkle said, suddenly quiet and serious. "About the quake. I have a favor to ask."

"Go ahead. God knows I owe you."

"That's not… It's—I'm asking you because I'm…" Sparkle trailed off and looked down at her desk. It rattled me—because in the year and a half we'd know each other, I'd never once seen her rattled.

She looked up and met my eyes. "It's my uncle. He's missing."

"Okay. Tell me what's going on."

"My uncle has problems. He's very ill, diagnosed as schizophrenic a long time ago. He bounces around addresses and sometimes goes missing for a while. My mom always finds him, though."

Sparkle had told me before that Baby Mike Bail Bonds had been founded by her mother—but that her mom proved too soft-hearted for the business. Sparkle, who was less prone to getting ripped off by sob stories, took over when she was barely nineteen, and had kept the place afloat ever since.

"My mom can do that, you know what I mean? Like, if somebody can be found, she'll find them."

"This uncle of yours is her brother?"

"Yes. On my Burton side. Curtis Burton."

I wrote it down. "Are you worried he might be dead?"

A sad smile crept up Sparkle's lips. "You don't beat around the bush, do you, Doctor."

"I'm sorry, honey. I—"

"It's okay. Lately Uncle Curtis has been living on the streets. He went off his meds again. He's done it before. This time, though—last we heard about him was before the earthquake. Now we can't find him."

"We...?"

"My mom tried. She couldn't track him down. She asked me to find him. Jessie, she's never done that before."

"*You* couldn't find him?"

Sparkle shook her head.

That was bad news. Sparkle did not fail to find someone. It was her business to track down people who did not want to be found, people who are desperate to disappear.

"I'll get on it. But, Sparkle—I work in the system. You know what I mean, right? I need any source of ID info you have on your uncle, anything that might turn up in a database."

Sparkle snapped out of her funk, swung her chair to the computer, and danced her manicured fingers across the keyboard. "He has an arrest record. Loitering, trespass, stuff like that."

"Threats of violence or self-harm?"

"None. But he's been fifty-one-fiftied a bunch of times."

A 5150 is a legal proceeding, an involuntary mental health hold. It meant that Sparkle's Uncle Curtis had been hospitalized against his will for seventy-two hours while mental health professionals established that he wasn't a danger to himself or anyone else. At the end of those three days, the law says the hospital has to let him go if they can't diagnose such a threat. If he was homeless when he was last fifty-one-fiftied, he was likely homeless again after the hospital had turned him loose, with nowhere else to seek help.

"Did you call our office already?"

"My mom did. They couldn't tell her anything."

"Who'd she talk to?"

"Whoever answered the phone."

I was about to chide her and ask why she hadn't just come to me in the first place—but the look in Sparkle's eyes stopped me. I knew why. She was afraid of what I might find.

"Give me his date of birth, medical record numbers, fifty-one-fifties, and I'll see what I can turn up through my channels. But don't jump to conclusions, okay?"

Sparkle was already up and heading to the printer. "Okay."

"I'll get right on it and let you know."

Sparkle handed me the papers. "It's probably just the quake, right? He's just lost in the shuffle, right? He'll turn up…"

I don't lie to the next of kin of decedents—but Sparkle was my friend, and I didn't know for sure that her uncle was a decedent.

"That's right, honey," I said.

———

Jones and Ramirez wanted to meet in a police interview room. It was small and white, with chipped laminate chairs, a cold silver table, and a camera mounted in one corner. At least it was quieter than the cavernous Homicide bullpen.

I spread out my notes and summarized the phone conversations with Natalie Haring and Jeffrey Symond, and my in-person interview with Oskar. It was a lot of material, but I sped through it. The two detectives listened and jotted the occasional note. When I finished, Inspector Jones said, "Thanks, Doc. We'll investigate this new material if need be, but none of it appears to be relevant to the case at this time."

That threw me. "How come?"

"It doesn't have anything to do with the person we've arrested for the murder of Leopold Haring."

"Arrested—? Who?"

"A man named Samuel Urias," said Inspector Ramirez. "We picked him up on Monday."

I remembered him. "The union steward at the job site? The one who pulled the pipes off the body?"

Jones smirked. "Showed us what a big shot he was, right? Well, a call came into the tip line saying that Urias had a major beef with our dead man."

Ramirez said, "Apparently he got in Haring's face at SoMa Centre the last time he was seen alive down there."

"When was that?"

"Day before he died. Urias is a heavy equipment operator, so it would've been easy for him to stage the scene after he killed Haring. All he had to do was put the pipes in place over the body, and give that band holding them a little snip, or a good twist till it snapped. We can get our lab to do a tool mark analysis, and I'll bet you that's what happened."

"But the body shows evidence of having been dragged. And there's no bloodstain evidence at the scene to show Haring was killed on that spot."

"Could be Urias stabbed Haring somewhere nearby and

dragged the body over there before dropping the pipes on him," Jones said. "Either way, he looks good for murder one."

Ramirez picked up the thread. "Urias has a lot of power as union steward. We went down and interviewed a bunch of the workers, and they all had stories about him. It's his job to be their advocate, and they all seem to think he's a stand-up guy, but from what they're telling us it looks like he was always making trouble, always in fights with somebody—usually management. We've got it in interviews that he was butting heads with the site superintendent, who kept hurrying the work while Urias was slowing it down to stick to union rules. We've also got his coworkers saying he fought with Haring whenever Haring showed up."

"We talked to the widow, Natalie, too," said Jones. "She's never met Urias, but she listened to her husband complain about him plenty. That's backed up by the workers at the site, who said Haring was constantly lurking around the place, seeing who he could piss off with his demands and complaints."

"And insults."

"Yeah, and insults. A swell guy, our Mr. Haring."

"Urias didn't take it well," Ramirez said. "The anonymous tipster on the phone line claims to be a worker on the site. He had some details to prove it, and they checked out. He said Urias told him that he'd really like to find an opportunity to get Haring alone and give him a pounding."

"Okay, so we pulled Samuel Urias's sheet," said Jones. "He's got a couple of calls for service on domestic disputes, and a couple of arrests for bar fights."

"No convictions," said Ramirez, "but the violence in his record and the specific nature of the threat reported by the tipster were enough probable cause to pull a warrant."

"We didn't turn up anything at his house."

"But then we tossed his pickup truck at the job site."

"Guess what we found there, Doc."

I just shook my head.

"Buried in the open bed, under a bunch of other tools, we turned up a bloody screwdriver."

I almost jumped out of the chair. "You're shitting me!"

"Just like you said."

"So now it's off our board and on to the DA," Jones said. The two detectives shared a smug smile between them.

"Does that mean it's not restricted anymore?" I said.

"Yup."

"So I can sign the death certificate?"

"Yup."

"Excellent."

That meant I could call back the lawyers and insurance agents and Haring's widow and his business partner and get all of them off my back. I didn't need to worry about Oskar Haring at all, since he wasn't even looking for the death certificate. He was looking for a receptive ear for his theories of the case—and that ear now belonged to some hapless assistant district attorney.

I offered my fist for bumping. The detectives obliged. Jones buzzed me out of the secure area, and I headed right down the hallway for my second police errand: Missing Persons.

The detective assigned to find Curtis Burton was a round man molded into his chair in a cramped office stuffed with over-flowing evidence boxes and overburdened manila folders. He had watched retirement age stroll past him a while back, and wasn't out looking for it, or anything else. He looked up at me through big square glasses and an air of unruffled permanence.

I pulled out a fresh notebook, expecting to gather plenty of data for Sparkle. The detective located the Burton file, which contained a single boilerplate form. It covered information I had already seen—date of birth, arrests, involuntary holds, etcetera.

"The last thing on here is his fifty-one-fifty release from the General on October twenty-eighth," I said. "That's the day before the earthquake. What have you turned up since?"

"What do you mean?"

I turned the single sheet over, hoping there might be an investigative report on the back. It was blank.

"I mean, what are you doing to find this guy?"

The round detective's cell phone pinged softly and lit up. "Hang on." He looked at it. While he was thumbing a response, he said, "We've put a flag on his name and DOB. If he shows up in the system, we'll alert the family member who made the report."

"You mean if he gets arrested?"

"Or fifty-one-fiftied again."

I laid my pen down. "That's it? That's your investigation?"

The round detective took the question as provocation—which, to be fair, it was. "You know how many new cases we have since the earthquake?"

"You're not the only ones. We're stacking bodies like cordwood in the morgue."

"Yeah? So did you bother to look for this guy in your own freezer before you came down here?"

Shit, that was a good question. I didn't answer it.

"Leave your card and I'll put it in the file," the detective said, and went back to typing on the little screen smothered in his hands.

I took the stairs down to the Hall of Justice lobby, rather than waiting for the rickety elevators. I wanted to burn off a little of my anger before heading back to work. To Missing Persons, Curtis Burton was just another homeless man. There are a lot of homeless, and a lot of families looking for them, and the earthquake has made more work for everyone, sure. Sparkle's Uncle Curtis had slipped through the cracks. The only way the round detective was willing to do his job was to wait for Uncle Curtis to crop up on his own, one way or another. I wasn't about to let him get away with that kind of bullshit.

One of our day-shift 2578s was working the public counter.

The other one was in the Ops Shop, swiveling back and forth between piles of paper and the computer screen. I interrupted him, and asked first about Uncle Curtis by name and date of birth. That didn't come up in our docket. So I asked the investigator to look at all the current John Does we had in house to see if any of them matched him up by physical description: male, sixty-six years old, African American, five foot nine, approximately two hundred twenty pounds, no distinguishing scars or tattoos.

The investigator rolled his eyes so hard I worried he might sprain something. "That's pretty open-ended, Jessie. We still have fourteen John Does right now, twelve of those from the viaduct collapse. Some have presumptive IDs, but you'll have to give us some time to see if any of 'em match this description."

"How much time?"

"A few days."

I gave him a copy of the missing-persons report and asked him to be on the lookout for Curtis Burton, and to make sure the other 2578s got the message too.

The report had a phone number for the reporting party. I called it. Sparkle's mom, Gayle, was, predictably, a sweetheart. I introduced myself and told her that Sparkle had asked me to help out, and that I would do all I could. I was careful to say only that I was a doctor friend of Sparkle's, without mentioning where I worked—but Gayle was already one step ahead of me.

"Sparkle's told me all about you, Dr. Jessie. I'm glad she reached out. Sparkle doesn't want to say it, but I know there's a chance my brother won't turn up among the living this time— and if he's in the morgue, we want to know."

"I understand."

"Please God, that won't be the news we get. But if it is, I'm ready for it. Don't feel like you need to hide anything from this old lady, please."

"I won't."

Sparkle's mother sighed. "Curtis. Curtis is my baby brother. He's…got illnesses. Been in and out of institutions, on and off the streets, since he was twenty-four. We do what we can for him, but it doesn't always help."

She didn't seem to have anything else to add. Or maybe there was too much there, too much to even start with. She thanked me again, and I promised I'd be in touch, and we said our goodbyes.

I thought of my own baby brother Tommy, and my own fucked-up family life. I gave him a call, but it went straight to voice mail, which meant he was deep in some secure chamber at some corporate office, doing whatever he does with computers.

I sat back at my desk and watched the phone. It was giving off that vaguely radioactive vibe again, trying to warn me away. I knew I had to do it, though. I had to pick it up and dial. My fingers went automatically to the buttons, starting with 1-781.

"*Halo?*"

"*Co słychać, Mamusiu?*"

"*Czesia! Jak się masz, kociątko?*"

"I'm okay. Everything's fine."

"What is this phone number?"

"My office. I'm in my office."

"You had an earthquake."

"We did."

"You didn't call me."

"Here I am, *Mamusiu*."

"Yes."

The phone line from San Francisco to Lynn still had some static. I listened to it while my mother and I said nothing else.

"Why are you calling?"

"Just to say hello."

"But you didn't call after the earthquake."

"*Mamo…*"

"Tomasz called."

"Good for Tomasz."

"Don't be clever."

My mother has lived and worked in the United States for forty years. Her English is good, if quirky.

"How's everything in Lynn?" I asked.

"Fine."

"How is the foliage?"

"All gone now."

"Oh, right. How's work?"

"I can't work."

"What d'you mean?"

My mother, a nurse, had always kept the family afloat while my father was busy getting fired from various jobs and drinking up the bank account. Then the hospital closed—or, rather, was consolidated into obsolescence—and she got a job at an old age home.

"I sprained my hand," *Mamusia* said.

"What—?"

"Well, my wrist. I broke my wrist."

"What—!"

"Stop that. You sound like a broken record."

"Why didn't you tell me?"

"For what? How you could help?"

"I'm a doctor!"

"If you were here you could take me to the doctor. Instead the neighbor took me, all the way to Salem hospital. They gave me a splint."

"*O mój Boże, Mamusiu.*"

"It's getting better."

"How did it happen?"

"I fell."

"Where?"

"What does it matter? At the stairs, near the driveway. The

neighbor spilled oil. The other neighbor, the *bałwan*. From that motorcycle he drives."

"Is the splint off? Are you doing physical therapy? With a broken wrist, it's very important that you—"

"Of course I do the therapy! I was a nurse in the OT at Union Hospital from before you were born, don't forget, *kociątko*."

Three thousand miles away, an MD to my name and a gold badge on my belt, and hearing my mother call me a kitten made me feel twelve years old and late for supper.

"When are you coming to visit?"

"I don't know. We're awfully busy here. Shorthanded, and the earthquake has made a lot of work for us."

"Thank God you weren't hurt." Her eyes went to the Divine Mercy plaque in the hall by the bathroom and she crossed herself, I was sure of it. "So when are you coming?"

"Kozła doić próżno, Mamusiu." You can't get blood from a stone. She didn't respond. So I added that I would be getting some time off after Christmas, and maybe I could come then.

"Why not Thanksgiving?"

"Can't do it."

"You have plans?"

"That's not why I can't fly to Massachusetts for Thanksgiving, *Mamo*."

"You have plans?"

"Yes. I have plans."

"With the lawyer? The Indian?"

"Yes, *Mamo*. With Anup."

"He isn't a vegetarian?"

"Listen, *Mamusiu*, I've got to get going."

"How come you gotta?"

"I'm still at work."

"It's eight o'clock!"

"Not in California, *Mamo*. Here it's only five."

She laughed the only way I had ever heard her do: dry as raked leaves. "I know that. I joke."

"Yeah. You joke. Very funny."

"Yes, it was."

"I've got to go."

"Wait, Czesława." Using my formal name: She knew something was up. Even if *Mamusia* didn't know who Sparkle was, who Sparkle's missing uncle was, who Sparkle's worried mother was, she knew her only daughter, her Czesława. "Why you called now? You never answered me that."

"I just wanted to make sure you're okay."

"Sure I'm okay," my mother said. "Don't worry about me, *kociątko*. Worry about you."

CHAPTER 8

The Haring case was off my desk and out of my hair for about a week, but I had plenty more work to do. So did Anup—though we did, finally, find time for each other on Veterans Day. The Court of Appeal was closed and so was the Office of Chief Medical Examiner, so we spent one whole Wednesday together as tourists in our own town. We went to eat chowder and visit the sea lions at Fisherman's Wharf, then climbed the stairs to Coit Tower, stopping midway to watch the wild parrots. We bought ridiculously expensive Italian groceries in North Beach. We went back to Mahoney Brothers #45 and made love and then made a late dinner out of the groceries and fell asleep drinking wine and watching some stupid show on his laptop. We woke up, walked the dog, ate breakfast, had a kiss, and each went off to work.

It was just like we were a regular couple. It was brief, but it was bliss.

I managed to hide the sari and the bangles from him. Sparkle and I had gone on a shopping excursion over the weekend. Neither of us knows the first thing about Indian fashion, but at least Sparkle has an eye for style. She and an energetic saleswoman in a Desi shop got me properly outfitted for the festival of Diwali.

Diwali week was coming up fast. The highlight would be the third night, Lakshmi puja, when you get decked out in your finest to gather with friends and family. Each community is different, and celebrates in different ways, but buying new clothes for the festival is one of the common themes.

So says Wikipedia, anyhow. I wanted to make sure I was preparing in the correct way to attend a Lakshmi puja, but had been left to do my own research; Anup seemed to consider the whole festival a colossal pain in the neck, and brushed me off whenever I asked him about it. Anup's parents and two sisters all lived an hour away on the Peninsula, and I'd never met them. I planned to be ready to wow the Banerjees when we drove down there together for the big night—but I also wanted my outfit to be a surprise to Anup until then, and so I'd hidden the special Lakshmi puja sari and the jewelry that went with it under my makeup table in a plastic tub with a sticker reading BIOHAZARD HUMAN REMAINS.

Professional perk.

Ted Nguyen and I found ourselves facing a full slate of autopsies on Thursday after the midweek holiday, but on Friday there was only one new autopsy. Ted took it, leaving me a paper day. I had a ton of old cases to close, so that came as a relief.

A relief—until I checked my cubbyhole mailbox and found the subpoena. It was from an assistant district attorney in *People v. Samuel Urias*, and it was directing me to appear at a preliminary hearing—on November 16.

"That's *Monday*!" I yelled. "*Bzdura!* They couldn't give me more notice?"

"The famous dead architect, right?" said a 2578.

"Yeah."

"We've been fielding a lot of press calls on that one. I mean, a *lot*. Good luck."

I stomped off to my office, leaving a fresh wake of curses in the Ops Shop. With that subpoena, the Haring case had pushed itself back onto the front burner. I started by calling Samuel Urias's public defender, a woman named Eva Yung.

"My client has not waived time," she told me. "He's been in the city jail going on ten days, and I want to get him out of there. Can we meet to prep for the preliminary hearing?"

"Good idea, but I haven't finished my report."

"What's holding it up?"

I scanned through the file. "Toxicology results and histology slides. No surprise."

"Why's that?"

"Tox and histo take forever. Our lab's overburdened."

"Tell me about it."

I admire the San Francisco public defenders. They do thankless, heroic work for bad pay and worse press. Each one of them I'd worked with had been juggling bunches of cases in varying stages of crisis. Eva Yung seemed no different.

She said, "By toxicology, you mean tests of the decedent's blood?"

"Right."

"Are you expecting to find anything?"

"You never know."

"Would it change the cause of death, though?"

"Maybe."

Heavy sigh from Eva Yung. Then she asked the same question about histology.

"Again—it depends. Sometimes I see things under the microscope that can inform me about the age of an injury—and establishing a timeline for Leopold Haring's injuries is going to be important in the case against your client."

I held the line through Eva Yung's thoughtful silence, waiting for her to ask what I knew she would ask.

"Any chance you could get your lab to put a hurry on it…?"

Chief Toxicologist Carlo San Pietro answered the lab doorbell. He was short and round and wore tortoiseshell glasses, and his outfits never failed to dazzle. That day San Pietro was decked out in classic blue pinstripe with a brick-red bow tie, an apricot-yellow shirt, and tritone wingtips.

I pitched my request. San Pietro rolled his head back and around in theatrical fashion, and he made the expected rejoinder.

"Dr. Teska, you must know this is not possible. Not possible! We have so many, many important needs here, and I cannot take yours out of the line."

I put on my sympathy face and nodded along. "You have a challenging workload, no doubt. But, you see, there's a working man, a construction laborer, stuck in jail over this case, and his lawyer is on me night and day to look at the slides—five slides, that's all. So I was hoping you might have my five slides…?"

San Pietro pointed past rows of lab benches and boxy machines under fume hoods, to a technician in a Tyvek clean suit.

"We are cover-slipping right now," San Pietro said. "Perhaps yours is in this batch. If so, we will give them to you as soon—"

"Ooh!" I declared, and brushed right past him in feigned excitement. "Lemme see."

"Wait!"

He was too late. I stretched my hips in great strides to cross the room.

"What's the case number on those?" I said to the technician before I'd even reached her.

"Um…" she said, and peered at a computer screen. "Fifteen eighty-four."

"Perfect! That's what I'm looking for." I grabbed an empty

cardboard flat from a pile and scooped the five slides off the lab table.

San Pietro was apoplectic. "They are wet still! They will glue to each other… You must wait…!" I ignored him, and kept my attention on the lab tech.

"Email me the tox on this case right now, okay?"

The tech, the poor flustered dear, made a jerky nod and returned to the computer. I plastered up a grateful smile and breezed past Carlo San Pietro with a song and dance thanking his team for helping to advance the swift administration of justice.

———

Back in my office, I fired up the microscope and read the toxicology report in my email. It was completely negative—no drugs of abuse, no alcohol, not so much as a Tylenol in Leopold Haring's system when he died. One more thing I could check off my list, anyhow.

I found neutrophils in the nasal tissue when I put that slide under the microscope. Neutrophils are immune system repair cells, and their presence meant that Haring had got clocked in the face more than four hours before his heart stopped beating. I couldn't time the trauma more precisely than that, but I *could* tell all the interested parties that he certainly hadn't suffered that bloody nose at the same time that he died.

Next I examined the tissues from inside the fatal wound track. The first thing that caught my eye in the scattered mess of blood cells was a clutch of jagged, ruddy-bronze foreign bodies. Near them I saw something else that didn't belong—the dark corkscrew of a strand of wool. I moved the visual field around the slide and found more. I also came across long, light-colored plant fibers. Those were cotton, no mistake. Leopold Haring had been wearing a dark blue business suit and white dress shirt. The weapon that killed him had gone through his clothes and carried traces of the fabrics into the wound track.

I zoomed the magnification in and out over the red-brown things, sharp and flaky and distinctly alien in the landscape of human tissue on those glass slides. Then I packed the slides into their cardboard tray and went down the hall to Ted Nguyen's office. Ted had a few years' seniority on me, and I figured he might be willing to offer a quick consult.

"I don't know," he said, after considering the slide under his microscope. "The color reminds me of hemosiderin. Did you get an iron stain?"

"I didn't. I figured they were foreign bodies."

"Training in Chicago, we used to do iron stains to diagnose siderosis in mill workers," Nguyen said. "Metal filings in lung tissue look just like this, but way smaller. These things are huge."

"Microscopically speaking."

Nguyen pushed his chair away from the scope. "Interesting case you've got." That's the highest degree of enthusiasm the man ever showed.

I typed up the histology and toxicology findings in my autopsy report, then called public defender Eva Yung to tell her it was almost finalized.

"Would you sit down to talk to me about your findings?"

"Sure. When?"

"How 'bout now?"

"Right now?"

"No better time," said Eva Yung.

I looked at the email inbox on my monitor, and the IRL inbox on my desk. Both were overloaded enough to inspire panic and despair.

I printed the report and said, "Oh, hell, why not."

My cell rang through the BMW's console while I was inching off the freeway. The screen read *No caller ID*. That would be Anup, from his office landline at the Court of Appeal on McAllister Street.

"Hiya, hotness," I said.

"Dr. Teska? Jessie Teska?"

It was a woman. Whether or not she was the hotness, I couldn't tell.

"Oh! I, uh…"

"I'm trying to reach Dr. Jessie Teska?"

"Yes, yes—that's me…sorry, I… I thought you were someone else…"

"Dr. Teska, this is Amber Bishop at KnowNowSF, I'm putting together a story about the death of Leopold Haring and the police say the cause of death is homicide and I'd like to know more about that—I've got witnesses telling me he was crushed under a bunch of pipes, so does that mean someone dropped the pipes on him, and if so do you know…"

Zajebiście. A journalist. One who didn't pause for breath. I cut in.

"This is my cell phone. How did you get my—"

"An eyewitness at the death scene said that Jeffrey Symond was asked to come down there and identify his friend's mangled body, was it you who made that decision?"

"No! I mean, that's not what happened…"

"Did Jeffrey Symond positively identify Haring's body at the death scene?"

"Yes—well, it was a preliminary ID—but nobody… Wait, who did you talk to at the PD?"

"Is it true the cause of death is now homicide?"

"Manner of death. The cause is… It's not the same thing."

"Okay, what's Haring's cause of death?"

"I can't talk about…" I reached the end of the off-ramp and swerved to a stop in a beaten building's loading dock to get my head together. "You didn't answer me. How did you get my personal cell phone number?"

"I've been talking to several people who worked closely with Leopold Haring and said that he was a volatile man, hard to work with, some are calling him toxic. Since you're now saying he was murdered—"

"I didn't say that. I ruled the manner of death as homicide. Murder is up to the DA."

"So this *isn't* a murder? Jeffrey Symond is on record saying he saw the body and it was clearly an accident, crushed underneath pipes that fell off a truck. Since you've ruled this death a homicide, aren't you saying someone intentionally dropped those pipes on him?"

"Listen to me. Ms….?"

"Bishop, Amber Bishop, KnowNowSF—"

"Yeah, okay. I'm going to answer you. Are you writing this down?"

"Yes."

I spoke slowly and deliberately. "The death certificate for Leopold Haring has been filed with the San Francisco Department of Vital Statistics. It's a public record now." I paused. "Did you get all that?"

"But did you—"

"The death certificate is on file. You can go request it. It'll cost you, like, twenty bucks, I think, and should arrive within two business days. Got it?"

"Oh, yes, Doctor," Amber Bishop said, with acid. "And before I let you go, I'm going to give you an opportunity to comment on another angle of the story I'm writing."

I didn't like the sound of that. She went on.

"Before you were raised to the position of deputy chief medical examiner, you were involved in the RICO action against Hector Marroquin, and I've spoken to people who say that you—"

An air horn blared, drowning her out. A truck, flashing his headlights, wanted me and my coupe out of his loading bay.

"Hello, Dr. Teska…?" said the voice through my dashboard speakers. "Can I get your reaction to the allegation that you—"

I hung up the phone. I put the car in Drive. I scooted out of the truck's way.

The cell rang again. I bumped it to voice mail.

———

Eva Yung shared a shabby, cluttered office with another public defender. He wasn't there, which was just as well; it would've been intimate for a party of three. The office had big windows and plenty of sunlight, and Eva's half was overflowing with potted plants and Hawaiiana, including a framed photograph of a house on stilts in a jungle. I asked her about it while we were exchanging pleasantries.

"That was my place on the Big Island, in Kapoho. I was going to retire there someday. But the volcano took it."

"Oh." I'd never met anyone whose house was taken by a volcano, and couldn't think of anything else to say.

Yung smiled. "It's all right. I keep the picture to remind me that nothing is for keeps."

Yung was in her midfifties, tall and slender, with long arms, long fingers, long silver-gray hair, and enviable long legs under her business slacks. Her face was long, too, tanned and freckled, with Chinese features. She perched reading glasses on the end of her nose while she flipped through my autopsy report, and dropped them to dangle on a classic silver-and-pearl librarian's lanyard when she finished.

"So, wait. This stab wound. Couldn't it be from a knife?"

"No. Knife wounds look completely different, and leave a different type of track. This penetrating wound was made by something round and relatively blunt."

"How do you know that?"

"Abrasions on the edge of the entrance."

"It was made by something blunt?"

"*Relatively* blunt. Compared to an edged blade like a knife's."

"If we presented you with a specific weapon, could you match it to this wound?"

"Possibly."

"Could you rule it out?"

"Also, possibly."

Eva Yung rummaged through one of the several neat piles of documents on her desk and came out with a stack of glossy photos. "Inspector Jones gave me these after he ran the search warrant on my client."

The first photo showed a screwdriver. It was awful gory— dried blood all the way up the shaft, right to the handle, which was plastic and garish orange in color.

"This is a cheap piece of chain-store off-brand junk," she said. "My client swears up and down it isn't his, and he's never laid eyes on it before. He's a professional, and only uses professional grade tools."

I spread the other pictures across Yung's desk. One showed the bed of a pickup truck, followed by a series with the bloody screwdriver in it, revealed under a pile of old drop cloths.

"Sam is meticulous about his tools. He's certain that the screwdriver was planted."

"It's your theory that your client is being framed?"

"That would explain this tool that doesn't belong to him being found by the police in the open and accessible bed of his pickup."

"Who would want to frame him?"

"Plenty of people. Sam is the union steward. He says the SoMa Centre project is way behind schedule, which is causing the developer to bleed money. Sam is getting heat for the delays—but he's not going to sacrifice the safety of his crew to protect a greedy developer's bottom line."

"So if your client says he didn't do it, does he have any idea who did?"

"No, but Leopold Haring was certainly not a popular man at that job site. He liked to show up unannounced, bullying and micromanaging everyone. That's not his role. The architect is supposed to hand off the plans and go work on a new project, and leave the building to the builders. Leopold Haring didn't operate that way, and he was getting under the skin of plenty of the contractors and subcontractors and engineers and managers on the site, trying to tell them how to do their jobs. *All* of them."

It sounded to me like Samuel Urias's defense lawyer was blaming the conveniently dead victim. Then again, I had to admit I'd heard the same complaints about the decedent, even from his own business partner.

"Plus," Yung continued, "Haring had a hell of a temper. Sam says he could see somebody stabbing him just to shut him the hell up. But it wasn't him that did it."

"Okay, but did your client ever cross swords with the victim?"

"Yes. He acknowledges that he and the deceased got into an argument the last time Haring came by the job site. Haring came barging through, didn't even bother to sign in like everyone is supposed to for safety's sake, and went straight to some corner of the site where he demanded to inspect something. Sam found him and reamed him out for being in a hazardous area with no hard hat."

"Okay. The detectives told me your client has priors. Violent priors. Is that true?"

"That's not at all accurate. Sam has one DUI on his record, and an arrest for defending himself against an aggressor during an altercation in a bar. He pled no contest to the DUI and was never even held to answer in the bar fight—the other combatant didn't press charges."

Yung leaned across her desk. "My client is on a green card, working his butt off and supporting his entire family here and half the village back home in Mexico. There's no way he would jeopardize that. Trouble with the law is the last thing Sam wants."

Public defenders juggle a lot of cases. Few go to trial. They're dealmakers—they try to limit the harm their clients face. Sometimes, though, a public defender gets a client who really makes her want to go to the mat. I could see that Samuel Urias was exactly that client for Eva Yung.

"Sam has been dry for two years. He's never been violent against anyone except that one time in the bar, when he was provoked. He has no reason to want to kill Leopold Haring. He thinks it's a setup. I think he's right."

I sat back. "Whew. That's your pitch, huh?"

"That's my theory of the case."

"So, here I am. You have my report. What do you want to know?"

"First things first." Yung held up the picture of the screwdriver. "Could this be the weapon? Does it match the wound?"

"No ruler in the photo," I grumbled. "Typical. Do you know its length?"

"No. These are all the DA gave me."

"Well—where is this thing right now?"

"The screwdriver?"

"Yeah."

"In police evidence, over at the Hall."

"Can I examine it?"

"I thought you'd never ask," Yung said. She picked up her phone and dialed the DA's office.

"Bring a ruler," I said.

When we reached the police evidence lockup in the B-level bowels of the Hall of Justice, Homicide Inspector Keith Jones was already waiting, scrolling through his phone and looking grumpy. So was the case prosecutor, an assistant district attorney named Jason Bevner. Bevner looked like a high school football captain gone to pot, squeezed into a conservative suit and sporting the sort of short, bland haircut that never goes out of fashion for meat-and-potatoes white guys. We made a round of cordial introductions.

ADA Bevner's first question for me, before the evidence clerk had even retrieved the screwdriver, was what I was doing there with the public defender.

"Ms. Yung called me to discuss the case," I replied. "I had some questions about the physical evidence that the photos you gave her couldn't answer, so I suggested we should get a look at it in person."

Bevner kept eye contact with me and cocked his head at Eva Yung. "But you aren't her witness."

"Of course not. I'm—"

"You're my witness. I am the one who is calling you. You work for me."

"What...?" Yung said. "No, she does not."

"No, I do not," I concurred.

"Sure you do," said the ADA. "You're on the law enforcement team."

"I'm a medical examiner, Counselor. We don't work for the police, or for you."

"Then what's that badge for?" The ADA turned to Inspector Jones and bumped shoulders with him. "Look at that thing. Her badge is bigger than yours, Keith."

Keith Jones managed a miserable masculine chuckle, then stared at his shoes and tried hard to melt into the wall behind him.

"Hey," I said to ADA Bevner. I was tempted to grab him by his stupid yellow power tie. "Are you kidding? Honestly—is this a bad joke, or are you serious?"

The poor thick bastard looked genuinely puzzled. "You're a

peace officer. That's law enforcement, and that means you're a prosecution witness. Why are you even meeting with the defense? You're going to screw up my case."

"I am a scientific expert from an independent agency. I'm not a prosecution witness any more than I am a defense witness. I offer my professional opinion to the *court*, in matters pertaining to the cause and manner of death, the death investigation, and evidence from that investigation." I pulled out my cell phone. "Do you understand my role here, Counselor, or do I need to interrupt Chief Howe's afternoon to have him explain it to you?"

Bevner didn't know it, but I was bluffing. Sort of. Would Dr. Howe have my back in a spat with an assistant district attorney? I wasn't sure. Dr. Emil Kashiman, my mentor back in Los Angeles, surely would have—but I wasn't so confident about Howe. I'd seen the respect he garnered from the DA and police, but I'd also seen him fold under pressure from city hall.

Lucky for me, the ADA, who had gone all hot and puffy over his undersized tab collar, didn't have an opportunity to call my bluff. We were interrupted by the evidence clerk, who appeared at his window.

"Here ya go," he said, and held up a slender cardboard box.

The glass door next to the window buzzed, and Keith Jones sprang off the wall to push it open. We all filed through, into a brightly lit room with a long white counter marked out in a centimeter grid. The clerk came through a door on the other side and handed the box to Jones, along with a roll of evidence tape, a utility knife, and a Sharpie pen. He offered us black latex gloves from a box labeled XL. Jones took a pair.

"I carry my own," I said, and pulled surgical gloves, size small, out of a pocket. I had learned the hard and clumsy way that the San Francisco Police Department still seemed to assume that all police were men, and that all policemen had hams for hands.

The table had a butcher paper dispenser on one end. Jones pulled a long piece off the roll and laid it out, then sliced the box open and produced out of it an ordinary Phillips-head screw-driver. He placed it carefully on the paper. It was covered in dry, flaky, black blood.

All eyes turned to me.

I asked Eva for her ruler and laid it down. "The length of the shaft is four inches. With the handle, the entire tool is seven and a half." I documented the evidence with my cell phone cam-era. From another pocket I produced my magnifying glass—a true antique, hand-ground Austrian crystal set with brass in an antler handle. It had been a gift from Dr. Kashiman when I'd joined his team in Los Angeles. Jones chuckled at it and made a Sherlock joke. I ignored him. That tool was the finest low-magnification lens for the naked eye ever devised.

I leaned over the screwdriver and said, "You've tested this?"

The assistant district attorney answered. "Presumptive posi-tive for blood. We're waiting on DNA. They say they'll have it for us by Monday for the preliminary hearing."

Under the magnifier, I could see, sticking out here and there in the dark dried blood, bright blue flakes. I paused to take more pictures.

"What is it?" asked the ADA.

"Fibers."

They weren't what I was expecting to find. These were the wrong color—a pale baby blue. The ones I'd seen under the microscope, sampled from Haring's wound track, were much darker. And these fibers weren't wool, or cotton. They came from a woody plant material, most likely dyed paper.

"Any fingerprints?"

"None," Keith Jones said.

"What do you think," said Eva Yung, "is it consistent with the wound on the body, or not?"

I flipped through my own report to review the findings. At autopsy I had measured the depth of penetration as five inches, and the wound diameter as a quarter inch.

"I'm skeptical."

"Wait a minute," the ADA said.

"How come?" pressed Eva.

"The shaft of this screwdriver is too short for the length of the wound." I stood the screwdriver on end and eyeballed its diameter with the ruler. It barely cleared an eighth of an inch. "And it's too slender."

"Wait a minute," Jason Bevner said again. "You're the one who told us it's a screwdriver that made the wound! Isn't that right, Keith?"

The detective agreed it was.

"*Maybe* it was a screwdriver," I said. "But this particular screwdriver is shorter and skinnier than whatever caused the fatal injury."

"You said you saw fibers on it. Those are from the victim's clothing. The clothing wraps around the weapon as it's going into the wound, and gets pushed along there. Then, when it comes out of the wound, it leaves a hole that's bigger than the weapon. That's what's happening here."

The ADA wasn't as dumb as he looked. That was a pretty good theory. It didn't fit this case, though.

"That's possible," I replied. "It could explain the mismatch between the girth of the weapon you're presenting as evidence, and the diameter of the wound—but it still wouldn't explain the discrepancy between the length of the shaft and the depth of penetration, and that metric is much more important. A wound made with this weapon would be too short to reach the heart, and the lethal weapon went fully through the muscle wall of Mr. Haring's left ventricle. You'll see that in my report. Plus there's still the fact that the fibers I'm seeing here are the wrong color and type. They aren't the dark wool and white cotton fibers I found in microscopic evaluation of tissue from the wound. That's in my report, too."

Eva Yung didn't let the ADA catch his breath before she said, "You have to release my client."

"Not so fast," said Bevner. "Your client has priors, and he's on a green card."

"What's that got to do with anything?"

"Connection to a foreign country. He has family in Mexico, right? He's a flight risk. On Monday we will show that he has motive. This weapon was at the scene of the crime, in his possession, and has blood on it."

"You don't know whose blood."

"The DNA is going to show it's Leopold Haring's."

"Says you. If it doesn't, or if it's inconclusive, then you've got to let my guy go."

Keith Jones couldn't stop himself piping up. "It's a bloody screwdriver collected with a warrant from the back of your guy's truck!"

Eva Yung glared at the detective, and he withered. Then she turned back to the ADA. "Don't forget that my client is stuck in jail, the sole breadwinner for his family, boss of the crew on a vitally important construction project…"

"Okay, okay," Bevner said, throwing up his hands. "We've got the DNA expedited already. You'll have it in your hands at the prelim, if not before. If the results don't match Haring— then we'll talk."

The screwdriver went back into the evidence box, signed and sealed by Jones, and we all shared an elevator out of the B level of the Hall of Justice together. Jason Bevner, God bless him, turned out to be a happy warrior. It was just about quitting time on a Friday, and he asked us all, in a chummy way, what we had planned. Jones grumbled that he was on call. Eva Yung was going out to dinner with friends.

"How about you, Doctor?" said Bevner.

"I've got to go home and get to bed early."

"How come?"

151

"Big day tomorrow."
"Oh yeah? What's up?"
"Lakshmi puja," I said.

CHAPTER 9

The makeup alone took me more than an hour, and I didn't even attempt half the things I found in the YouTube tutorials. The jewelry was pretty involved, too. I settled on a few striking pieces of gold and goldish things: dangly earrings, a layered necklace, bangle bracelets, one anklet, and—a reach for me—a faux nose ring. I trawled through half a dozen videos of women wrapping themselves in saris before I finally found one that I could follow with success.

The end result was worth the effort. The sari hugged my curves so that the folds of bright silk positively sashayed as I practiced in high heels, making the five-pace parade back and forth across Mahoney Brothers #45 under Bea's skeptical gaze. I watched myself do a turn, and another, in the full mirror, my heart racing. I was gorgeous. I was going to make a stunning first impression. I was going to let Anup's family see how much I wanted to be a part of his life—their lives.

Five o'clock rolled around, but Anup still hadn't texted. Traffic down the Peninsula on a Saturday is unpredictable, and Cupertino's a long haul. I called him.

"When are we planning to leave?" I asked.

"For what?" Anup said.

"The Lakshmi puja."

"The *what*?"

"The Lakshmi puja. Tonight."

"What are you… Where did you learn about Lakshmi puja?"

"Wikipedia."

"Oh. Well, my family doesn't really do Lakshmi puja."

"All right. What do we do?"

"Um…" said Anup, "We… I…go down and pick up my sisters, and then we meet our folks at the temple."

"All right," I said again, and wondered why he was being so obtuse. "Time is wasting. Want me to come over to you, or are you picking me up here?"

"Jessie," said Anup, "you're not invited."

It's not easy to stun someone who cuts up dead bodies for a living. We see the very worst things that people do to one another. We have thick skins.

Why?

I didn't say it. For the first time in the eight months of our progressively and steadily more intimate life together, I had stumbled across a question I was afraid to ask Anup.

He broke the silence. "I'm sorry, Jessie. I didn't realize you… I should've been more clear. This is a stupid family obligation—for *me*. It isn't anything you need to bother with. Let me tell you, you're lucky you don't have to go—every Diwali, my sisters do nothing but complain about the hours they've spent shopping, and having to get their hair done, and then getting all dressed up in their saris and stuff."

I sat in my tiny house at the other end of the phone line, alone in my sari and stuff, and tried to sound worldly and blasé. "Sounds like a hassle for them. Yeah."

"I can't… It's kind of out of my hands, you know? And it's just for tonight. Tomorrow, I promise, we can spend the whole day together. We could go for another hike, maybe."

"Sure," I said.

"Okay. Thanks for understanding. I oughta get rolling."

"Yeah, traffic. Have a good time."

"Unlikely. Love you, bye."

"I love you too, Anup," I said. My voice was small.

My cell phone told me the call had ended. I sat there for a while, my head running circles around itself. Then I got up.

I unwrapped the sari off my body. I folded it carefully, and laid it back in the biohazard tub where I'd been hiding it. I went to the cable car's tiny bathroom and dug through the medicine cabinet over the sink, looking for makeup wipes. I found them—but it'd been so long since I'd had any reason to use them that they'd gone dry. A little jar of cold cream crouched in the back, though. I grabbed it and swung the cabinet's mirrored door closed.

There I was, staring back. The makeup regimen I'd worked on so hard for Anup, for his sisters and his parents, made my eyes pop and gave my lips way more flair than I usually managed, even for a special occasion. The jewelry added to it, amplifying without distracting. I uncapped the cold cream and scooped some.

My eyes returned to the mirror. I stood there over the sink and did nothing. Then I wiped the cold cream off my hand and put the jar away.

I went to my closet and raked through the hangers till I found a dress: navy blue and elegant, with a V-neck bodice trimmed in yellow lace that would work with the gold jewelry. I slipped it on and checked myself in the full mirror again. Then I speed-dialed a familiar number.

He answered.

"Tomasz," I said to my brother, "it's Saturday evening, so I'm guessing you're at work."

"Yup."

"Here in the city?"

"Yup."

"Wrap it up. We're going out to dinner."

I met Tommy at a Korean barbecue place on Geary Boulevard. Tommy eats like a machine and burns off the calories with massive daily brainwork, I guess. I don't know how else he does it, because he doesn't like exercise and he doesn't do much else than sit in front of a computer and work. Work is always some top-secret tech start-up that he's been called upon to rescue from the terrible coding skills of lesser beings. I hardly even bothered asking anymore. I never understood a damn word of what he said about any of these jobs, and he certainly didn't like to hear shop talk from the ol' autopsy suite, so we generally ate in silence unless we had something important to say.

After we had been seated and placed our order, Tommy found a question worth asking.

"Why you so dressed up?"

"Because, damn it, I look *pretty*."

The waitress brought a draft beer for me and a root beer for teetotaler Tommy, and I told him all about the Diwali fiasco. Tommy was sympathetic to me, of course—but also wasn't as hard on Anup as I wanted him to be.

"Pleasing parents from the old country can be challenging," he said with grim irony.

"No shit." I raised my beer. *"Na zdrowie."*

"Sto lat."

We clinked.

"I spoke to *Mamusia* yesterday," I said.

"I know. She called to tell me."

"Hold on—she called you to tell you that I'd called her?"

"That you'd *finally* called her. She's been calling me every day since the quake to tell me you hadn't called yet."

"That's not why she was calling you."

"I know."

"It was your reward for being a good boy."

"Jessie, I know."

"Did *Mamusia* tell you she broke her wrist?"

"She *what*—?"

"Yup. Splint and everything. She hasn't been working."

"Then how's she buying groceries?"

"Tommy. You think I asked?"

He sighed. "No."

"Because...?"

"She wouldn't have told you."

Our meal came in the nick of time—before I lost control of my temper and lit into my brother. He'd offer money to support *Mamusia*, sure. He made more than I did, lived frugally, and had no debt load. He could afford it. Tommy never offered our mother anything other than checks, though. He had left Lynn before I did. He ran off to California right out of high school, with nothing but his mad coding skills and a pile of chutzpah. He had never been back.

Part of me didn't blame him and part of me hated him for his ability to shut our entire childhood into a box and lock it away. Somebody had to take care of *Mamusia*. She was going to be aged out of the workplace soon enough—or fall out of it, if she was injuring herself without telling anybody. She had one brother and two sisters in Poland. I'd never met those aunts and that uncle, and *Mamusia* had never met their kids. She was a US citizen and had been for decades, but she held no passport and had no interest in going back to visit the old country. Danuta Repczynska had left Poland as a young woman, landed herself an American husband, and never looked back, even after Arthur Teska started beating her. Beating us.

Tommy got it the worst. *Mamusia* never fought back. She never went to the cops, to the social workers at the hospitals where she worked, not even to the priest. Then, one day when he was barely fourteen, something in Tommy made him hit back—and once he started swinging, he didn't stop. Dad went out the door, I changed the locks and arranged for the restraining order, and Arthur Teska, her husband, was out of *Mamusia*'s life.

But then her children left, too. Our mother was living alone in the middle floor of the three-decker on Pinkham Street in East Lynn where we'd grown up, her only loved ones thousands of miles away. I had been a Californian for more than ten years, Tommy for two or three years longer than that. I went back to Lynn every year around Christmas. Tommy? Not once. I had harangued him to go visit, but he made excuses, or just flat out refused. Sooner or later, we were going to go nose-to-nose about it. Sooner or later, somebody was going to have to go back to Lynn, and not just for a visit.

Sooner or later, I knew from professional experience, that old immigrant lady would likely die alone in her Lynn three-decker, and then Arthur Teska was going to come roaring back into the picture. He was out there somewhere. I knew he was, because I knew his Social Security number, and I have access to the federal Death Master File. I check it monthly. If he died first, no problem. But if his wife did—and, yes, *Mamusia* had let Tommy and me kick the sadistic bastard out of our lives, but she hadn't divorced him—then we were going to have complications. I had seen those kinds of complications firsthand, at work. Happy, healthy families get into fistfights over real estate and the disposition of a loved one's remains; I didn't even want to think what would happen if our mother passed away and our father came back to Pinkham Street.

He would, too. That would be just like him, waiting for his

chance to get back under our skin as soon as the danger of violating a permanent restraining order was lifted by the more lasting permanence of death.

"Mmm. Garlicky."

I watched my brother Tomasz tuck away the barbecue. *Which one's the hollow leg,* a neighbor's mom used to ask, when he stayed for supper. My little brother is a slender man. He isn't slight, though. Not in any way. He and I had always relied on each other. Tommy had put himself between me and the leather belt many times. I learned how to tell from Dad's footsteps on the stairs how drunk he was—and how deep in the house we should hide. Tommy had lied to protect me and I had dressed his wounds. Most kids grow up, but we didn't. We survived.

I ordered a fresh beer and lifted it. Tommy hoisted his own glass.

"A toast," I said. "To playing dress-up."

Tommy put down the soda without drinking. He pushed his food around, said nothing. I stopped before the beer reached my lips.

"What is it?"

"Nothing."

"Come on."

He went back to shoveling the food in silence, and I knew I was going to have to do the work for both of us, like I always do. It's the way he's been since he was a kid, keeping his trap shut, avoiding trouble—trouble with words, at least. My brother, my flip side.

"Don't make me drag it out of you."

He just shrugged. The routine was getting on my nerves, and I told him so.

He stabbed the fork into his bool kogi and left it there. "Who did you think you were fooling, playing dress-up in a sari?"

"That's it? Lighten up. Bad joke, I take it back."

"It's no joke. That's the problem. What did you figure would happen?"

"Happen…?"

"When you got done playing dress-up. What were you trying to show the Banerjees? How easy it is for somebody—anybody— to throw on the threads, toss on the jewelry, and join the club? You were going to fake your way into their *temple*…?"

My brother contemplated the bubbles in his root beer for a minute, while he tried to piece together words like he pieced together strings of code all day long.

"Let me ask you this, Czesława," he said finally. "How many times have you had to spell out your name? *C* as in cat, *Z* as in zebra, *E*, *S* as in Sam, etcetera. How many dumb-Polack jokes can you repeat by heart? Do you remember trying to explain to your friends that it wasn't really your birthday till it was your name day?"

"Gimme a break."

"Imagine all the stupid hassle we've put up with all our lives— only in Anup's skin, not yours. Anybody ever tell you to go back where you came from? Anybody ever spit on you and call you a terrorist? Did we take up a collection to hire security guards at St. Michael's? I dare you to ask Anup. Gimme a break, she says. Give *him* a break. He'll come around—as long as you let him, and you don't do stupid shit."

Easy for you to say, I thought. "That's your advice?"

He tore into the beef again, and shrugged. "You asked."

"Only because you were sitting there doing your silent but judgy routine."

"Like I said, you asked."

"My mistake."

Tommy looked back up at me—and grinned. "You know I'm right, though."

"Fuck off. It's entrapment."

"Admit it. I'm right."

"You're a *głupek*."

"But I'm right."

He had a piece of his dinner in his hair. I reached across the table and flicked it away. "You might be."

He held up his root beer. "I'll drink to that."

I clinked it, and we drank. Tommy returned his attention to his meal. I pushed mine away.

"I was only trying to do the right thing, you know?"

Tommy nodded. "But it wasn't the right way."

"So now what?"

Tommy just shrugged. He was all out of deep thoughts.

"I don't know if I can do it."

"Do what?"

"Wait for Anup to come around."

"Yeah," my brother said, and speared a bit of food off my plate. "If I were in your shoes, I don't know if I could, either. But you ought to try. He might be worth it."

We got the check and returned to our customary silence for a little while. I drank my beer and Tommy tucked away every scrap of food on the table. He yawned.

"I better go," he said.

"You're kidding. It's not even nine!"

"You know me, *siostrzyczko*." He rose. "You want a ride home?"

"No," I said. "I could use the walk."

The cool salt air made its way up Geary Boulevard from Ocean Beach. I pulled off the high heels and went barefoot, concrete under my toes. I wasn't ready to go home, to go to bed alone and lie there thinking about Anup.

After a couple of blocks, I found myself standing right outside Trad'r Sam, the battered tiki bar. I'd driven past the place a thousand times in my year and a half in San Francisco, but had never been inside. I don't much like tiki bars, and this one looked especially dumpy—fake palm fronds over a Dutch barn door, a novelty sign boasting of *Polynesian Drinks*, a limp green awning keeping the gull shit off the clutch of scruffy smokers. I went in anyway.

It was squat and dim, with a handful of small booths, more fake palms, and a horseshoe bar lined in bamboo and trimmed with tiki heads. The bartender was a young dude in a backwards baseball cap who looked about as Polynesian as I am. I got a Mai Tai.

The TV over the bar had the local news on. It caught my attention when a mug shot of Samuel Urias emerged over the shoulder of the Botoxed anchor.

"New developments tonight in the investigation into last month's death of prominent international architect Leopold Haring. San Francisco police have arrested a worker at the South of Market construction site where Haring was found crushed underneath building materials on October twenty-eighth. Samuel Urias, thirty-eight, has been charged with murder and other crimes, including special circumstance charges that sources say stem from an attempt to disguise the killing as an industrial accident. Our team will bring you special live coverage Monday morning from the Hall of Justice, as the trial enters its preliminary phase..."

I asked the bartender if he would please change the channel. He did, to college basketball. I tried to watch it and nearly succeeded. Anything—anything at all—to take my mind off the Hall of Justice. I watched and sipped and started to feel a little more relaxed as the game wore on and I reached the bottom of the Mai Tai.

"It is a small world, isn't it, Dr. Teska?" said a voice behind me. It belonged to a man. With a brogue.

Denis Monaghan cleaned up nicely. He was in a houndstooth suit with a Savile Row cut, complete with peaked pocket square, and his hair was styled to match. He had one hand in a jacket pocket, slid flat up to the knuckles, with his thumb hooked just so. He looked like he ought to be appearing in black and white.

"It's a small town, anyhow," I said.

"May I join you?"

Old World chivalry again; he didn't just plonk himself in the empty stool next to the lady without her permission. "Please do," I said.

He sat, mindful of his pleated trousers. "If you don't mind my saying so, Jessie—you look gorgeous."

"I know. But thank you for noticing, Denis. You smell wonderful."

Which was true. He beamed. "It's not too much, like? The cologne?"

"Perfect. What'll you drink?"

He seemed surprised. "You're buying?"

"Why not?"

"What do you got there?"

"It's a Mai Tai." I shook the ice. "Was a Mai Tai."

"Maybe just the one, then."

I waved over the bartender, who indulged the dapper couple with a heavy pour.

"Fruity rum drinks are underrated," I said.

Denis held up his. "To Trad'r Sam, whoever and wherever he be."

"Cheers," I said. We clinked our oversize cocktail glasses. "Why you dressed so fancy?"

"It's my Twinning Day."

"Your what?"

"I have a sister in Galway, you see…well, Tuam, now. I have a sister and three brothers, actually, but it's me sister in Tuam's birthday today, and—"

"You dress up for your sister's birthday? That's the sweetest thing I've ever heard!"

"It's not altogether for her. It's for me, too. I'm a twin now."

"Is that a riddle?"

"She turns forty-two today. I'm forty-two. I turn forty-three next month, on December sixteenth. So, for the next month, I'm…"

"A twin!"

"No flies on you, Doctor."

"Back in Boston we have a term for your condition. We call it Irish twins."

"Funny," Denis said. "In Ireland we have a term for it, too."

He waited. So did I. He won; I just had to know.

"Well…?"

"We call 'em Yankee scamps."

It wasn't a terribly good joke—in fact, it was a terribly bad joke—but I was just tipsy enough to find it uproarious. I lifted my fruity drink.

"To your sister. *Na zdrowie!*"

"*Sláinte.*"

Denis had turned glum all of a sudden. I recognized the look. I'd seen it on my mother, after she'd hung up the phone with one of her sisters back in Poland.

"Tell me about Galway," I said. It was the right call; Denis sat up and brightened. He told me about his sister's house in Tuam, a cathedral town of tight brick fronts and stone pavers. They weren't from there. They had grown up on a farm in the middle of nowhere, a crossroads with a church and a pub and a war memorial and not much else.

"My brother Rory, the eldest, he got the farm. The rest of us had to fend for ourselves. Mick to London, Sean to Dublin, myself here to America, and our sister Kate, who married a fella from Tuam."

"Your twin sister Kate."

"Today she is."

He went on for a while, waxing nostalgic about the west of

Ireland. I enjoyed hearing it. I'd heard it before, growing up, from some of the Ould Sod neighbors.

"Tell me about Boston," Denis said.

"Lynn. Outside of Boston. Outside of Boston…story of my life." Lynn had been on my mind, after my unexpectedly deep dinner with Tommy. "It's a tribal place. Parochial. Like, literally. I come from St. Joseph's parish in East Lynn, but we went to St. Michael the Archangel in West Lynn, 'cause we're Polacks and that's the Polack parish. The Italians had their parish, and the Puerto Ricans theirs, and the Irish, of course. The Cambodi- ans and the Haitians shared a church, but alternated Masses on Sunday. Nobody mixed, except in school. Where I come from you are defined by the color of your skin, the town you grew up in, and your religion, in that order."

Anup might be worth it, Tommy had said. But Anup had shut me out. He had shut me out for the same nearsighted, small- minded reasons I thought I had left behind. All I had wanted was to show him I wasn't an outsider, or I didn't have to be one. I wanted to impress his family. I wanted to join his parish. But Anup didn't want me there—? Not tonight, not for Diwali he sure didn't.

Then again, I reminded myself, Tommy really was right about my little stunt. I had bought the sari, the bangles, the makeup, without talking to Anup about it. A few YouTube tutorials later, I was ready to crash the party. It was careless—thoughtless. It was all about me. I'd wanted to play dress-up and surprise him.

Mission accomplished, Czesława.

"Ah, the hell with it," I said to Denis, apropos of nothing, as far as he knew. I rattled my empty Mai Tai. "It's your round, Monaghan. And I've had enough of this fruity shit."

"Whiskey, then."

"Fine idea. Which whiskey, though?"

"An Irish whiskey, of course."

"Of course."

"Jameson is the cliché, but I drink Paddy's."

"An Irish whiskey called Paddy's isn't a cliché?"

"Not if you're drinking it with a bog-bred culchie."

The bartender had a bottle of Paddy's. He poured us shots. I lifted mine. *"Sto lat!"*

Denis lifted his glass. "Who's that, when he's at home?"

"It means, *May you live to a hundred.*"

"Ah…! *Saol fada!*"

"What?"

"Drink up and I'll tell you. One drink per toast. Hard and fast rule here at Trad'r Sam's."

"Aye, aye, cap'n!"

Hard and fast indeed. Monaghan was no dummy. But I didn't want to go home—and if I felt like getting plastered with a handsome man in a sharp suit on a Saturday night, then, goddamn it, I would. We knocked back the whiskey.

"God, that's awful!" I yelped.

"'Tis," said Denis.

I begged the barkeep for peanuts. "What was that thing you said?"

"*Saol fada?* A short toast to a long life, in Irish. The whole thing goes, *May you have a long life, a wet beak, and die in Ireland.*"

"Man," I said. "It's not often that I'm on the delivery end of this sentiment—but you're kind of a downer, Denis."

He did look down, genuinely. "Not for me," he said. "No death in Ireland for this man."

"Don't tell me you're a sad drunk."

He forced a cheery face. "So, then."

"Think the rain'll ruin the rhubarb?"

"Not if it's in cans," he shot back, without missing a beat. Denis was sharp. Sharp, funny, and just uninhibited enough for my liking.

We got into shop talk, comparing notes—what's it like to be a contractor versus a medical examiner—and discovered that, in terms of workflow, it's much the same. Denis explained that he's always juggling multiple projects, in different phases of completion. I described how I'd do an autopsy in the morning, talk to the family the same day and maybe the police the next, if it's a criminal case—but then would wait weeks for toxicology and lab results, all while starting new autopsies, new cases.

"So it's the same for me," I said. "Only I'm not building anything."

"No. You're in demo."

"Demo…?"

"Demolition, my dear Doctor."

Denis explained that he was now a general contractor, but had spent years doing subcontracts—like fixing the climate control at the OCME—on different buildings all over the San Francisco Bay Area. "Jack-of-all-trades. I've done drywall, electrical, big demos, small rebuilds, from foundation on up to the roof cladding. Whatever the city, in her wisdom, throws my way."

"What's your favorite type of job?"

"Them old clay chimney pipes in the houses here in the Avenues. You go down in the basement, whack the yoke with a sledge, and watch it drop into the cellar in a million clinking smithereens and a *massive* cloud of dust."

"Sounds messy."

"That's half the fun! How about you? What's your favorite type of autopsy, dare I ask?"

"I like really complex hospital cases, the ones the other doctors can't figure out. I have to be a jack-of-all-trades, too, you see—I have to have a working knowledge of every branch of medicine, plus what kills people, and the changes the body undergoes after death… Ugh. Sorry. Never fails—talk to me long enough, and I'll end up on the subject of decomposition. Tell me more about Ireland."

But he didn't want to. He kept steering the conversation right back here to America. He wanted to know more about my life outside the morgue. And I didn't want to get into that—at all.

"It's my round," I said. I called the bartender over. "What kind of fruity drink can you make with that awful Irish whiskey?"

"I could do a Shark Eye."

It took him a few minutes. He served the cocktails in plastic imitation skulls, each with a shark-shaped stir stick.

The drinks were actually pretty good, but the skulls weren't anatomically correct. I rotated one around and pointed out all the reasons why. Denis and I nearly fell off our barstools laughing. The rest of the crowd at Trad'r Sam took it in stride.

A toilet flushed and I woke. God, the light was blinding. I was in a strange bed, in a strange room. Sounds of traffic outside, and a bathroom sink running. It stopped, and a door opened, and out of the bathroom came Denis Monaghan. He was naked, and looked as hungover as I felt.

The room wobbled. I lay back down. My mouth tasted like bad whiskey and sticky fruit juice.

"Boże mój…"

"Morning," said Denis. I squinted in his direction. His hair was ruffled and his face pale and sour in the aftermath of drink, but he carried his builder's muscles on a broad, solid frame, and from the neck down was altogether buff and beautiful in that dazzling light. Seeing him dangling there brought it back to me—our romp through the night, after leaving Trad'r Sam, in the sheets where I found myself lying, undone by alcohol and debauchery and the cruel bright sunshine of California in November.

"Good morning," I said, but didn't mean it. I scanned the rest of the room. One of my high heels was lying on its side in a corner, and the other was AWOL. My special-occasion navy blue dress was hanging on an actual lampshade. I snatched it and held it in front of myself as cover while I scurried toward the bathroom and scanned for my underwear, which was also AWOL.

I slid past Denis with an effort at a demure smile, and barricaded myself in the john. I used the toilet and splashed cold water on my face, then hazarded a look in the mirror. My hair was a dirty blond thicket, and the meticulous makeup I'd spent so much time on the day before was blurred and smeared in grotesque streaks.

In place of bath linens Denis had only a roll of contractor's paper towels, the heavy-duty blue kind, so I scrubbed my face with a couple of those. When I kicked open the trash can to throw them out, three used condoms stared back at me. I concentrated, which hurt my head. The first time—I remembered that vividly. The second one? Also yes, for sure. But the third...? Oh, wait. Oh, yes. Yes indeed.

Holy moly.

I caught myself in the mirror again and found that I was wearing a goofy grin. I wiped it off and wiggled naked into the dress, then opened the bathroom door and came slinking out. I scanned the room for my panties. And my bra. Shit—where was my phone?

Denis had put on jeans and was pulling a T-shirt over his head, but he paused to watch me pad around his apartment, rumpled and barefoot and bare-assed under my fancy dress. The sight pleased him.

"Make yourself useful and help me find my phone."

"Oh, I can be useful. Handy, even."

"Don't I know it. Now help me look."

"I'm one step ahead of you, love."

I turned. He was wearing a poker face and my panties on his head, cocked like a beret.

Yes, I was hungover. I needed coffee. I was embarrassed, and felt exposed in the glaring sunlight. But, damn it, Denis's stunt was really fucking funny—and I found myself sprawled on his bed again, losing myself in giggling hysterics.

Denis took the opportunity to bounce down next to me. He started caressing me and nibbling my ear. I pushed him away and grabbed the panties off his head.

"That's unfriendly," he said.

"Leave me alone, you. I have to get home before my dog tears the place up."

"You have time enough. We'll be efficient." He started to undo my dress.

I pulled away from him. "No."

His fingers stayed on the dress. All the playful had gone out of his eyes.

"Not time enough?" he said.

"No."

Denis didn't move. He watched me and I watched him back. Then he let go. I slid off the bed and got to my feet. I pulled my hair up.

"Right," said Denis. He sat up, ran a hand through his own hair, and rose to go toward the kitchen. "But surely you have time for a cup of tea."

"I can't. Believe me—this dog won't wait."

"Ah, now," he said. "Jessie, honest, I do not make a habit of picking up women in bars. Let me make you a civilized breakfast before you go. I would hate for you to think…"

"Denis," I said, "you've been a perfect gentleman. Now, would you please help me find my phone."

He reached into the back pocket of his jeans—and pulled it out. He tossed it on the bed.

"You sneaky bastard," I said, scooping it up.

Denis produced that ready smile of his. "I'm only bold, love."

My phone still had plenty of juice—but, of course, there was no signal. Cell service had been spotty before the quake, and turned shitty after. I asked Denis for his Wi-Fi password.

"Can't give you that, love," he said. "I have secrets."

"Don't we all. You have nothing to fear from my hacking skills, believe me."

He acquiesced. "It's Janina."

"Oh, really," I said, arch as hell.

Denis held up a palm in self-defense. "Not what you think! It's my toothpaste."

"Sure. Sure it is, Denis."

"It's true, I'm telling you! Hang on…" He popped into the bathroom and, true enough, came back with a tube of something called Janina Whitening Toothpaste.

"Ye don't use it here," he said, cradling the tube in both hands like a sleeping kitten. "I have to order it special. Bloody expensive, but worth it." He bared his mouthful of bright teeth in a predatory grin.

I entered the password and got my phone connected to the internet. Denis offered to drive me home, but I demurred and said I'd get an Uber. I had enjoyed our romp, but had no intention of repeating it. He didn't need to know where I lived. It occurred to me, though, that I didn't know where the hell I was, either. I opened the ride-share app and looked at the blue dot.

We were in the Richmond District. If I weren't knackered and hungover, I could walk home. I ordered an Uber anyhow, to save face, for both of us.

———

As soon as I clicked the seat belt, my cell pinged with a text. It was Anup.

Sorry again bout yesterday. I'll pick u up 4 a hike? Whole day free, would love to spend it w/u.

The Uber ride was all of five minutes. I burned four of them thinking about a response.

Can't do it, under weather.

He came right back: Can I get u anything? Come over, nurse u?

No thx, I typed, gonna just lie down & drink tea.

That wasn't even a lie. The car pulled up in front of 892 41st Avenue and Anup replied:

Kk. Feel better.

I could hear Bea the beagle's frantic yelping as my key scraped into the gate's lock. The phone pinged again.

Maybe nxt weekend we catch up. Love u.

I paused, half in the gate, phone in my hand. Then I typed, Love u 2, and fought down a wave of hungover regret and shame. Shame, because that was no lie, either.

CHAPTER 10

The preliminary hearing in *People v. Samuel Urias* took place in one of the Hall of Justice's older courtrooms. There's no jury in a prelim. It's usually a brief and straightforward affair, presided over by a judge. This one was a graying woman with the air of a grumpy umpire.

I was on the witness stand. Oskar Haring, the son of the man Samuel Urias was being charged with killing, sat in the public gallery, keeping himself apart from the ruck of journalists with open notebooks. He was unkempt and fidgety, and had his eyes locked on me. Another man, also alone in the crowd, watched me from a pew on the opposite side. He had tightly curled brown hair, thick at the top and shaved at the sides, and a reddish mustache and goatee. His skin was freckled and wrinkled beyond his years: he spent a lot of time in the sun. He saw me watching him and flicked a shy smile, then caught himself and looked away.

Assistant District Attorney Jason Bevner lifted his blocky self to approach the stand, and launched into the direct examination by asking me if I had performed an autopsy on Leopold Haring on October 29.

"Yes," I replied.

"During the autopsy did you collect a blood specimen for DNA, for identification purposes?"

"Yes."

"What was the cause of death?"

"Penetrating trauma to the heart."

"Did you determine the manner of death?"

"Yes."

"What was that?"

"Homicide."

"You did not determine that this was an accident?"

"It was not an accident."

"How do you know that?"

I addressed myself to the court reporter and described, slowly and clearly, the many postmortem injuries to the body and the single fatal one, a penetrating wound through Haring's back, between his fifth and sixth ribs, straight into his heart.

"The scene was staged with the fallen pipes to appear as an accident. But that wasn't what happened. The body had been moved. There were drag marks in the dirt that matched evidence on the clothing and the body, and the lack of vital reaction in the wounds caused by the fallen pipes indicates that Mr. Haring did not die there."

"Someone killed him somewhere else, and then placed him under the pipes and dropped them on him?"

"That's what the physical evidence shows."

"What kind of weapon would have caused the penetrating trauma that you determined was the cause of death?"

"Something at least five inches long and about one-quarter inch thick, with a round shaft."

"Did you tell the police that the wound was consistent with an injury caused by a screwdriver?"

"I did."

"No further questions."

Bevner swiveled and returned to his seat. The judge looked to the defense table and said, "Cross."

Eva Yung came in front of me, nodded in a staged, impersonal way, and asked if I had examined the screwdriver the police said they had recovered from her client's truck. I answered yes.

"Isn't it true that you said, after handling, examining, and measuring that screwdriver yourself in the police evidence room, that it was not the right size to have caused the fatal injury in the deceased?"

"Yes."

Eva walked me through a couple of questions about the fibers I'd found on the screwdriver's shaft—whether they matched the fibers I'd found in the wound track. They did not, I said. Did I find any fibers on the screwdriver that *did* match the fibers I'd seen under the microscope, or any that matched the clothing Haring was wearing? I did not.

"Isn't it true, Dr. Teska, that you cannot state with reasonable medical certainty that the fatal wound was caused by the screwdriver that was recovered from my client's truck?"

"That's true."

Eva Yung told the judge she was finished with cross-examination, and the judge asked the ADA if he wanted to redirect. He did.

"Dr. Teska, if you were provided with evidence that the screwdriver in question, the one Inspector Jones recovered from the back of Samuel Urias's truck, had blood on it that matched the DNA of the victim, would it change your mind that it might be the murder weapon?"

"Maybe. Depends on what kind of evidence."

Jason Bevner went back to his table and held up a document.

"Your Honor, I'd like to approach the witness with people's exhibit three, the police criminalistics lab's DNA report on the blood from the screwdriver—"

Eva Yung sprang back out of her seat. "Objection, Your Honor—hearsay, lacks foundation. Dr. Teska isn't a DNA expert."

"She is a board-certified forensic pathologist and she is more than qualified to interpret DNA," the prosecutor shot back. "Heck, she could be running the criminalistics lab. She's been qualified as an expert witness, and as an expert she can rely on hearsay like this report."

"I'll allow it," the judge said.

The prosecutor smirked and Eva Yung sat. Then he got permission from the judge to approach me on the witness stand, and handed me a copy of people's exhibit three. I read it over. I had reviewed DNA laboratory reports like it a hundred times, but this one held a surprise. I said nothing, and took the time to read it again carefully before I looked up at ADA Bevner.

"What does the report say, Dr. Teska?"

"That the evidence marked as 'screwdriver recovered from truck' was positive for human blood, and that the DNA was a mixed specimen of two contributors, both male."

"And was one of the contributors matched to the decedent, Leopold Haring?"

"Leopold Haring cannot be excluded as a contributor."

"That means yes?"

"Yes."

"It says that the DNA on the screwdriver was matched to the blood specimen you took from the body of Leopold Haring during the autopsy, correct?"

"Yes, that is how I would interpret this report."

"No further questions."

Eva Yung was still scrutinizing the defense copy of the lab report when she approached me. She kept her eyes on the paper and said, "Isn't it also true that my client Samuel Urias was *excluded* as a contributor?"

"Yes, that's correct."

"That means his DNA is not on this screwdriver that the police say belongs to him?"

"Yes."

"How is that possible?"

I opened my mouth to expound on the complexity of extracting DNA off a piece of forensic evidence, but the prosecutor cut me off.

"Objection, Your Honor. She hasn't been qualified as an expert in DNA methodology."

"She's exactly just such an expert, Your Honor," Eva Yung argued. "Dr. Teska works with DNA all the time. Besides, the ADA just handed her the report and said she's an expert in interpreting it!"

"Your Honor, I plan to call Dr. Shirley Shimamoto back to the stand. As the expert who authored this report, she alone is qualified to answer questions about methodology at the crime lab."

"Yeah, you're right," the judge said. "I'm allowing the people's objection." She peered down at me over the tops of her half-moon glasses. "You are instructed not to answer that question, Dr. Teska."

"Yes, Your Honor," I said dutifully. Then the judge asked Eva Yung if she had any further questions. She didn't. Same question to Bevner. Nothing coming from him, either.

"You're excused, Dr. Teska. The court thanks you for your time."

I tucked the DNA report into my case file, thanked the judge back, and made my way to the door at the rear of the courtroom. As I walked down the aisle through the public gallery, two men watched me—Oskar Haring from one side, and the man with the red goatee from the other. Both looked perturbed.

A couple of reporters followed me out of the courtroom and started barking questions as soon as we were in the hall. I told them I had no comment. They barked more questions, with more urgency. I said nothing. I made for the stairs, knowing they wouldn't follow. If I wasn't talking, the next witness to take the stand in the prelim, whoever that was, would be more interesting to them. I was right—they stayed behind as the heavy metal door clanged shut on the stairwell.

I wove through the familiar old corridors of the Hall of Justice, and mulled. Eva Yung was pursuing the theory that someone had planted that screwdriver in the open bed of Samuel Urias's truck. Now the DNA report showed that the screwdriver, which did not match the fatal wound, seemed to have the dead man's blood on it. Plus it had another, unidentified man's blood mixed in. No, wait—not blood; DNA. Just because there's blood on the screwdriver doesn't mean that the DNA came from blood. The blood could belong to both of the two contributors, or only one of them. That one didn't necessarily need to be Haring. It could be the mystery man's blood on the screwdriver, and Haring's DNA that got onto it somehow other than by being plunged into his back.

I was contemplating how much scotch I would go through every night in order to make it into work each morning as a DNA analyst when I nearly bumped right into Denis Monaghan. He was coming off the line of people cramming through the metal detectors in the Hall's main lobby, and looked as surprised as I was.

"Small world," I said, barely beating him to the punch.

"Small town, anyhow," he replied, grinning wide.

Denis was wearing another suit, this one more conservative than the Twinning Day outfit I had stripped off him on Saturday night. With his brawn stuffed under its seams, it made for another sharp piece of business attire.

"What are you doing here?" I asked.

"Ara," Denis said, and waved his hand toward the crowd behind the security checkpoint. "Business nonsense. You get to see me in my other suit!" He struck a pose. "That's the full formal wardrobe for Denis Andrew Monaghan, the complete and entire collection."

I did a quick double-arch of my brows, which I hoped was a suitable display of appreciation, given the public setting. "What is it, a lawsuit?"

"Always. A carpenter makes lawsuits like a pig makes shite."

"Another colorful Irish saying?"

"No—my own poor personal slogan, I'm afraid."

"But you aren't a carpenter."

"Sure I am."

"Carpenters don't fix HVAC, I know that much."

Denis sidled carefully into my personal space. The smell of his cologne brought me back to his bedroom, and a flush spread across my collarbones. "Ah, Doctor," he said. "I thought I'd already demonstrated that I'm a jack-of-all-trades and master of some."

"Um-hm," I said. I didn't trust myself to say more, but I didn't back away.

He made sure no one was in earshot, and then he murmured, "Come out with me again."

"No," I murmured back, and cold shame pushed the flush right off my skin.

"Why not?"

"Denis… I misled you the other night. I never told you I'm in a relationship."

The spell broke. Denis straightened. "No ring on your finger," he said with a defensive twinge. "I checked."

"You're right. But, still—no."

He smiled in a rueful way and shrugged. "That's a shame, really it is. We had a good time together, didn't we? You had a good time—didn't you."

"I did. Oh yes I did… But it was only a one-time good time."

Denis started to say something, but it never came out. He looked off and shrugged, then stepped back, clapped his hands, and rubbed them together as though we'd just settled a building contract.

"Right, so," he said. "Be well, Jessie." And he slipped right into the stream of people heading for the elevators. I watched Denis go, and decided that there are worse ways to hammer home the coffin nail in a one-night stand.

I crossed the lobby to put myself into the line for the exit onto Bryant Street, but stepped back out when I saw beyond it, to the parade of news vans out there. The crowd at the doors was enormous, and it had cameras. Cameras, and the hungry look of murder-trial reporters. Muscle memory took me another way, across the lobby to a side corridor, where a sheriff's deputy guarded a pair of glass doors marked *Authorized Personnel Only*. I showed my badge and he waved me through, outside to the gray concrete cloister of the police parking lot.

I hustled down the walkway that skirted the parked cruisers, congratulating myself for my cleverness, until a young woman appeared from the corner off Seventh Street and started straight at me. She had her phone thrust out like a microphone.

"Dr. Teska," she said before I could dogleg into the parking lot, "when you testified up there about the DNA on that screwdriver—"

"Who are you?"

"Amber Bishop, KnowNowSF, did you mean that the weapon the police found in the back of the defendant's vehicle should be—"

"No comment."

The walkway was narrow, and I didn't want to shoulder past the reporter, but I didn't much like being ambushed, either.

"Are you aware that the prosecution has called witnesses who will testify that Samuel Urias repeatedly threatened Leopold Haring at the work site?"

"No comment."

"You're saying the bloody screwdriver doesn't match the wound you found during the autopsy, but they know the blood belongs to Haring. How do you account for that?"

"One of the DNA profiles can't be ruled out as Haring's. That doesn't mean it's his blood. DNA and blood aren't the same thing."

Mój Boż, Czecia, ucisz się, I heard my mother tell me from inside my skull. She was right: I should shut up. I slid past the reporter, brushing against her on one side and a patrol car's dirty fender on the other. She followed as I power walked toward the street.

"If that isn't the screwdriver that killed Leopold Haring, then how come it's covered in his blood?"

"No comment."

"There's another man's DNA profile on that sample, but it isn't Samuel Urias. Who'd it come from?"

"No comment."

"You've seen that report, Doctor. Who's the other man with DNA on that screwdriver?"

"No comment."

"Oh come *on!*" Amber Bishop swooped past me on the sidewalk and planted herself in my path again. "What's with this stonewalling? Why won't you talk to us? That's your job!"

"I have no comment, Ms. Bishop."

"You're the deputy chief! Mike Stone always talked to us…"

I stepped up but didn't step around her this time. I put my nose right into the reporter's, till I could smell the hustle and the Coco Mademoiselle coming off her pores.

"You take Mike Stone's name right out of your mouth," I said carefully and quietly. "I have no comment for you."

When I walked away again, Amber Bishop had sense enough not to follow.

I was back at my desk, clearing out backlog cases, when the phone rang. It was the veteran day-shift 2578, saying he had a caller on hold for me—and that the caller wouldn't give his name.

"Sure, put him through."

The mystery caller was a man with a Spanish accent. He wouldn't give me his name, either.

"Why do you want to talk to me, sir?" I asked.

"You were in court today, in the case of Samuel Urias. I have information."

"What kind of information?" The first thing I do when I testify as an expert witness is to state my name, occupation, and place of work. It's not hard to track me down. The caller could be another journalist from the public gallery, and I was not going to put up with any anonymous-caller shenanigans.

"Samuel didn't kill that man," he said.

"Okay."

"I know he didn't."

"How do you know that?"

"A lot of people want Samuel off that job site where he's working. *A lot* of them. He gets blamed for this killing, and now he is off the site. You see?"

"Sir, the police are really—"

"No. They will not. You must help Samuel, Doctor. There must be something you can do—because the way they blame him, it cannot be true what they are saying, and it's your job to find that out. Yes?"

"You haven't answered my question. Why do you say you know Samuel could not have committed this murder?"

"I was...with him that night."

"What night are you talking about?"

"October twenty-seven."

"What time were you with him?"

The mystery caller was silent. I waited.

"All night."

"Okay," I said, flat. "Can you prove it?"

"No."

"But you can swear to it. Samuel has a lawyer. Her name is Eva Yung. I'm going to give you her number, so you can call her and testify to this alibi. Even if you—"

"No. I cannot."

"But your friend is in serious trouble here—"

"I cannot. You have to stop them."

"Who?"

"The police. You said this screwdriver is not the one. That's right. It cannot be. What the police are saying Samuel did, he didn't do it."

"You were there today? You saw me testify?"

I waited out another itchy pause. "Yes."

"What you saw was only one small piece of the trial. The evidence—all the evidence, taken together—looks pretty bad for your friend. But if his lawyer can establish that he was with you that night, it would prove he didn't do what the prosecutor—the police—say he did. You understand that, right?"

"I understand. But I cannot testify."

"Can you tell me why?"

"No."

I guessed the caller must be the curly-haired guy with the red goatee who had been watching me so intently when I took the stand.

"Okay, look. You called me out of the blue. How do I know you're telling the truth? What do you expect me to do?"

"Fíjate en la sangre," the man said. "The blood—look at the blood."

"What about it?"

"You said that the screwdriver has the dead man's blood, and someone else's, but not Samuel's. You have to find that other person, the other blood. That must be the killer. It is not Samuel."

I started to explain that the presence of another person's DNA doesn't necessarily point to the murderer, but the damn guy got agitated and cut me off again.

"I am telling you that Samuel was with me that night and he didn't do it. *Fíjate en la sangre.*"

And he hung up.

Son of a bitch. I found Eva Yung's email address and fired off a quick message giving her a heads-up about the call. If the guy called her, and if he was legit, then she might be able to establish an alibi for her client. Then again, Eva Yung had given me a song and dance about Samuel Urias being a warrior for his brother workers, a solid family man, a pillar of his community. This guy was trying to push the story that he was Urias's secret lover. Yung might have been leaving that part of her client's biography off for my sake, or she might be ignorant of it. The mystery caller might be lying.

Nie mój cyrk, nie moje małpy. Not my circus, not my monkeys.

Except, I realized with a sorry sigh, alone there in my office, they were my monkeys. The mystery caller—Redbeard, if that's who it was—had a good point about one thing, damn him: Who was that second DNA contributor? The prosecutor had mentioned the specialist who produced the report. It was a Japanese name, something moto. Wait—it would be on my copy of the lab report. I pulled it out. Shirley Shimamoto, PhD.

I called the police crime lab and asked for her. I got a secretary, who told me that Dr. Shimamoto was still stuck in court at the Hall of Justice, but that she should be back at the lab by four or four thirty.

If Redbeard was telling the truth, whoever belonged to that second set of DNA alleles might be able to help Eva Yung keep an innocent man out of prison. The bony finger on the minute hand on the novelty death's-head clock I keep on my desk started inching toward 4:00. I looked up the police criminalistics laboratory's address. Turned out it was in the disused shipyard at Hunters Point, not far from my office. I decided to head home early, and pay a quick visit on the way to DNA expert Shirley Shimamoto.

My BMW's navigation system gave up somewhere in the shipyard's ruined plain of rusted cranes and rotting warehouses. Internet mapping apps on my cell phone fared no better. I found the criminalistics lab only because it was the sole structure lit up in the gloomy autumn dusk. It was a newer building surrounded by a moat of parking lots, empty but for a cluster of half a dozen cars huddled together.

"The unnamed contributor could be nearly any male person," Shimamoto told me as we clattered our way through the echoing building to her office. "Anybody who touched the thing. It could be someone who handled the screwdriver at the store, or another worker at the site—it was found in an open-air truck bed, remember."

"They wouldn't have to bleed on it?"

She shook her head. "DNA don't care."

"That's a good slogan."

"We like it. What's the OCME's?"

"They'll still be dead tomorrow."

Shimamoto snorted a laugh.

I looked over the report again. "Is there anything unique about this DNA profile?"

Shimamoto went to her computer and poked around. Then she swiveled the screen to show me a graph, and pointed. "See these STR loci? They're more common in African Americans."

"How accurate is that measure?"

"Eighty percent likelihood."

"Hmm. What are the ways you would match this sample to an individual?"

"If he gets arrested on a felony, his DNA would get entered into the FBI database, and it would be flagged here. We check it automatically on any unidentified human sample."

"So that means he hasn't been arrested for a felony in the past."

"Not since we started collecting DNA."

"And how long's that?"

"Thirty years, more or less."

It was a dead end. I don't like dead ends. I asked Shirley Shimamoto if there was anyplace else she could look, any other resource where she might find a match for this DNA profile.

Luckily for me, Shirley liked a challenge. "Let me see," she said, and fiddled with her computer. "There's another database that might... Aha! We have a match here..."

"Really? That's great! So who is it?"

"It's not a name. We have a match to an internal sample from the medical examiner."

"You're kidding."

"Nope. Case number SFME–1556."

"What's the name on the case?"

"John Doe number fifteen."

"Ugh," I said. "Should have thought of that. Somebody in my office must have submitted the DNA for identification."

Shirley typed some more. "Let me look... Yes. Says here a C. Teska, MD. Two weeks ago, on November second. Wait, C. Teska? Any relation?"

"Yes," I said, "I know her a little." I sighed and leaned back in the office chair. "That's me. I go by Jessie, but my name's Czesława."

"It's what?"

"Czesława."

"Oh," said Shirley. "So this is your John Doe."

"That's what it looks like."

"Convenient!"

"Isn't it, though."

"You don't seem thrilled."

"What was your first clue, Shirley?"

It was a little easier to get out of the shipyard than it had been getting in, and I made it back to the Office of Chief Medical Examiner just after five. The 2578s had completed their shift change, and Cameron Blake was at his desk in the Ops Shop.

"Just the man I want to see," I said.

"Oh no."

"That's right. I need an ID on a Doe. John Doe fifteen, case number fifteen fifty-six. Do we have any leads on who—"

"Wait, wait," Cam said, and clicked around on his computer. "You told me his name was Curtis something, and you wanted to match him to a Doe, right? Now you're saying he's a Doe and you want...what?"

"No, not that one. John Doe number fifteen. Different guy. This one matches a DNA profile in one of my homicides."

"Which homicide?"

"Case 1584, Leopold Haring."

Cam found the computer file and scanned his monitor. "Oh, the architect. Right. High profile. That family is a pain in the ass. They can't decide what to do with the remains. First they wanted direct cremation, then somebody sent a legal order halting direct cremation, and then another legal order from somebody else, about foreign removal..."

"Where?"

"Hell, I don't remember. Australia?"

"Austria?"

"Sure. They keep switching funeral homes, and every single thing about this body has lawyers attached."

"Wait," I said. "We still have Leopold Haring?"

"No one has picked him up yet."

"That's going on three weeks. He must be getting pretty ripe."

"Crazy rich people," Cam said, and rubbed his gleaming scalp with one hand. "They're the worst. Four hundred bucks a day in morgue storage fees doesn't bother them, so they stiff us with the cadaver till they're good and done fighting over what to do with it. By the time this bunch figures it out, Mr. Haring will be a soupy bag of bones."

"So what have you done on this case so far?"

"Which case?"

"John Doe number fifteen!"

"Okay, okay, hold your horses."

He bounced around the computer database again. Case file SFME-1556 came up. "Oh, I remember this one. From the King Street rubble, way down the bottom. His face was no good for a visual ID, and we couldn't get fingerprints—one hand was never recovered, and the other one wasn't viable." He clicked on the computer again, and pulled up a photo of the mangled body. "Blunt trauma, blunt trauma, blunt trauma...disarticulation of the extremities, starting to bloat."

"You're right about the face," I said. It was not recognizable as human, except that it was attached to something that was wearing clothes.

"Yeah. So we sent his DNA to the lab, and we're waiting to hear back if they get a hit."

The circular irony of this made my head spin. Our 2578s had sent John Doe #15's DNA to the police criminalistics lab to see if they could identify him when their other methods failed. Instead, the crime lab had connected John Doe #15 to the Haring homicide when they discovered that he was the second DNA contributor on the bloody screwdriver...and still nobody had a name to hang on him.

"Damn it," I said to Cam. "I need an ID on this Very Important Doe."

"What's the hurry?"

"There's been an arrest in the case, but I'm skeptical that the guy did it. Very Important Doe here is connected to a key piece of physical evidence."

"Very Important Doe." Cam chuckled. "Since it came in as a decomp, you must've done a full-body X-ray, right?"

"Yeah."

"Have you looked at the films for something unique—a skeletal deformity or a healed fracture, maybe?"

I thought about it and realized I hadn't. We'd been so swamped after the earthquake, I had just performed the autopsies and handed the John and Jane Does off to the investigators to worry about.

"Maybe you'll get lucky and find something on radiology that we can use for an ID, at least a presumptive one," Cameron said. "Get a presumptive ID, and we can try to contact the family, collect a DNA sample from them, get a comparative going, and bingo—we got him."

I sat down at another Ops Shop computer, logged in, and opened the radiology images I'd taken before starting the autopsy, looking for anything that might stand out. It wasn't hard—a bright white line jumped off the X-ray of the dead man's right forearm. It was something metal. I clicked on another view and saw that the metal object was actually two separate surgical plates used for repairing badly broken bones. John Doe #15 had one on the surface of his radius and one on the ulna. I never saw the plates when I cut into the body because you don't dissect limbs during an autopsy unless there's a good reason to, like the presence of a wound.

This was a good reason. Medical devices have serial numbers. I was going to have to go find John Doe #15 in our cooler, open him back up, and retrieve the two plates. Maybe I could track them to whatever hospital put them into my Very Important Doe. Then I could get comparative radiology and see if the patient's X-rays from the time of the surgery matched the autopsy X-rays. If they did, I'd have the patient's name.

A lot of ifs.

Cam thought this was a hilariously bad idea. "That corpse was already ripe when we brought it in, and now it's been sitting in the cooler for two weeks! Yarina's gonna love you forever, Doc."

"She'll be fine with it."

Cam laughed wickedly. "And she's got a long memory, our Yarina Marchenko. I'm telling you."

I found Yarina cleaning up the autopsy suite, getting ready to close down for the day. I told her we needed to pull out a body.

"Now?"

"Afraid so."

"It cannot wait until tomorrow?"

"Believe me, I wish it could. It has to do with a homicide, and I need to do it before we get new cases in the morning. Will you help me?"

She didn't want to, of course, and started grousing.

"I promise I'll clean up by myself," I said. "You can go home as soon as we're done."

She groused some more, but didn't refuse—Yarina was nothing if not conscientious. She went back to fixing up the autopsy suite for the next day's work, and I hustled to the locker room and got suited up in my PPEs before she could change her mind. Cam was right: two weeks is a long time for a body that came into our office in a state of pronounced decomposition to continue to marinate in the cooler. Better Yarina find out what we were doing at the last possible moment.

The state of the cooler took the wind right out of my sails. It was crammed—absolutely crammed, floor to ceiling—with body bags.

"What the hell...?" I said.

"Earthquake dead." Yarina squeezed in there and started examining toe tags. "They must go somewhere."

"Yes, but…" The cadavers were stacked two or even three to a gurney. It was horrifying.

"We wait for funeral homes to come and collect. Meantime, every morning, more cases. More bodies. They come faster than they go. We have surplus."

Yarina was unfazed by the catacomb cooler. She is unflappable, that woman. She had been some sort of clinician back in Ukraine. I could only imagine her bedside manner.

It took a while, but we found John Doe #15. His nylon pouch sat on top of another, both of them sharing a single gurney. I asked Yarina whose body was the one underneath my Very Important Doe.

She peered at the toe tag. "Haring, L."

"You're kidding."

"This is your case, also, yes? The architect."

"Yes."

Yarina found this morbid coincidence absolutely hysterical. "Look! Now they are like brothers, sharing a bed!"

I took the head and Yarina took the feet, and we started to move John Doe off of Leopold Haring. As soon as we shifted the pouch, a wave of stench billowed up. It was so strong I could taste it. I swore in Polish, and Yarina agreed in Ukrainian. We tried again, and discovered the hard way that a greasy mess had been leaking out of a seam in John Doe's body bag and slicking onto Haring's. We freed up another gurney and slid John Doe onto it. When we did, some of his decomposition juice dribbled onto the cooler floor.

"You clean," Yarina said. "This you promised."

"I know what I promised!" I snapped.

It was a whole lot of nasty, sweaty, gagging effort to get John Doe #15 out of the cooler. We managed it eventually, and rolled him over to the Decomp Crypt.

The Decomp Crypt is what we call the Advanced Decomposition and Virulent Disease Vector Isolation Vault, a small room with a single autopsy table and an exhaust system that's separated from the rest of the morgue. It's claustrophobic and loud. Yarina and I crammed ourselves in there with the remains of John Doe #15. She maintained a steady stream of bitching and moaning about the double-stacking of bodies. The investigators should be working harder to get them out! The Haring case came in before the earthquake, and new earthquake cases were still coming in, when the injured died under hospital care. Why's this completed case still taking up room in our morgue…?

I kept my mouth shut and ground my own gears. I was deputy chief medical examiner, and it was supposed to be my job to manage cadaver storage so we didn't end up stacking them like cordwood in the cooler. Yarina was right about Leopold Haring, too—and I resolved to call Natalie and prompt her to deal with her dead husband's remains, like it or not. What if the press caught wind of—

"Co tak jebie!" I yelped, and gagged, and turned away.

Yarina had unzipped the nylon pouch but didn't even attempt to shift the body off the gurney and onto the table. It was just too soupy. Even she was appalled. This thing that had once been a man had gone beyond bloating and had collapsed in on itself. The skin hung on the bones like wet paper. The fat had melted, spreading and resettling in fetid blobs. An oily sludge heaved around the bottom of the vinyl pouch. John Doe's head was still attached. It looked like a December jack-o'-lantern.

The right arm was still attached, too, and that's all we needed to access. I told Yarina we'd work on the body in the pouch, on the gurney, and not even try to get it onto the table. There was no point—and I was not confident it would hold together if we tried.

Yarina said, "Okay, good luck," and left the crypt for the regular autopsy suite before I could object.

I reached into the mire, pulled out the right forearm, and

went to work with my scalpel as quick as I could, slicing and scraping through the soft tissues till I reached the two surgical plates. They had been there a long time—stout bone calluses had grown around them, like an old tree swallowing a fence post. There was only one way I was going to get the plates out of John Doe's arm. I put it back in the body bag and pushed through the pressurized door to the autopsy suite.

"No," said Yarina. "You cannot have my bone saw."

"But it'll only take me a few minutes…"

"You will break my bone saw."

"No, I will not."

"You will. Plates are titanium. Saw blade is stainless steel. Titanium is more hard. You will break my blade."

"I promise I will not break the blade, Yarina. Now, please go get the thing so I can finish this unpleasant job."

Yarina went off to find the bone saw, muttering darkly to herself.

The electric handsaw's rattling din filled the tiny, airtight Decomp Crypt. I aimed the blade for the distal end of the ulna and plunged down. The tool bit into bone and made a neat line all the way through.

"Świetnie!" I declared to no one, and made the same cut at the proximal end. I made two more to free the smaller plate, and emerged victorious from the Decomp Crypt with two pieces of a dead man's rotting bones in one hand and Yarina's precious power tool in the other.

All I had left to do was to pull off the metal plates. I clamped a dura stripper to the longer piece of bone to hold it, readied the bone saw again, and pressed it forward, bone dust flying, ripping smoothly along the edge of the surgical plate—

Until, with a sickening grind, it stopped.

Across the room, Yarina sighed. "You have broken my blade."

"Don't worry, it's just jammed…" I said, and wrenched the saw out of the bone.

She was right. I had snapped the damn thing clean in half.

I admitted fault. I begged Yarina's forgiveness. I asked, "Do you have another blade?"

"Yes," she said, and held out her hand for the saw. I gave it to her. "But not for you, Dr. Teska."

She shuffled across the autopsy suite, and returned to my table with a hammer, a set of chisels, and a hacksaw. I took the tools without a word.

Yarina left, and I was alone in the morgue. It's something I don't like to do; not because I'm afraid of a room full of corpses or because I believe in ghosts. I don't. I believe in people. I believe people are capable of doing violent, evil, stupid things to one another if they convince themselves they have to, or simply that they really want to, as long as they have also convinced themselves that they can get away with doing those things. I had faced such a person in another morgue once. I didn't want to do it again.

I aimed a chisel perpendicular to the bone and whaled away with the hammer until the plates were free, then put the bigger one under my magnifying glass and peered at the inner surface. Engraved there was a figure, an *O* with an *X* overlapping it— probably a corporate logo—followed by something that looked like a serial number: *L-418 S-C88D46M*. I checked the other plate and found a similar pattern, cut into the metal, clear and complete.

It had been, as I imagined it would be, a whole lot of sweaty, nasty work—but I had found the information I hoped I would find, buried as deep as it could possibly be buried inside my Very Important Doe's right forearm. Whether or not I would be able to make use of it remained to be seen.

Bea was going bananas by the time I got back to Mahoney Brothers #45, but she hadn't shat the rug or torn up the furniture, so I rewarded her with a nice long romp down the beach. She enjoyed it, but I sure didn't—it was pitch dark already, and a soggy little north wind was blowing. California was making me soft. Back in Lynn it would start getting dark around four o'clock this time of year. Any given day in November is grim and cold and likely to sleet. The foliage has blown away and the snowy postcard days are still weeks off. Thanksgiving can be the gloomiest time of the year.

Thanksgiving. It was, what, ten days away? Anup and I had never finished planning for the holiday—the last time I'd raised the subject, we were sharing soup dumplings at House of Shanghai Taste and the earthquake interrupted us. When Bea and I got back to the house and I'd settled into bed, I called him.

"How you feeling?" he asked, right off the bat.

"Fine. Why?"

"Yesterday you said you were laid up. Is it a cold?"

"Oh—no. A stomach bug. Or maybe something I ate. I'm fine now."

I'd forgotten that I'd lied to him on Sunday morning to beg off going hiking, his way of making up for Saturday night, the Lakshmi puja I wasn't welcome to attend—the Saturday night that had turned into an off-the-hook debauch for me and Denis Monaghan.

"I tried calling you earlier," Anup said.

"Yeah, sorry—something came up last minute at work."

"But your stomach is okay?"

"Fine now."

"Well, try to take it easy tomorrow, will you?"

I promised him I would, compounding lies with more lies. I had a sudden flash of panic that I would trip up—or he would catch on—so I changed the subject to my testimony at the preliminary hearing. It worked; Anup knew both Jason Bevner and Eva Yung and was eager to hear about their sword-crossing in a murder case. I curled up under the duvet with Bea at my feet, and we gossiped.

It was no use trying to blame the drinking. I could've pulled the plug on Denis's advances at any moment, there in Trad'r Sam's, but I didn't. No use trying to pin blame on Anup, either, with his rejection of me on Diwali. He had pissed me off and I had gone and cheated on him, first chance I got. One man I hadn't lied to was Denis, when I told him I'd enjoyed my night with him. I had. But it was a stupid and spiteful betrayal of Anup's trust and I regretted it. I couldn't take it back. Anup would never know the story of my one-night-stand with Denis Monaghan. Not if I could help it.

I never did raise the subject of Thanksgiving, either. We still had time enough to put the plans together. When I hung up, though, a notion entered my sleepy head and worried around in there. It was the realization that the spark I'd felt for Anup ever since I'd first fallen for him had faded. It was still there, but it was dim. That dark night, it felt like it was dying.

CHAPTER 11

After autopsies the next day (two naturals: advanced heart disease in one, and liver failure from chronic alcohol abuse in the other), I brought the bone plates I'd dug out of John Doe #15 to Dr. Howe, looking for his advice about tracking down their provenance.

Howe loves a challenge. He put the battered plates under his reading light and examined them without comment. I waited— I knew better than to interrupt the chief on a consult. Finally, without looking up, he spoke. It wasn't what I expected to hear.

"Why do you keep dodging the press on the architect thing?"

"I…what do you mean?"

"I've got a pile of messages from KnowNowSF, demanding I tell them what we're hiding over here. Are we hiding something over here, Dr. Teska?"

"No! Of course we aren't…"

"Then why are you giving reporters the impression that we are?"

"I didn't! I mean, I just gave no comment, is all. If they want to read into that—"

Howe fixed his small sharp eyes on me. "Oh, they will. Believe me, they will. They take 'no comment' as a provocation."

"I'd just come off the stand. I figured my testimony should speak for itself—the reporters were in there watching it, after all."

"They won't give up. I'm surprised Emil Kashiman never taught you that. A high-profile case, with the unusual—even lurid—circumstances in which that body was discovered, they're not going to take 'no comment' for an answer. Come up with a better one. I'm certainly not going to do it for you."

He returned his attention to the surgical plates. "Now—to this little puzzle. Orthopedic device manufacturers get gobbled up by one another all the time. This company might not even exist anymore. If you do manage to figure out who the logo belongs to, call their regulatory department. The bean counters might know which hospital purchased it, and when. Be careful, though—you could fall down a rabbit hole trying to secure an ID this way. Don't burn too much time on it."

"Is there a database for these devices?" I asked.

"No, too much HIPAA. The surgeon might talk to you if you can track him down, but I doubt anyone else will."

Dr. Howe handed me the plates and repeated the admonition not to spend too much time on a search that was unlikely to produce a name to hang on this John Doe.

That reminded me of another thing I wanted to ask him. "We need to come up with some provision for temporary body storage until we can clear out the remaining quake victims. The cooler is full of pouches stacked on top of each other. This John Doe was leaking decomp fluid onto a gurney and the cooler floor."

Dr. Howe went suddenly officious. "The problem isn't body storage—it's turnaround time. Get those deaths processed and certified, and the bodies released to funeral homes, and we won't have a storage problem."

I managed, for once, not to speak my mind. The gray-haired day-shift 2578 out in the Ops Shop must've overheard, because he motioned me to join him at his desk on my way out.

"No way the boss is going to bring in a refrigerated trailer, Jessie," he croaked quietly in his cigarette-scarred baritone. "Imagine if the press caught wind? Nobody can see the state of the cooler from outside these walls, remember."

He had a point. Even if the FEMA money were available for an auxiliary morgue trailer—and it might well be, after the quake—Chief Howe wouldn't request it. He prided himself on running a tight ship. As far as he was concerned, we were just going to have to work harder to process those John and Jane Does, and clear the cooler faster than new arrivals could fill it.

The investigator asked to look at the bone plates. There was a trick to interpreting the information stamped onto them, he said. One of the codes was the lot number—a batch of devices produced and shipped from the factory together—and the other was the serial number, individual to each one. He didn't recognize the corporate logo, but brought up a web page and his screen filled with a riot of medical-device company banners and badges. We scrolled through together—and found it. The X overlapping an O belonged to OstereonX Devices. The 2578 Googled them. OstereonX had been bought out a few years before by, sure enough, a bigger device company called Moss Medical.

And then the Ops Shop hotline rang. It was police dispatch, reporting a fresh body. The veteran 2578 said, "Okay, just a sec," into the receiver and put his hand over it. "We gotta go fetch this. Sorry I can't help more."

I mouthed *I owe you one*. The investigator winked back. "Good luck working the phones," he said. "You're gonna need it."

I went straight to my office and called Moss Medical, Inc. and navigated the phone tree until I got the regulatory department. The lady on the other end told me they had inherited the old records from OstereonX on paper, and had put them all in storage.

"Don't you have anything on this serial number?"

"No, ma'am."

"How about the lot number?"

"No, ma'am."

"I'm sorry," I said, as sweetly as I could, "I guess I'm confused. You sell these things, right?"

"Yes, ma'am."

"So somewhere you have a record of those sales. Right?"

The lady sighed, and told me she would transfer me to the sales department.

The man in sales wished he could help me, he really did—but then he repeated over and over again in slightly different ways that he didn't know anything about serial numbers for specific products made by one of the companies that his conglomerate had glomerated at some point in the murky past.

"How about lot numbers?"

"Well, now, maybe. Why don't you give 'em to me."

"L four one eight."

"For both of 'em?"

"Yes."

"Four one eight, four one eight," the salesman muttered. "Hang on just a tick, will you, please…?"

He put me on hold. I put him on speakerphone and bathed my office in the Muzak while trying to multitask by filling in the details on another autopsy report. But I'm no good at multitasking, so I was glad to hear the salesman come back on, jaunty as can be.

"It just so happens that the lot numbers for those OstereonX products were recorded in a PDF database. I can tell you that lot number four one eight went to the San Francisco Department of Public Health in California."

"When?"

"Ten years ago."

The Department of Public Health meant San Francisco General Hospital. Surgery at the General meant the recipient of the two bone plates would likely have been an indigent person. I knew my Very Important Doe had been homeless, at least at the time of his death. So next I called up the General and asked for Orthopedics.

"We don't keep those records," said the nurse who answered, and transferred me to someone in the hospital stockroom. I had a hard time hearing the guy—he had a heavy accent across a fuzzy phone line—and we took to barking block sentences back and forth like sailors in a gale. He shuffled through his records, then told me which operating room had taken those two devices, on which date—and the name of the surgeon.

I barked my gratitude, hung up, and called Orthopedics again. I got the same nurse, and asked for the surgeon.

"He's in the OR right now."

"Can I leave a message?"

"We don't do that. He doesn't check in with us."

"Well, can you give me his cell phone, or email or something?"

"No."

"So how do I get in touch with him?"

"After he scrubs out, he heads straight over to Mission Bay for clinic. If I was you, that's where I'd go looking for him."

Next on my agenda was another irritating task: I had to call Natalie Haring and tell her it was time to get her husband's corpse out of our cooler. I watched my death's-head clock while I mulled ways to get that message through. The clock's tiny pirate cutlass had cut through fifty-seven seconds when I came up with a tactic.

"It's come to my attention that your husband's body is still being held in our storage space," I said, after Natalie and I had exchanged phone pleasantries.

"Yes?"

"It's been three weeks. That's quite a bit longer than we typically store bodies. Is there anything I can do to help you get your husband's remains to a funeral home? Is it a matter of cost…?"

"Of course not."

Bingo.

"Oh," I said. "Then I'll be happy to have our own mortuary professionals prepare things from this end. Please tell your funeral home they can arrange for transportation anytime today."

"I…wish it were that simple, Doctor. You see, we're having some differences of opinion in the family, and my husband's will was unfortunately imprecise as to the disposition of his remains."

"I understand, Mrs. Haring—but the decedent's will is not the authority in these matters. The desire of the next of kin is, and that's you."

"Again, if only it were that simple." I waited and said nothing. So did Natalie. Eventually, she seemed to have a new idea. "If you would be kind enough to find the time to come to our business office, Dr. Teska, I'm certain you could help us resolve the matter."

Fat chance, lady. I had thirty-something open cases to contend with. I couldn't say that, though. So, seeking another excuse, I asked where their business office was.

"Two Bridgeview Way."

"Where's that?"

"Right by the hospital complex in Mission Bay."

That's where I was headed to track down the surgeon who had fixed up John Doe #15's arm. I could kill two birds with one stone; if I actually showed up, in person, to mediate the Haring family dispute, maybe I could get that high-profile corpse out of our office, and please my boss.

"What time?" I said.

The orthopedic surgeon was older but not old; important and impatient. I had barely landed in the ergonomic chair opposite his gleaming silver desk when he said, "Did the patient sign a waiver allowing device tracking for research?"

"I don't know."

"Well, if he didn't, then I can't talk to you. HIPAA."

"Doctor," I said, "your patient is dead. He has no HIPAA."

"You're sure I did the surgery?"

"That's what the operating room record says. The devices came out of a John Doe, and I need to ID him."

I handed him the bone plates, and before he'd even turned them over he said, "OstereonX! That's a good solid product." He ran his fingers over the warped metal like a jeweler with a pawned masterpiece. "I think I remember this procedure—it's not often I do both a radius and ulna in the same patient. Why didn't you just unscrew them? I did such careful work on those bones, and now, look at this."

"Like I said, I'm trying to put a name on a dead man here. Can you help?"

"It was about four years ago, I think. Let me look at my database." He swiveled his computer monitor so I couldn't see it. Okay, fine. I took the opportunity to daydream out the window at the sweeping southerly view, with San Bruno Mountain on one side and the bay on the other. It occurred to me that I was looking down on my own little dumpside office, out there somewhere. Closer, right below us, a crane was swiveling back and forth. Mission Bay is usually crawling with cranes. What struck me about this one, as I watched it, was that it seemed to be running in reverse. It was demolishing a building, not erecting one. Mission Bay is landfill—and landfill turns to jelly in an earthquake.

"Hope they were insured," I muttered.

"Who?" said the surgeon.

"Down there. Quake damage, right?"

"Oh. I don't know."

"Was it bad around here?"

"I don't know. I was home in Marin. Ah—here we go." He pointed a steady, slender finger at the screen. "Oh, yes. Patient came to the ER at the General. He had fractures of both bones of his distal right forearm. Usually I can stabilize the ulna, and the radius reduces on its own. Not this time. That's why he needed both plates."

He laid them out on his desk and fiddled with them. "I really had to squeeze this screw in right here. And the end piece had to go nearly to the condyle of the wrist." He beamed. "I did a great job with this! Textbook."

"Doctor," I said.

"Yes?"

"What is the patient's name?"

"Oh. I don't know. In my spreadsheet he's Trauma Blue 1343."

"What does that mean?"

"It's hospital admissions shorthand for a John Doe."

"You've got to be kidding me. You admitted this guy to the hospital and did surgery on him, and you never found out his *name*?"

I'd offended him. "This is trauma service at the General. I fix them up and send them off. The only reason I kept this spreadsheet was for my own personal research into complication rates. No disrespect, Dr. Teska, but the way we work might be a little different than what you're used to down at the morgue, where your patients lie around and don't get any deader. We deal with emergencies."

No disrespect? *Pocałuj mnie w dupę!* But instead of telling the surgeon to kiss my ass, I took a deep breath, kept my voice even, and asked him if he could describe the patient.

"I have him down as a sixty-two-year-old Black male."

"How about radiology?"

"What do you mean?"

I pointed at the backside of his paper-thin computer screen. "Is his name on the radiology report in the chart?"

"I don't know. I don't have his chart on hand. If you want to look at the films, you'll have to go ask radiology to find them."

"I don't have a name for the patient, Doctor."

The surgeon made a show of flipping the cuff of his lab coat to consult an expensive watch. "It's my clinic day, and I have patients waiting. If you'll give me your email, I'll see if I can get somebody from records to look for the full file."

He seemed awfully blithe about it. So I gave him my card, and then I pulled out my heavy gold Deputy Chief Medical Examiner shield and slid it across his desk.

"This is my badge number. Please make sure you reference it in the correspondence."

It spooked him. "Hold on…what kind of case is this? Am I going to get subpoenaed?"

"Right now, this is a simple matter of identifying a John Doe. Further steps will depend on how quickly we can get a name on this individual. If the radiology images you took in the operating room match the images I took in the autopsy suite, we will have a positive identification. Those X-rays are crucial to this open case, which is part of a homicide investigation."

The surgeon displayed a good deal more animation. He declared he would get right on it, and wrote the badge number on a notepad. Then he wrote it again on his desk calendar—and underlined it. Twice.

I pocketed my shield and thanked the surgeon for his time. We shook hands. I put a good tight squeeze on him.

It was a short walk along a sterile street to the offices of Haring & Symond, in a twenty-story building at number 2 Bridgeview Way. The entire district around the new hospital complex had sprung up all at once, with planned-city efficiency, and the place had a raw feel to it, like walking through the set of a dystopian sci-fi movie.

Haring & Symond occupied the penthouse. Natalie Haring greeted me in the lobby with more warmth than I expected, and walked me down a series of hallways until we were outside a glassed-in conference room with a stunning view of the Bay Bridge. The chairs were filled with men and women in serious dark suits. I was surprised when Natalie stopped there, opened the door, and invited me to enter.

The serious suits were lawyers. They jumped out of their chairs and we shook hands in a frenzy of self-introduction. Jeffrey Symond, the late Mr. Haring's business partner, was seated at the head of the table. He didn't get up. Natalie positioned herself to stand beside him. Everyone in the glass room directed their attention at me. They meant business.

I had come there expecting a private conference with a widow. Instead, I'd walked into a shiver of sharks. Natalie saw that she'd caught me flat-footed, and pressed her advantage.

"The reason we've invited you here today, Dr. Teska, is because we have some questions about the medical examiner case surrounding my husband's death."

"What kind of questions?"

"They involve insurance matters." She settled herself smoothly into the seat next to Jeff Symond and nodded to one of the suits, who pulled out a chair for me at the other end of the table. I sat; what else could I do, except maybe turn tail and run? Besides, I was curious to see where this interrogation was going to go— and I wasn't under oath. I didn't have to answer a damn thing.

"You see, Doctor, my husband Leopold was a conservative and prudent man, and carried several life insurance policies. He also had separate policies through the corporation, as riders on our umbrella insurance, which have provisions to provide payment if he were to die unexpectedly while at work. Even though we have filed all the proper death claims paperwork with the holders of these policies, none of those companies has released the money they owe us. Owe *me*, that is. As the beneficiary. We find this...puzzling."

I asked Natalie, with as much courtesy as I could muster, what exactly she wanted me to do about it. "I have closed the case and have issued the death certificate. That's all the insurance companies usually require. After that, I've seen families wait six months or more for the payout."

"This is a special case, you see. It's not just about me personally. It's about us, Haring & Symond, as a business. Our cash flow—"

A lawyer cut her off. "Mrs. Haring would just like to know from you, Doctor, how you can aid us in expediting the payout process for—"

And a different lawyer cut off that lawyer. "Just a minute. If the corporation is having cash flow issues, an insurance payment is not a fitting vehicle for—"

The first lawyer cut off the lawyer who had just cut him off, and they got into a muddled little spat. Yet another lawyer tried to mediate, but it wasn't working. I looked to Natalie. She had clammed up. I didn't like it.

I cast my voice loudly and directly at the dead man's lifelong friend and partner, who clearly did not want to be in the room at all.

"Mr. Symond—what is your role here?"

Symond went from miserable to alarmed, and stammered a half answer before his lawyer stopped him. Another lawyer stepped up and encouraged Symond to answer the question, and Symond's lawyer jumped down his throat.

It was becoming clear that this meeting had been Natalie Haring's idea, and that Jeffrey Symond thought it was a terrible one. So did all the lawyers, who had probably tried and failed to talk her out of it. They were all there for damage control. Natalie wanted something out of me. I figured, since I was already there and all, maybe I could get something out of her, too. Maybe she could help me further my investigation.

I ignored the squabbling attorneys and fixed my attention on Natalie. "Mrs. Haring, do you know a man named Samuel Urias?"

"No."

I couldn't tell if that was the truth. She was certainly holding something back.

"How about you, Mr. Symond."

Jeffrey Symond sat up in his chair. "The union guy? Yes, I know him. I'm down at that construction site most every day, so I guess you could say we work together—"

The lawyer looming over Symond put a hand on his shoulder. "Mr. Symond is here in his role as a corporate officer only," he said, "and will not be answering any questions about the criminal case that involves Leopold Haring's death."

"Hey," I replied coldly, "you people asked me here. Now you want to stop me asking questions?"

I shifted my focus to Natalie's lawyer. "Then why should I stay? You don't have a subpoena and this isn't a deposition. You can't compel me to do squat. I'm only still sitting in this chair because Mrs. Haring lost her husband, and it is my ethical duty to help answer any of her questions that are germane to my investigation of that death."

And I need to get that dead body out of my overcrowded morgue, I did not add.

I looked right at Natalie. "I can't go outside the bounds of that investigation."

She didn't respond. The meeting was definitely not following the script she had drafted in her head.

"We don't want you to exceed the limits of your investigation, Dr. Teska," a man said. I hadn't noticed him there, in the recesses of the conference room—and he hadn't approached to offer his hand during the feeding frenzy. He was older and more expensively dressed than the other lawyers. A young female colleague, in a tailored wool suit that radiated institutional power, flanked him.

"We just want to ask you one thing," the older lawyer said.

"What's that?"

"Did you receive any calls from any insurance companies, asking about the cause and manner of death in this case?"

"Yes," I said.

"And what did you tell them?"

"I never called them back. I closed the case before I even had the chance to."

The older lawyer affected an expression of puzzlement. "How did that happen?"

"They called me while the case was still pending, and now it's closed. The death certificate is finalized. I assume they will receive my report through the usual administrative channels."

The older lawyer nodded to his colleague. She stepped forward and held out a slender folder. "We want you to contact the insurance carriers directly, please."

I didn't take the folder. It hung in her hand over the table, then she put it down in front of me.

The older lawyer spoke again. "We request that you make it clear to the claims officers that your investigation has concluded, that you have certified this death as a homicide, and that Samuel Urias killed Leopold Haring. That's all."

"Oh, is that all? You're confusing me with a police detective. And I don't believe we met, Mr....?"

"Berwick." He strode over with hand outstretched, and I rose to shake it. "Douglas Berwick."

I knew that name. It was the middle one in a set of three that adorned the masthead of the biggest and most powerful law firm on the West Coast.

"I don't determine who is a suspect, Mr. Berwick. You want to talk to Homicide Inspector Keith Jones."

"Inspector Jones is a busy man, and he's moved on to other cases."

"Oh, that is a lie coming out of your mouth, Mr. Berwick." The lawyer recoiled in surprise, and his colleague almost toppled off of her Zanottis. "You know exactly why these companies won't pay out."

The room went dead silent. Then, finally, Jeffrey Symond said, "Why?"

I turned to him. "All these lawyers know why, Mr. Symond. I'll let one of them explain it to you."

"No," he shot back. "Tell me what you mean by that. You know why the insurance companies won't pay out? Well, I don't, and it's my ass on the line here."

The lawyer closest to Symond whispered something in his ear. Symond brushed him off and shot up out of the chair.

"No. My best friend is dead—murdered, brutally—and our company, his *legacy*, needs that insurance money, or else we're going to go under. Like, next month."

The lawyers sat there with their mouths clamped shut. Jeffrey Symond leaned over the conference table and continued.

"Did you know that Leo and I started our first company together when we were twenty-six, Dr. Teska? In a garage. Literally. Leopold didn't even have a work permit—he was here from Austria on a student visa, and I had to pay him under the table, mostly in pizza. So, please. Tell me why the insurance money hasn't come through, because I have already lost Leo and I am on the brink of losing our company."

Mr. Berwick and his aide stood stock-still and stony, but all the other lawyers looked like their heads were about to explode. I knew why: they couldn't stop me from speaking up if I wanted to. I also knew that if I didn't speak up, then nobody else was going to. I decided that Jeffrey Symond deserved to know the truth.

"In my professional experience, Mr. Symond, there is one clear category of circumstance when the insurance companies would be dragging their feet like this. I've seen it happen before—when the beneficiary of the insurance policy is considered a suspect in a homicide."

I turned my gaze to Natalie Haring. She shot daggers back.

"But the union guy killed Leo!" Symond cried. He seemed to be sincerely shocked. He also seemed to be either naive, or dumb as a box of rocks.

"That's why all these attorneys are here, Mr. Symond," I said. "They're worried that I may not be convinced the forensic evidence supports the accusation against Samuel Urias. That's why they really asked me here—to conduct their own little cross-examination."

I turned to the lawyer at my elbow and said "How's it going so far?" Someone in the room swallowed a snicker.

Symond sank back into the chair. "What reason did they give you for calling this meeting, Mr. Symond?" I asked.

He started an honest answer, but then, dumb or not, decided better. He took a beat and said, "Business reasons."

"Ah, yes. Business. These insurance policies that your company took out against Leo's death—if they pay up, who benefits? Who controls the company now, with Leo deceased? Is it you and Mrs. Haring?"

Symond's lawyer leaned down again, and again murmured in his ear. The lawyer was just covering his ass, though. Anyone could see there was no way Symond intended to answer me. After all, as Leopold Haring's business partner, Jeffrey Symond was beneficiary of any life insurance policies that paid out to the company. In the cold, clear eyes of the claims adjusters, Symond would be a suspect in Haring's homicide, too. He might not even have known it until I pointed it out to him.

I rose. I didn't see anything good coming for me in staying in that room. Before I could even turn around, though, Mr. Berwick asked me if I had fielded any calls from Oskar Haring.

Kurwa. It was a simple trap, but a tight one. If I said nothing or refused to answer, it would serve as confirmation that I had interviewed the dead man's troubled son. Saying no would be a lie, and even though I wasn't under oath, I'm not a liar unless I need to be.

"Yes, I have."

Natalie Haring leaped up and flipped out.

"*Why*—? Why would you drag Oskar into this? He's not responsible for anything he says! What did he tell you?"

Two of her lawyers tried to reel her in, but Natalie wasn't letting up.

"My son is bipolar. He was off his medications when he assaulted his father. He's been…difficult to manage. Recently he's started fantasizing. And…and he's getting worse…"

I looked at Berwick. He wasn't smiling, exactly—any more than a computer chess program smiles when it puts you in check.

Natalie's voice returned to an even timbre, but the anguish was still behind it. "It's not his fault, the lies he tells. It's not his fault. But, Doctor—that doesn't mean he isn't lying to you, all the same."

Heads turned toward the glass wall that looked out to the hallway. There was a ruckus coming from the direction of the lobby—indistinct raised voices, something banging.

The sound froze Natalie Haring. Jeffrey Symond bolted upright in his seat. He said, "Oh, no."

Oskar Haring appeared from behind the plate glass, striding for the conference room door, the receptionist, flustered, in tow.

O wilku mowa, a wilk tu.

Speak of the Devil.

Oskar threw open the conference room door. Jeffrey Symond jumped out of his chair and moved behind his lawyers. "Call security!" he yelled at the receptionist.

"I did, Mr. Symond," she said. "They're—"

Oskar reached into his pocket.

"Oskar, no—!" Symond cried, and cowered. The lawyers crooked their arms and crouched sideways in panic.

Oskar's hand came out. It held a plastic card.

"I have the key, Jeff—remember? I work here too!"

The lawyers released a collective breath and brushed at their suits, trying to look unfazed. Jeffrey Symond was still hiding behind them. "You used to!" he sneered back.

"Jeffrey—" said Natalie Haring in a warning tone. She had snapped out of her spell.

"He can't keep doing this!"

"Not now, Jeffrey."

"Go get security," Symond ordered the receptionist. She nodded and started out the door.

"Laura," said Natalie Haring quietly. The receptionist stopped. "No police. Tell Duane that too, you understand? No police."

Laura the receptionist nodded again, then left, keeping her nervous eyes on Oskar as she retreated down the hall.

Natalie turned to her son and calmly asked him if he was carrying the gun.

"No!" Oskar spat, and pointed at Symond. "He has it! And I want it back!"

"I do not," said Symond.

"Do so!"

"Jeffrey does not have the gun, Oskar," Natalie said. "You don't either?"

"Of course not, Mother! But it's mine, and I want it back."

"It's your grandfather's gun, you brat," said Symond.

"It's mine! It's *mine*!" Oskar was in a full-body clench, like an electric current was coursing through him.

"Shh," said Natalie. Oskar relaxed immediately at the sound.

"Papa had the gun when he left us, Mama," he said. Then, for the first time, he noticed me standing next to him. "You're that doctor. What are you doing here?"

This time I was confident I should keep my mouth shut, and I did. One of the lawyers spoke up and said the meeting was to address business concerns involving the death certificate.

"The death certificate that says it's a homicide," Oskar replied, fixing me with his unblinking eyes. "Did you know about the gun, Doctor? It's a Rast und Gasser, an antique revolver from Austria, but it works just fine. I take it target shooting just to make sure. Beautiful machining, never fouls. My grandfather gave it to *me*, and my papa took it away. He had to fight me for it, and I lost. He was a strong man, my papa. Did you know he was armed when he was murdered?"

I didn't respond.

"Did you find a revolver on his body?"

"No."

Natalie's lawyer said, "You don't have to answer his questions, Doctor."

"My autopsy report is public record. There was no gun."

"He had it when he was murdered," Oskar said. "When he was stabbed in the back. Do you think a stranger could have snuck up on my papa and stabbed him in the back? Not while he was armed. Not my papa."

There was action in the hallway again. A couple of uniformed security guards and a gorilla-shaped man bursting out of his business suit were coming in a hurry. Natalie caught the eye of the gorilla, and made the tiniest shake of her head. The gorilla stopped the other two. They hung back, just outside the conference room.

Natalie turned to her son. "Oskar, maybe Papa locked the gun away somewhere before he went to the construction site. Maybe he—"

From the corner where he still lurked, law partner Douglas Berwick cut her off. "Mrs. Haring, I'm going to have to instruct you to stop speaking now."

Oskar sneered. "Yeah, say no more, Mother." He wheeled back to me. "Do you know why Mr. Berwick over there wants my mother to shut up, Doctor?"

Then, when again I didn't answer, he hissed, *"Because she killed my papa."*

He raised both arms to shoulder height, fingers thrust with violence at Natalie Haring, and at Jeffrey Symond.

"They killed my papa!"

Symond pushed his way past his lawyers. "How dare you! You lunatic! How dare you...!"

Oskar ignored him and addressed himself, perfectly calmly, to me again. "The man they arrested had no reason to kill my father. It's a setup. Mama and Uncle Jeff killed my papa."

"And you'll inherit everything if we're in jail, won't you, you lying little psycho!" Symond yelled.

He was still standing with his lawyers, livid but clearly frightened of Oskar. Natalie Haring had frozen up again.

Symond went on. "Even if we're only arrested, that's probably enough for you. You're secondary beneficiary on all those policies. You'll get everything, won't you? You'll get the company! *Our* company—!"

One of the lawyers surrounding Symond grabbed him by the arm and hauled him to the back of their scrum, talking to him in a low voice about possibly shutting the fuck up already.

Mr. Berwick stepped forward and came to me. "All right,

Dr. Teska. Thank you for coming. We're going to ask you to leave now."

I didn't.

Natalie nodded to the security squad outside the door. They entered and flanked it.

For a moment nobody did anything. Natalie didn't actually want to throw me out, of course; she was hoping I would take the hint. I didn't want go, but didn't want Dr. James Howe getting an angry call from Douglas Berwick, either. So I stood.

"I'm a principal in this company too, don't forget," Oskar suddenly yelled, in the general direction of the clot of lawyers that had swallowed Jeffrey Symond.

Symond elbowed his way out of it. He noticed the security guards. He stood tall, took a single step in Oskar's direction, and said, "You're a figurehead, Oskar. A fucking garden gnome."

Oskar turned his eyes to the ceiling and started to mutter. Nobody tried to stop Symond this time.

"Your father was the smartest man I ever met, and he knew just how dangerous you are—to your mother, to our company. To yourself! He gave you harmless busywork tasks around here so he could keep an eye on you."

Oskar was fidgeting, his feet moving in something more than a shuffle and less than a pace line, his gaze shifting from ceiling to floor and back. He was talking to someone inside his own head. He ended up toe to toe with Symond, a lawyer at each of their shoulders.

"Leo used to complain that he always had to make sure you were taking your pills," Symond said. "Looks like you aren't. Again." The lawyer closest to Symond put a hand on his shoulder and tried to get him to back him away from Oskar, but Symond only leaned closer. "Looks like, with your daddy gone, you've taken a dive off the deep end, and now you're…"

From the mists of memory, my clinical psychiatry rotation in medical school came back to me, and I saw what was happening.

"Wait—!"

I was too late. The other lawyer had already raised his hand and put it firmly on Oskar Haring's shoulder. The moment he did, Oskar swiveled, grabbed the man, and threw him across the table. Then he attacked Jeffrey Symond.

Symond tried to fight back, but it was no use. He was angry, but Oskar had gone haywire. He was flailing, striking out at everyone around him, but mostly at Jeffrey Symond. Two lawyers made the mistake of trying to pull him off. He bit one and laid the other one out with a punch to the jaw.

As the security team pushed their way through the suits, my ear isolated a strange sound behind the yells of the lawyers and Natalie's screaming (Natalie was screaming) and Symond's grunts under the frenzy of blows. The sound made its way through the others because it was so...wrong. It was laughter. Hyena laughter. Oskar Haring was laughing while he savaged Jeffrey Symond.

The security team succeeded in clearing away the lawyers and getting a grip on Oskar's windmilling arms. He kicked at them, but they were big men, and professionals. It took some effort, but they got him pinned, face-down, on the floor.

I was taking shelter behind my chair, but couldn't stay out of the situation when I saw that. I've watched countless closed circuit television tapes from jails and bus stops and outside convenience stores, of security professionals pinning frenzied people face-down that way. Those frenzied people end up on my autopsy table.

"Hey! Duane!" I shouted, guessing the gorilla in the suit was the one Natalie had instructed the receptionist to talk to about keeping the police away.

It worked. Duane the gorilla looked at me, puzzled. I said, "You're going to kill that man if you don't get him up."

"Shut up, lady," Duane said. He had a bright red welt on his cheekbone where Oskar had landed a punch, or maybe a kick.

"I'm a doctor. I'm telling you, he can't breathe that way. He is going to go into respiratory arrest, and it's going to happen quick. Get him on his feet or sit him up, *right now.*"

Duane ignored me. One of the uniformed guards had a knee between Oskar's shoulder blades. The other one produced a set of flex-cuffs, and fastened his arms behind his back.

That was the last straw. The clock was running out. I pulled out my phone and scanned the flustered crowd until I found Douglas Berwick. "I'm calling 911 right now unless those goons get off him and let him breathe," I said to the alpha lawyer.

Berwick was no fool; or, at least, he had read forensic case studies about the lethality of prone restraint in people undergoing a psychotic break. "Get him up," he said to Duane.

"We don't work for you," Duane growled.

"Do what she says!" It was Jeffrey Symond. He was being tended to by Natalie and some of the suits. Someone said something about first aid, and an ice pack.

Duane and the rest of the Haring & Symond security team grudgingly obeyed the chain of command. They dragged Oskar up and sat him on the sofa. Oskar was disoriented at first, but then he lolled his head around, saw the huge men looming over him, and started laughing again. One of the uniformed goons looked like he would sincerely have liked to punch Oskar's teeth down his throat.

Natalie leaped to her feet. She left Symond's side to go to Oskar's. She smoothed his hair and started talking to him in a low, comforting voice.

Oskar stopped laughing and started crying. He collapsed, hands still bound behind him, into his mother's lap. Natalie lowered her lips to his ear and continued to soothe him.

Oskar's voice came muffled, out of his mother's lap. "Why, Mama…? Why did you do it? Why did you take him away?"

Natalie didn't say anything to deny it. She just stroked and murmured.

Douglas Berwick touched my sleeve to get my attention. "Thank you for your time, Dr. Teska."

He didn't seem the least bit ruffled. I nodded, and moved to the conference room door. I looked back. Oskar Haring was going catatonic. Natalie Haring stroked his hair mechanically, mechanically repeating that mommy loved him. Jeffrey Symond was back in that chair at the head of the table, slumped again, with an ice pack on his face.

"Excuse me."

Mr. Berwick's aide was coming through the door, and I was in her way. She carried another first aid kit.

I was relieved to be on neither the delivery end nor the receiving end, for once.

CHAPTER 12

Anup had texted me earlier that he wanted to cook me dinner, but when I arrived at his place, he wasn't even there yet. He'd had to work late. We got takeout. It wasn't terribly good, but we were both hungry enough and worn out enough that it didn't much matter.

I had a splitting headache again, and couldn't find any Tylenol in my bag. I asked Anup for some. "It's your concussion," he said, "and the earthquake was like three weeks ago. I keep telling you, you have *got* to go back to the doctor, get a scan—"

"It's been too long to blame this headache on that. I have a headache because…well, because lawyers."

"Because lawyers?"

"Lawyers and John Does."

I told him all about my search for John Doe #15's identity, about chasing down the orthopedic surgeon with the bad attitude, and then all about Natalie Haring and her attorney ambush that turned into a catastrophe of shouted accusations, unhinged violence, and forcible restraint.

"Ugh. Every lawyer I know has had a nightmare client like your architect's wife," Anup said. "I guarantee she's told them that she's paying the bills, so she runs the show. She won't listen to reason and they can't say no to her. Douglas Berwick, in the flesh, on short notice...? You know how much that meeting must have cost?"

"Don't tell me."

Anup got that thousand-yard prosecutor's stare I'd seen before. "They *really* want to see this guy go down for it. If he's acquitted, then the insurance company—companies—might find grounds to refuse payment on the policies. If that happens, and the architecture firm goes belly-up, then the lawyers will never see a red cent of their fees. If, on the other hand, the policies pay out, then the lawyers get paid, too."

"You think they might've been getting ready to offer me a bribe, before Oskar barged in?"

"No way."

"That's too bad. I could do with a nice juicy bribe."

Anup's expression turned grim. "Oskar sounds dangerous."

"Yeah, well. All three of them are more than a little off."

"You should've got out of there the minute he showed up. You put yourself in these hazardous situations—"

"Oskar is not a psychopath, Anup. He's bipolar. People with bipolar disorder are not any more dangerous than any of the rest of us."

"Tell that to the people with ice packs on their bruises. Why'd you even agree to show up at that meeting—?"

"I wanted to get the body out of my morgue."

"And did you?"

He was getting under my skin. "What do you care?"

Anup stood, exasperated, and started collecting the takeout

boxes. "Jessie, seriously. Your job is to do autopsies. Go do them, then do your paperwork and come home."

I got up, too, and banged some dishes around, clearing them. "Don't you tell me how to do my job, okay? It means a lot to me."

"Apparently."

"Yours doesn't?"

"Mine isn't *dangerous*. And yours shouldn't be! How many concussions has Ted Nguyen had from climbing around a collapsed bridge till a piece of it landed on his head?"

"That again...? Give it up, will you. And, for the record, you couldn't pick a worse example of a happy professional living his best life than Sunshine Ted."

"You have to set boundaries in your work life. Do you want me getting a call from Dr. Howe one day, telling me that you're dead because you—"

"Anup—!"

"I'm serious! You go out and pull these stunts, and you get *hurt*. No job is worth that."

"Easy for you to say."

"Yes, it is! I apply my skills and training in the law to the job that fits the situation in life I find myself in, whatever that is. If the situation changes, I find a new job. But you...? Your job is a crusade. It's messing with your life."

"Thanks for your concern. I can take care of myself."

"Yeah? How's your headache?"

I was tired of arguing. I rifled through his kitchen utensil drawer and found a way to change the subject.

"Where do you keep the turkey baster?"

"Why?"

"For the *turkey*, Anup. I want to make sure we have all the tools we need, and that they're lined up properly when we start the Thanksgiving cooking. Which we'd better do soon. We can get all the pies and most of the side dishes done and into the fridge, and then we only need to heat them up while the bird is in the oven…"

Something was wrong. He wasn't tuning in. At all.

"Anup?"

"I've told you—I don't want to talk about Thanksgiving, okay?"

"It's a week away! We have to get started with—"

"Not right now."

"Then when? What is going on, Anup?"

He sat down again. Anup Banerjee, in his crisp lavender shirt, conservative sky blue tie gently loosened, his lightweight wool blazer hanging neatly across the chair. Not a crease on him. Not on his clothes, anyhow.

"It's my parents," he said.

"What about them?"

"They aren't coming."

"What…? Why not?"

"I haven't invited them."

I was floored.

"You… But, it's a week from this Thursday. You know that. So why haven't you…?"

He didn't answer. He didn't have to.

"This is just like Diwali. You're…ashamed of me."

Anup whipped around, all false surprise and feigned assurance. "No! No, of course not, Jessie. I love you."

"Then why are you… Why don't you want me to cook a meal for your parents, sit down, and get to know them?"

"It's not you. I just don't think my parents…"

"What?"

"My parents aren't big on Thanksgiving."

"Bullshit."

Anup had told me before that his family always had a re-laxed, stress-free Thanksgiving, enjoying the turkey and stuff-ing in front of the television, watching the parades. His mother called it "the American holiday." I remembered that distinctly— because my *mamusia* called it the same thing, and approached the day with the same attitude. We had joked about it, both of us wondering if it was in the Immigrant Handbook or something.

I moved around to sit beside him. "I've already ordered the turkey. It's off a free-range farm in Sonoma, never been frozen. It has a *name*, Anup."

He was shifting his gaze off. I wanted to grab him by the ears and force him to face me.

"We've been working on this together for weeks. I *thought* we were working on it together, anyway."

Anup looked miserable. He still said nothing.

"You really are ashamed of me."

Finally he met my eyes. "I'm not," he said.

After that, I was the one who had to look away. I didn't want him to see how much he had hurt me. He was lying.

"Look, my parents are…conservative. There are things about the way I live my life that they disapprove of. I don't want to get you mixed up in the issues I have with them."

"I'm one of the things they disapprove of. That's what you're telling me."

"That's not it, Jessie! It's not about you—it's about them."

"It's because I'm not Indian."

His big dark eyes went wide. It shocked him that I would say it out loud. Jesus—after eight months of the deepest intimacy, Anup Banerjee didn't know me at all.

"How could you say that?"

"How could I…? Am I wrong? It's because I'm not Indian, and you don't even want to admit that to yourself."

"For once it's not about you, okay?"

"Then what is it? I'm a doctor. Your parents are doctors. I'm not married. Neither are you. I love you and you love me. So what is so shameful about this woman you love, that you don't want to bring her home to the folks?"

"You really want to know?" He wasn't trying to shift his eyes anymore, and a fire had come to them. "It's questions like that! No filter. You just open your damn mouth and let whatever's in there pop out, without thinking about the consequences—the collateral damage to people around you when you drop those bombs."

"*I* drop bombs? When were you planning to drop yours on me? When were you going to tell me you've been lying to your parents about us, that you aren't ever going to let them meet me. Either you're stone blind or a fucking coward, take your pick!"

"Go ahead, make my point for me! You're right—I *don't* want my parents exposed to your temper tantrums. They wouldn't be understanding about it, let me tell you."

"You don't like the way I talk, huh…? Tough shit. And that's rich, coming from a guy who *never* says the hard things."

"Untrue."

"Look where we are right now! You always have to control the narrative, like you're still in court. Always put together, always on guard, like someone is watching you, even when it's just the two of us. At least now I know why—your *parents* are watching you, from inside your own goddamn skull! And here you've been, lying by omission all this time, to all of us. You want to protect your poor, impressionable parents from me? Then what kind of woman do you want, Anup?"

"Not this kind, I know that much!"

"Good for you."

Part of me, the spiteful, whole-truth part, wanted to throw Denis Monaghan in his face. I didn't, though. I wouldn't. There was no point. I had slept with Monaghan because another part of me, the buried part that knows the truth before the rest does, had seen on the night of the Lakshmi puja that my life with Anup Banerjee was already over. Anup was never going to choose me over his family if his family was telling him that his love for me was wrong.

But he hadn't even made that choice! If he was telling me the truth, then he was working off a set of assumptions about his parents—that they would reject me because I wasn't the right kind of girl for their son.

"Anup—have your parents told you they don't approve of me?"

"They don't have to. I know them. You don't."

"Not for lack of trying! You've kept me away from them, and them from me. You're trying to protect us from each other, right? That's so fucking stupid—"

"There you go again—"

"Fuck you, I'm angry. I deserve to be! You're putting your family—or your *idea* of your family—ahead of you and me. Why can't you be a little selfish, just once? Just for shits and giggles, Anup, give it a try. Stop shielding your parents from me, with my foul mouth, warts and all. Stop trying to take care of all of us. Let's see what happens!"

He was furious. So furious that, for once, it showed. He spoke in a strangled snarl. "That's so easy for you to say, isn't it. Like you would know what it's like to walk in my shoes. How can I even begin to…? You don't know them, and it's clear you don't know me, either. You don't know what it's like."

"Go ahead, pick a fight with me. Has it not occurred to you that maybe they'd be happy to hear you aren't as lonely as they probably think you are?"

I gave up. It wasn't my job to tell a grown man how to talk to his goddamn parents.

Anup said nothing. That was enough for me. He had pulled on the prosecutor's inscrutable mask. Before we were lovers, back when he was an assistant district attorney, Anup had cross-examined me in court. At that moment, I felt like I was back on the witness stand, the only one in the room who was sworn to tell the truth, the whole truth, and nothing but the truth, so help me God.

I went to the bathroom and took my toothbrush out of the glass on the sink, then to the front hall and grabbed a shopping bag. I went to the bedroom and collected the clothing I'd left there for the mornings when I'd spent the night and wanted to go right to work. There wasn't much.

Anup hadn't moved from the kitchen table. "The wok," he said, when I came back, bag in hand.

"What?"

He nodded to the pot rack hanging over the kitchen island. "The brass wok. It belongs to you. You bought it at that place on Grant Street, remember...?"

"You can keep the fucking wok," I said.

His laugh made my hair stand up. It was short—but boy, was it nasty. "You think you can just waltz into my family and be your own authentic self, right? Well, you can't. You won't fit in—and you and I both know you won't change, either. This won't work. I don't see how it can work."

He rose and took the wok down off the pot rack. "I don't want anything from you," he said, and handed it to me.

Anup and I spent a long moment separately scanning the apartment for my other stray belongings. I found a couple of small things—house slippers, a half-read novel—and added them to the plastic shopping bag. He pointed out an expensive candle I'd bought at the Berkeley farmers market, and handed me that, too. As a reflex I thanked him, and a bitter taste came to my mouth.

"I'm sorry, Jessie," he said. "I have to—"

"You don't mean that."

"What?"

"*Sorry.* You don't mean that. You're never sorry about anything."

"Fine. Whatever. It doesn't matter anymore. I have to think about my family. I'm the only son they have. We can't make this work."

I nodded. "*We* aren't trying to. Good for you, though, finally having the guts to tell me the truth."

Anup Banerjee opened his mouth to get the last word in, like he always does, but then just shut it and shook his head. I dropped my key to his apartment on the kitchen table. Then I walked out. He closed the door behind me. Neither of us said goodbye.

CHAPTER 13

I read the email from the orthopedic surgeon over and over, but each time it said the same thing.

RE: SFGH Trauma Blue 1343/SFME badge #202

Dr. Teska,

I have, as you requested, made inquiries into the identity of patient Trauma Blue 1343, which you brought to my attention by presenting me with two OstereonX plates used in a surgical procedure to repair broken bones in patient's right arm.

I have located patient's medical record number and chart, which I am having sent to your office. Enclosed please find, per your further request, a computer disk from our radiology department with the relevant perioperative X-ray images.

Patient's MRN is SFGH1428087. Patient's name is Curtis Roland Burton.

My Very Important Doe was Sparkle's Uncle Curtis. Sparkle's

Uncle Curtis was the second DNA contributor, along with Leopold Haring, on the bloody screwdriver the police had pulled out of Samuel Urias's pickup truck, which formed the basis of the criminal charges against him for Haring's murder.

I popped the radiology DVD into my computer and found the images taken after surgery. I went to my own file for John Doe #15 and opened the full-body X-ray I'd done before starting the autopsy. I zoomed in to the right arm, then moved the images so they were side by side on the screen. Those surgical plates mending the bones were identical on both X-rays.

It was proof. I had an ID on John Doe #15, and I had found out what had happened to Uncle Curtis.

I called Sparkle and told her we needed to talk.

———

When I got to Baby Mike Bail Bonds, I found the man himself filling the office sofa. Sparkle sat behind her desk. She and Baby Mike both greeted me solemnly, and I sat, too. I told them everything I knew. They weren't shocked to hear that their uncle's body was in my morgue, but they were horrified to learn how he'd died—crushed in the homeless camp under the infamous King Street viaduct.

"How could we let that happen to him?" Sparkle said.

"Come on, Sparks," said Baby Mike.

"I mean it. We should've—"

"Uncle Curtis was never going to die in his own bed, cool and comfortable," Baby Mike said. "That wasn't ever going to be the way he was going to go, and we all knew it."

"Oh, Michael." Sparkle sighed and dabbed her eyes with a tissue. "That's terrible to say."

"It's true, Sparks. We all knew it, didn't we?"

"It didn't have to be that way."

"Maybe. I don't know." The huge man reached over and

crushed the tissue box in his hand, trying to tease one out for himself. "I just don't know."

"I'm so sorry for your loss," I said.

I stayed a while longer and offered practical advice about collecting the body and arranging for the funeral. I also offered to break the news to Gayle, Sparkle's mother, myself, but Sparkle felt it would be better if it came from her. I warned them, in the gentle way I had practiced with other families, that, whatever type of memorial service they planned, it would have to be closed-casket.

Baby Mike got up off the sofa when I said that. He went to Sparkle behind her desk, lifted her up, and held her tight.

After leaving the cousins alone to make their hard phone calls, I walked down the block to Caffè Zeffiro, my go-to escape hatch when I'd worked at the Hall of Justice. I needed to sit down and process the morning's news over a cup of coffee.

Uncle Curtis Burton's DNA was on the bloody screwdriver, and Samuel Urias's wasn't. Did that mean that Uncle Curtis was the killer? He had one hell of an alibi: the medical chart said that Curtis Burton, record number 1428087, had been hospitalized under a 5150 at the General Hospital on October 25. He was still locked away on that three-day involuntary custodial hold on the morning of the twenty-eighth, when Haring's body was found. Jeffrey Symond, Natalie Haring, and Oskar Haring didn't agree on much, but they'd all asserted that Leopold had been alive on the late afternoon of the twenty-seventh, when he'd been in a fight with Oskar before heading to the SoMa Centre site. And if I were to ask Inspector Jones, I would bet that he could produce other evidence—phone records, texts, more eyewitnesses—that Haring was still alive and kicking when Curtis Burton went into the locked psych ward against his will.

Curtis Burton didn't kill Leopold Haring. So how did his DNA get onto a bloody screwdriver along with Haring's DNA, and what the hell did any of that mean, if the screwdriver didn't even match the fatal hole in Haring's heart—?

"Dr. Teska," someone said behind me. It was Eva Yung, Samuel Urias's public defender, in the café's snaking counter-service line. I waved her over to join me. She was having some latte sort of thing and we chitchatted about the pros and cons of soy milk versus almond milk versus oat milk until I told her about Curtis Burton, the second DNA contributor on the screwdriver, who could not possibly have killed Leopold Haring.

Eva saw a silver lining—for her side, at least. "I guess it inserts still more reasonable doubt into that weak piece of physical evidence they're trying to use against my client. Still, though… that's a deeply weird finding."

"You're telling me," I said—and *didn't* tell her that the dead man with the new ID was also the uncle of a good friend of mine. With lawyers, even ones I like personally, I try to maintain a need-to-know protocol.

I asked Eva if the man who had phoned me claiming to be a friend of Samuel Urias had contacted her, as I had urged him to do.

"He called me. We set up a meeting, but he never showed."

"Damn. But, over the phone—did he tell you the same thing he told me, that he could provide an alibi?"

"Yes. Sort of. He was oblique about it."

"If you can get him on the stand, he won't be."

"Doesn't seem likely. He called from a blocked number and wouldn't give me his name. If he won't testify, he's not much good to Samuel."

"Did you ask Samuel about it?"

She smiled ruefully. "Did I ask my client, a married, church-going man with children and a reputation in his community both here and back in Mexico, if he had, in fact, spent the night in question involved in a sexual liaison with a man? Yes. I asked him something like that."

I pinched the bridge of my nose and nodded. "He got offended and denied it."

"The very idea that some man would offer a lover's alibi made him sick to his stomach. Those were his exact words—'sick to my stomach.'"

We drank our coffees in silence. Then Eva said, "What if the blood isn't even Haring's?"

"What do you mean?"

"We have isolated two sets of DNA alleles on a screwdriver shaft that is covered in blood. We have confirmed that the blood is human—but we can't say for sure which of those two DNA contributors it belongs to, right?"

I thought about it. "The blood could belong to both of them—*each* of them, that is. Some from Curtis, some from Leo. Yes…but that's not necessarily the case. The blood on that shaft is human blood, which means human DNA, which means it definitely belongs to at least *one* of them. We've been assuming that, if that were the case, the blood must belong to Leopold Haring—because this is supposedly a weapon that was used to stab him to death. You're asking if the blood could instead be *only* Curtis Burton's blood, with some of Leopold Haring's DNA that somehow got on there. Could that blood on the bloody screwdriver belong to Curtis Burton and only Curtis Burton…? That's an excellent and puzzling question, Eva."

"Thank you. I try."

"If the blood doesn't even belong to Haring, then it isn't possible that the screwdriver was the murder weapon."

"I would certainly like to establish that."

"Interesting. Outside my realm of expertise. But you know what? I owe that DNA scientist a call, to tell her about the positive ID. I'll ask her."

"That'd be great." Eva Yung looked worn out, even with half

a latte in her system. "You know what would make my job a lot easier? A goddamn alibi. Sometimes your clients make it hard to help them out, you know what I mean?"

"No," I said. "Mine are generally pretty compliant."

———————

Eva headed back to the Public Defender's office to work another case, and I took advantage of the relatively good cell signal and mellow noise level inside Caffè Zeffiro to call Shirley Shimamoto at the criminalistics lab. I told her that we had secured an ID for my John Doe, and I wanted her to help me explore the possible ways his DNA could have ended up on that screwdriver.

"For starters, does the DNA have to have come from his blood? Is there, like, a marker for that?"

"No. It could have come from blood, or it could have come from lots of other sources."

"Like what?"

"Any nucleated cells—could be semen, skin, epithelium carried in mucus secretions, or even in stool. It could also be touch DNA, meaning he just handled the screwdriver and left the alleles behind."

"Really?"

"Could be."

"Is that…likely?"

"Could be. DNA is specific to an individual, but it can't tell me how it got on there or when. Though there is one peculiar thing about this sample."

"What's that?"

"There are two DNA profiles, as you know. They seem to be present in roughly equal amounts—but one of them is more degraded than the other."

"Huh?"

"I've never seen this before, in mixed samples. Typically each set of alleles is equally degraded if there's been decomposition. Here, the data suggests that the DNA came from two people, but one of them was decomposing faster than the other. Well… not faster, exactly. For longer."

"Hang on. The DNA that's more decomposed—"

"More *degraded*—"

"—the DNA that's more degraded…belongs to which sample set?"

"John Doe's."

"Curtis Burton's."

"Okay."

"So Curtis Burton's…blood, snot, whatever, got onto this screwdriver before Leopold Haring's blood, snot, whatever did?"

"That's what it looks like. Both of them were collected at the same time, when the screwdriver was taken for evidence—but that doesn't mean they had been laid down on the screwdriver at the same time."

Shirley Shimamoto was overlooking another possibility. It was one that I, who have spent many hours around decomposition and degradation, am steeped in.

"What if Burton's DNA sample is more decomposed than Haring's because Burton was already a couple of days dead when his sample was laid down on the screwdriver?"

Shimamoto thought about it. "Well, I guess that would look exactly the same, wouldn't it. Yup. Could be. Kind of gross, but could well be…"

I called Eva Yung, got her voice mail, and left a message with the rough outlines of what Shirley Shimamoto had just told me. Then I called Jason Bevner at the district attorney's office, and told him I wanted to talk to him, with Jones and Ramirez, if possible.

"When?"

"I'm at Zeffiro's and can come right over."

"Now…?"

"If that's convenient."

He pushed aside his surprise and said, sure, why not.

I like face-to-face meetings. I spend too much time with the cold, stiff dead, after all. Why talk on the phone, or video-conference, or whatever, when you can meet in the flesh? We should all enjoy the flesh while it's still warm. Take it from me.

"What's up?" Bevner asked from behind his desk. Inspector Ramirez sat opposite him. He said Jones couldn't make it. He didn't rise to shake my hand, and neither man offered to find me a chair. They didn't want me to linger.

I told them all about Natalie Haring's attempt to get me to change or at least soften my opinion on the screwdriver, ending with Oskar Haring's outburst, and the melee that ended the meeting. Then I told them about Curtis Burton, the impossibility of his having anything to do with Haring's death, and Shimamoto's weird lab finding that Burton's DNA was more degraded than Haring's. I didn't tell them about the possibility of an alibi for Samuel Urias; I figured the ethical thing to do was to let Eva Yung try to track Redbeard down, and let her present him as a witness if she could, rather than to offer him as a target to the prosecutor before it was even established whether or not he was credible.

"Okay," said Bevner, when the dust had settled on my spiel. "So what?"

"So now you have a whole bunch of new suspects in this homicide, that's what. Plus it looks even more strongly to me that your prime suspect had nothing to do with it."

"What new suspects?"

"Natalie Haring stands to collect a life insurance windfall, including a double-indemnity rider from her husband dying on the job site."

"Everybody always blames the wife."

"Then there's Jeffrey Symond. He'll collect enough *separate* insurance money to keep his firm in the black for years to come. That's why there were so many lawyers in that room—there are multiple, overlapping stakeholders, corporate and kin. Jeffrey Symond is now the sole partner in Haring & Symond, and he doesn't have to put up with Leopold Haring's troublesome antics anymore."

"That's ridiculous," Ramirez said. "Symond said himself that he can't run the business without Haring. Haring was the creative genius."

"Maybe," I said. "For sure he was an asshole, everyone agrees on that. And there are other creative geniuses out there. Symond can hire one, or a couple, even—and he doesn't have to split things fifty-fifty with those new hires, the way he had to with his bosom buddy. From what I can see, Symond will be much better off now, as long as Samuel Urias goes to prison for killing poor old Leo."

"Crocodile tears from Jeff Symond, huh?"

"I'm just saying."

Ramirez turned to Jason Bevner, warming to the idea. "Natalie is tied up in the business, too. What if she and Symond conspired to off Leopold? What Oskar said to the doc, about how hard it would be for somebody to sneak up on Leopold if he was armed—? That's a good point. If one of them was distracting him, the other one could've stabbed him."

The look Jason Bevner was giving Inspector Ramirez told both of us that I wasn't getting through to him. So I pushed some more.

"Let's not forget Oskar. He went into a psychotic state in that conference room as soon as some schmuck attorney laid a hand on his shoulder. We know that Oskar and Leo exchanged punches the day Leo died. He's not denying that. Oskar could've followed Leo to the construction site, right? Leo was a violent man. Don't you think he might have struck his son again, and set off exactly the sort of frenzied attack I just witnessed out of Oskar, an attack that ended with a fatal stabbing—?"

"With what?" said Bevner. "Oskar's DNA isn't on the screwdriver."

"That's exactly my point. You already know my scientific opinion about that piece of evidence. It doesn't fit the wound, the trace evidence doesn't match, and the new DNA findings only make things worse for your case. Dr. Shimamoto's report is going to inject a shit ton of reasonable doubt."

Bevner shrugged. "Maybe. Let's say you're right about this new—very confusing—DNA data. Maybe you've done your job too well, Doctor. If the screwdriver gets thrown out, then we won't be able to proceed with a case against Mr. Urias. That's true. I'm sure that Ms. Yung will insist that we release him from our custody. I'm telling you, though—going to trial might be the best thing for that man."

"Why?"

"Because he'll have the chance to get acquitted, that's why."

"He's only just been charged!"

"Yeah. And sometimes that's as good as done. You know what I mean?"

"No," I said honestly. "I don't know what you mean."

Bevner shrugged again and eyed Ramirez. The detective looked away from both of us and grunted, in what sounded like disapproval.

"Well, Doctor," said Jason Bevner with an air of finality, "we disagree. I say we had enough for the prelim with that screwdriver, and it'll hold up at trial, too. The way it was brought into evidence—the warrants, the search of Urias's truck—is unimpeachable. That's a good piece of evidence. It's a *great* piece of evidence! I've won cases with way less. I can see no reason to reopen the investigation so we can bat around a bunch of your theories about the dead man's family and business partner. Leave them be."

Them, and their well-heeled lawyers, he meant. Assistant District Attorney Bevner wasn't about to go bugging a bunch of rich, connected people when he had an easy patsy in his pocket.

I heard Bevner crack wise behind my back after I rounded the bend out of his office. Detective Ramirez didn't join in.

I left work on time for a change, and managed to make it home and get the leash on Bea for a good solid beach run while we still had some daylight. It was shaping up to be an award-winning sunset, with no fog and some high clouds, so Bea and I climbed the sand ladder to Sutro Heights Park. Working her stubby legs up that cliff face tuckered the dog out. She lay down in front of me on one of the benches on the parapet of the park's ruined mansion, and we gazed out over Ocean Beach and the wide Pacific as the sky turned gold, then red, and deepened toward violet.

Curtis Burton had been in custody, in the General's psych ward on a 5150, when Leopold Haring was killed on October 27. He was released on the twenty-eighth and died in the collapse of the King Street viaduct on the twenty-ninth. So how did their DNA get commingled on the bloody screwdriver the police had recovered out of Samuel Urias's truck—a screwdriver that didn't have Urias's own DNA on it?

I was thinking about it the wrong way. The screwdriver wasn't the murder weapon. It didn't match the wound, and no amount of finessing by ADA Bevner was going to change that. Its dimensions were wrong, and it had fibers on it that didn't match the decedent's clothing. And I believed Redbeard, the alibi lover, even if he refused to meet with Eva Yung. Nobody had killed

Leopold Haring with that screwdriver, but somebody had bloodied it and dropped it into Urias's pickup bed to frame him for
the murder. So maybe the screwdriver had nothing to do with
the killer at all. It could be someone else trying to set up Urias,
right…? I mean, if I were the killer, and I stabbed the guy with
a screwdriver, and I wanted to pin it on someone else, then I'd
just dump the actual goddamn murder weapon in his truck!

"Somebody is screwing with us, Bea," I said. She snuffled in
the patchy grass. The bluish band on the Pacific horizon was
mellowing, and shrinking. The day was at its end.

"Who gains?"

Sutro Heights was clearing out of dog-walkers and sunset en-
thusiasts. I took Bea down the granite stairway off the parapet,
across the wide lawn, and onto the gravel path toward Anza
Street, toward 41st Avenue.

Toward home. Such as it was.

CHAPTER 14

I didn't get to catch up on my sleep. I was on call, and got sent out to a bar on Union Street in the Marina District at around 2:30 a.m., in the wake of some last-call mayhem. Two men had got into an argument, apparently about an old girlfriend who was long rid of both of them. The argument turned into a fight, and one of them ended up braining the other one against the brick frontage of the bar. The suspect stayed put and was in custody. He was fully soused when first responders arrived, and pretty badly busted up himself. But he was still alive, and his buddy wasn't.

There wasn't much point in my being there, at the scene, but that's the way it goes sometimes. Blessing the body, Dr. Kashiman used to call it back in Los Angeles. I told CSI to examine the brick wall for blood and hair samples, but they already knew that, and took offense with my reminding them. The most interesting thing about the scene was the drinks menu posted outside the bar. It was creative. Donna suggested maybe we should all come back sometime, after work. Cam thought they were overpriced, even for the environs. The two of them had this discussion while they zipped our dead guy into his nylon pouch.

I got back to bed around 4:00, but was up again at 6:30 to walk the dog and get into work. Besides the homicide, I also caught two naturals, though one of them was only an external. Ted Nguyen took three solid cases of his own—an apparent suicide, a decomp probable-overdose, and a motor vehicle accident. It was busy for a Thursday. We were delayed a bit, too, after Ted put his decomp through the Quiznos 5000 full-body X-ray rig. The machine tripped the damn circuit breaker again, plunging the morgue into a blackout.

"At least the HVAC came back," I said, when the power returned. It had been working without a hitch since the last time Denis Monaghan had tinkered with it. I thought back to my bleary morning in his bed, with him joking about how handy he was.

"What is funny?" Yarina asked.

"Funny?"

"You are making a smile."

"Oh…it's nothing. Private joke."

Yarina grunted and went back to her handsaw. When the power went out, so did the electric bone saw, while she was right in the middle of popping the skull on my homicide. Not knowing how long till the juice would come back on, Yarina took the opportunity to pull out the hardware-store saw we hardly ever had occasion to use, and was cutting into the dead man's skull with it. She did so with vigor, but much griping.

Eventually the lights came back on, and I wheeled the homicide case into the cooler. It was still crowded, but not nearly as critically as it had been the week before, when I'd gone in search of John Doe #15. After stowing my homicide, I helped our young day-shift 2578 move some gurneys around so he could get access to a body he had to release to a funeral home. The fellow on the gurney turned out to be none other than Leopold Haring, finally vacating our morgue. I wanted to wish the 2578 luck dealing with that family, but restrained myself.

Back at my desk, before ducking out for lunch, I checked my phone messages. I had one from Homicide Inspector Daniel Ramirez, time-stamped first thing that morning. I got ahold of him on his cell, somewhere with a good deal of traffic noise and wind.

"Oh, yeah," he said. "Listen, uh…about yesterday. If you're right about the screwdriver, I don't want to see this whole case fall apart. There's a spotlight on it as it is, y'know what I mean?"

I did. The story was still bouncing around the local news, and occasionally hitting the national media. Amber Bishop at KnowNowSF wasn't the only reporter leaving me voice mails, especially now that they had Samuel Urias as a villain for the story.

"So, look," the detective continued. "This ADA, Jason Bevner, I've worked with him before. He isn't going to give up on the screwdriver. If he's right about it, we have a good case against Mr. Urias. If you're right, though—"

"Inspector, if you're going to try to talk me into changing my stated expert opinion about—"

"No, no! That's not what I meant, Doc. I wouldn't do that, don't worry—I've worked with *you* before too, don't forget. Here's the thing. The only way you're going to get that screwdriver thrown out is by producing another murder weapon. One that'll stand up better at trial. If this one had Urias's DNA on it, I might feel different—but you're right about the thing. It shouldn't be this complicated, right? If you came up with a weapon that fit the wound better, and maybe had the right fibers, and definitely had somebody's DNA on it who doesn't have a solid alibi like this 5150 guy…"

"Fifty-one-fifty guy, Curtis Burton, was already dead and decomposing when his DNA got on that screwdriver, Daniel. The whole thing is nuts."

"That's what I'm saying. It's always bugged me that we got that warrant off an anonymous tip. I was surprised the judge approved it. When we told her the doc said the wound came from a screwdriver, I think she decided we had enough there to pursue the search, since the building site was bound to have screwdrivers, right? Between the tipster and your statement about the type of wound, it was enough for the warrant, but I always thought it was pretty thin."

"Bevner likes it."

"Yeah. But he… Well, like I said, once that guy sets his mind to a theory of the crime, you won't convince him otherwise. But if you can come up with another weapon that matches the wound, you might have a chance."

So why aren't you out there searching for the goddamn thing, *Detective*, I wanted to ask. I didn't, though. I knew why he was turfing it to me. Daniel Ramirez and Keith Jones had delivered Samuel Urias to the assistant district attorney, and the ADA liked Urias for the murder. If the ADA didn't want to listen to reason in light of new scientific evidence, Ramirez couldn't go reinvestigating the case on his own, especially considering that he and Jones were probably juggling half a dozen other homicides by now. Still, Inspector Ramirez felt bad for Samuel Urias. I had managed to inject reasonable doubt about his guilt into one man's head, anyhow.

I heard a truck barrel past wherever Ramirez was standing, and a distant voice call his name. "I gotta go," he said into his cell. "Think about what I said."

And he hung up.

"Cops," I muttered. Ramirez claimed the judge had approved

the warrant because I had told him the murder weapon was a screwdriver. I hadn't said that. I had said that the wound was made by a penetrating weapon with a round shaft, at least five inches long and approximately one-quarter inch in girth. If the detectives had gone to the judge asking to look for crossbow bolts, she would've laughed them out of her office. They didn't. They told the judge that this body found on a construction site had been stabbed with a screwdriver. And now one of them was having second thoughts, while a man who was probably innocent of the murder sat waiting to go to trial for it. What did Ramirez expect me to do about it? Go find the murder weapon, he says. Sure, I'll get right on it.

Zasrane to życie. I would, too. I knew it. I couldn't help myself.

A text from Sparkle pinged onto my phone, asking if I was free for lunch. It was unexpected—I figured she would be tied up with funeral plans for her uncle.

Need a break from all that, she replied.

We got tacos, as usual, from the El Herrador truck, and walked them over to the only park anywhere near Baby Mike Bail Bonds, a grassy rectangle with some basketball courts, a kiddie playground, and picnic benches set in a little garden. The garden sometimes had people passed out or sleeping in it, and I had once accidentally interrupted a sex act taking place in a stall in the public bathroom, but on the other hand the park had sunshine on even the foggiest day, so I liked it.

It wasn't foggy that afternoon. The high clouds were back, wispy and distant. The wind was light. It was a lovely autumn day. Sparkle looked worn out. I had to prompt her to eat her tacos.

"I keep thinking about him," she said. "But only the good things. He was the fun uncle. He didn't have kids of his own, so he had all this energy for us—chasing us around when we'd all get together, putting one kid on his shoulders, one piggyback, while grabbing two more under each arm, you know? Like that.

He had this terrible illness, and it dragged him down—but he never let it drag us down. He was always there for us when we were kids. That's what makes it so hard that…we let him down. We weren't there for him."

"Hang on to those good things, honey. Is your mom holding up?"

Sparkle looked away. "No. This was always her biggest fear, and now here it is. But she's…she'll be all right. Funeral's gonna be hard." She shook her head and sighed. "Thanks for asking—but, like I said, I need a break. Tell me what you're working on."

"You really want to know?"

"As long as it's not too graphic."

"Okay. Well, I have this problem case…"

When I'd finished telling her the whole tale, Sparkle said, "Wait, this is the one with those weird rocks you were asking about, right?"

I nodded. "You sent me to see your friend the cement expert. He confirmed what a guy at the Department of Building Inspection said about the rocks, that they were a special type of fast-setting concrete, not something you'd find on a job site like the one where we recovered the body."

"But your dead man was carrying them."

"In a zippered pocket."

"Why would he do that?"

We both thought about it. Then I said, "He was collecting evidence of something."

"Okay…"

"Haring was infamous for micromanaging his jobs, and he was always hanging around, yelling at the builders. Maybe he'd found that rocky aggregate somewhere that he didn't like seeing it, and he was…what was he going to do with it?"

"Bring it to Department of Buildings and make a huge stink," Sparkle said.

"Could be."

"You showed it to the guy at the DBI, right?"

"I did."

"And…?"

"He…he clammed right up."

"Oho now. You don't say."

"His name was… Peter? He had these horrible pointy sideburns. I showed him the rocks and he told me right away what they were. Then he asked me where they came from. When I told him it was SoMa Centre, he handed me some bullshit form to fill out, and made himself scarce."

"What was the form?"

"He said it was so they could start their own investigation."

"And you never heard back from them again."

"That's right."

"He's on the take," Sparkle said with an offhand flip of her napkin. "All those guys at the DBI are on the take."

"Come on, Sparkle."

"Oh, I'm serious. You know how much money is getting spent on a new skyscraper in San Francisco? *Money.* Lots and lots. Yeah, I'll bet your Peter with the pointy sideburns is taking a bribe to sign off on this special cement getting used there."

I chewed and thought about it. "I have to go back to the scene. To do that, I need either a police warrant, which I ain't gonna get, or a pass from the Department of Building Inspection. If I go into the DBI to ask for one, they're going to hand me off to Pointy Peter again, since he's in charge of that job card. He's just going to give me more runaround."

"Why you want to go back to the scene?"

"I'm sure that screwdriver is not the murder weapon, but I can't point to what *is*."

"So you want to go poke around and look for…what? A screwdriver that fits the wound?"

"Maybe. I don't know exactly."

"Well, honey, that's not good enough. I mean, it's been weeks since the murder, there's been an everloving *earthquake* in the meantime, and you don't know what you're looking for."

"I know what I'm looking for. A rod-shaped weapon a quarter inch in diameter, maybe with blood on it, and maybe with fibers. Ideally, the blood will belong to Leopold Haring and *only* Leopold Haring this time."

"You think you're going to find another screwdriver somewhere?"

"I don't know, Sparkle! I have to *try*. Otherwise, Samuel Urias might go to prison over a piece of false evidence that someone planted in his truck. If that happens, then I will have played a part in putting him there. I'm not going to let that happen if I can help it."

Sparkle nodded in a sage way. "This is Anup rubbing off on you."

That knocked me back. "What…?"

"Anup. With his appeals of factual innocence. Those are people like this Samuel guy—like he's going to be, anyhow, if they go ahead with the trial and if the ADA is right about the screwdriver evidence convincing a jury."

Psiakrew. Sparkle didn't know about the breakup. I hadn't had a chance to talk to her about it. If she had known, she never would have thrown that in my face.

She was right, though, just the same.

"What's Samuel's last name again," Sparkle asked.

"Urias."

"He have an accent?"

"Yes."

"Brown skin?"

"Kinda."

"Okay, then. You're right. He's going to prison." Sparkle wiped her fingers, pulled out her phone, and started thumb-typing while she talked, as she does. "I guess I don't blame you for wanting to help him—or to try, at least," she said, "considering the wrongful-conviction horror stories Anup probably tells you over dinner. I've seen some of my clients go down like that." She pressed something on the phone with satisfaction. "I'm gonna hook you up."

"What do you mean?"

"What you need is someone who knows how DBI works. Even better, a DBI contractor who can go into their office with you and pull some strings. It would be a further bonus if this contractor was, say, a physically imposing individual who is hard to ignore."

"Sparkle, what are you—"

My phone chirped.

"Group text," Sparkle said.

I pulled it out. She had included me in a miniature conference with a number my phone didn't recognize.

"My cousin Michael," she said.

"Baby Mike?"

"That's right."

"He works for the Department of Building Inspection?"

"He's a security contractor with them."

"I thought you said he moves refrigerators."

Both our phones chirped, and Sparkle started texting again. "He does that, too. It's a gig economy, honey, ain't you heard?"

Baby Mike was working on some of their uncle's funeral arrangements, but agreed to meet me at the DBI as soon as he could. I texted that he didn't have to come if he was busy, but he replied that he was eager to help. I got the impression that, like Sparkle and her call for tacos, Baby Mike was eager for some distraction from the family's grief.

I headed right over to the Department of Building Inspection. With the slew of earthquake demolitions and repair jobs the city still had ahead of it, the place was busy. Sure enough, it was Peter with the sideburns who met me when my turn came at the permits counter. He didn't seem to remember me right off—but he sure did once I mentioned SoMa Centre.

"Oh, right. You came in with a chunk of HAC concrete."

"I did."

"What can I do for you today?"

I told him I needed to get back onto that site as part of an ongoing death investigation.

"Okey dokey," he lied, and turned to a computer monitor. He made a serious face while he pretended to look something up, then made a frowny face, and turned back to me. "I'm afraid I can't let anyone onto that site. It's under investigation."

"I know. I'm investigating it."

"No, I mean *our* investigation. We don't open sites to other agencies when we're conducting an inspection audit."

I laid my badge on the permits counter. "Peter, I am investigating a homicide. I promise I won't get in the way of your engineers down there. In fact, if you can point me to the spot at the site where they're looking into this HAC stuff, I'd certainly appreciate it."

His folksy facade was slipping. "Why would you want to do that?"

"I suspect the HAC that I pulled out of the pocket of a dead man might have something to do with the way he ended up dead. You see, the dead man was Leopold Haring, the architect on the project—"

"I know who Leopold Haring was."

"Great! Then you might have heard rumors about what a stickler he was for things being done the way he wanted them done. It could cause some real headaches for the nonarchitects who actually had to implement his plans..."

"Ma'am," Pointy Peter said, nodding toward the mob beyond the reception window. "You might have noticed how much the earthquake has impacted what we do around here. I've told you that I can't let you onto that site, so now I'm going to ask you…to…"

He trailed off, with a look I've seen before when Baby Mike fills a doorway.

"Hey, Doc," the big man said, and held out his massive hand for me to shake. I did. He was wearing a generic SECURITY jacket, with an ID lanyard around his oak-trunk neck.

"Hey, Peter," Baby Mike said to Peter. He didn't offer his hand.

"Um," said Peter.

Baby Mike scanned the empty permits counter. "You get what you came here for?"

"No. Peter here says he can't help me."

"Oh," said Baby Mike, and nodded slowly. "It's like that."

Baby Mike glared at Peter, then slid his immense form across the length of the permits counter while running his fingers under its lip. Something clicked, and Baby Mike lifted the counter's pass-through hatch.

He passed through.

"Wait…" Peter clucked. Baby Mike ignored him and strode straight past the desks behind the counter to a frosted-glass door with somebody's name on it. He threw open the door without knocking, and closed it good and solid behind himself. We heard raised voices through the door and saw shadows moving back and forth. The voices got louder, and it sounded like flesh got smacked a few times. The shadows merged, and one of the voices went on for a minute. Then the frosted-glass door opened.

Baby Mike emerged, a sheet of paper in his hand. An older man followed him, beaming. "Fill that out however you need to, Michael," he said. "Great to see you!"

"You too, Jerry," Baby Mike said. Then he stopped and swiveled back, and gave this guy Jerry a slap on the shoulder. Jerry

251

returned the slap to Mike, and grinned even wider, and the two of them went in for a brief, manly hug, with more slapping.

Baby Mike went back around the desks and across the pass-through, ignoring Peter, and cocked his head at me. I followed in his wake as he carried right on into the lobby, plowing through the crowd to a counter supplied with pens on dirty string leashes.

"Fill this out and I can get you a walk-on." He handed me the form. It was specific for the SoMa Centre job card and listed Haring & Symond, Architects, right up top.

After the display of violence I'd seen in the conference room at Haring & Symond, I couldn't discount Oskar as a suspect in his father's murder. But, apart from his volatility, there was no evidence against him—and Pointy Peter's stonewalling about the job site in general and the yellow block of HAC in particular had pushed another theory to the top of my list. Peter was covering for somebody. Natalie Haring and Jeff Symond had money. If something had gone awry in the construction of SoMa Centre, something they wanted buried, they could be paying him off. And if Leopold Haring had tried to expose the construction flaw, then Jeff and Natalie had a good motive to shut him up—and to cover it up with the pipes, as an accident. Natalie could file for double indemnity on that workplace fatality rider, after all.

The screwdriver still didn't make sense, though. Why would Natalie and Jeff frame Samuel Urias with such a sketchy piece of manufactured evidence? Why not drop the real murder weapon in the back of his truck?

Baby Mike broke my trance. "You almost done? I told my aunt Gayle I'd be back by four, and if I'm late, she'll worry. I'm not going to let her worry."

"Sorry," I said, and went back to the form. It had a release of liability and a list of boxes for a conflicts check, with the site superintendent listed as representative for the general contractor. Under his name were a bunch of others, the subcontractors. One of them jumped out at me.

Monaghan, Denis.

I put down the pen.

"What's the matter?" asked Baby Mike.

I thought back to what Denis had said, about our jobs being similar. He always had balls in the air, multiple projects on multiple sites, just like I always had autopsies, lab results, and death certificates to juggle on multiple decedents. Denis had been working at SoMa Centre at the same time he came in to fix our HVAC. Facilities maintenance had given him key-card access to the Office of Chief Medical Examiner. I had seen him tag himself into the autopsy suite—the very day I met him, when I jumped down his throat about wandering in there without any PPEs. Once he was in the autopsy suite, he had access to the cooler.

"Doc, are you gonna fill this out, or what?" demanded Baby Mike.

"I need a minute. I promise—just one minute." I pulled out my phone and dialed Inspector Daniel Ramirez.

"Hey," I said, as quietly as I could in the crowd. "That anonymous tipster, the one who pointed you to Urias—he told you that Urias was a pain in the ass, right?"

"He said Urias beefed with lots of folks down there, especially Leopold Haring."

"Is that true?"

"For sure. We interviewed everyone at that place. The laborers, the guys who spoke Spanish, loved Urias. They all told me he looked out for them, and he was the only one. Management, though—they hated the guy. The site superintendent was always rushing the pace, and Urias was always pushing back, to slow it down for safety's sake. I got the impression there was a lot of friction."

"What about the subcontractors? How did they feel about Urias?"

"Hated him."

"They all did?"

"Yup. The subcontractors were all real clear about that—Urias was slowing them down, and that meant he was going to cost them. Time pressure is serious on these big jobs, they said. There's a per-day bonus, big money, if you deliver the project early, and penalties if you're late. It's written into all their contracts."

"And how's the time pressure on the subcontractors now that Urias is out of the picture?" I asked.

There was a pause. "That's a good question."

Well, I thought—there's an easy way to answer it.

I hung up, went back over to the counter to join Baby Mike, and rushed right through the rest of the job site inspection form.

CHAPTER 15

I got lucky and found parking not far from the SoMa Centre site at Sixth and Folsom. The space was right in front of a combination laundromat and pickup bar where the clientele were preening and flirting while they nursed cocktails and watched the dryers roll.

Jack-of-all-trades and master of some, Denis Monaghan had called himself, the shifty bastard. *He* was the one who set up Samuel Urias. Denis had planted the bloody screwdriver in the union steward's truck as an expedient way of getting him off the SoMa Centre site. Monaghan had been in the morgue working on the HVAC when I did Haring's autopsy. Up in the ceiling, he'd pretended to be out of earshot, but I would bet he had overheard everything we said about the architect's true cause of death—that it wasn't a load of pipe that killed him, and it wasn't a shooting. It was a stabbing, with a weapon shaped like an ice pick or a screwdriver. During the investigation, Jones and Ramirez had put the case under restriction, with the assumption that only the killer knew Haring didn't die from the pipes, and only the killer knew what kind of weapon was used to stab him in the back. But Denis Monaghan knew, too, because he had been present in the inner sanctum of the autopsy suite when we were discussing that evidence.

Monaghan knew who Haring was, and he knew how he could make the Haring homicide useful to him. He saw his opportunity to fuck with Urias when he watched Yarina wheel Haring's body into the cooler on October 29. The next day, when he came back to fix the HVAC again, he came up with a pretext to go alone into the cooler with his toolbox. Hell—he'd probably sabotaged the HVAC to make sure it would go down again.

Samuel Urias insisted that the bloody screwdriver was not his. It was a cheap piece of hardware-store junk. Monaghan had probably bought it brand-new to make sure his own DNA wasn't on it, and stored it in his toolbox. Once he was alone in the cooler, he found Haring's body, zipped the pouch open, and bathed that screwdriver in Leopold Haring's blood.

But there was a complication. Haring wasn't alone on his gurney in our cold storage room. He was sharing it with Curtis Burton. Decomposition fluid from the homeless man's bag had followed the pull of gravity and leaked into the famous architect's. Their DNA mingled there. When Monaghan smeared Haring's blood on the screwdriver, Burton's DNA came along for the ride. That was how Shimamoto had come up with such a strange lab result—she was measuring a sample taken from two bodies at different stages of decomposition, sharing the same felonious fucking dipstick.

And the fibers—those baby-blue plant fibers on the screwdriver shaft. I had seen that color in Monaghan's bathroom, on a roll of heavy-duty paper towels. Monaghan must've wrapped the bloody screwdriver in one of those. If Jones and Ramirez could get a warrant for Denis Monaghan's toolbox, they might find that very same commingled DNA in it, and that would be enough to exonerate Samuel Urias. Assistant District Attorney Jason Bevner was going to shit himself. I hoped I could be there to see him get the news.

As long as he wore gloves and kept his own DNA off the screwdriver, and as long as he stayed anonymous when he called the crime tip line, it was low risk for Denis. Low risk, and, if Inspector Ramirez was right, high reward: get the pesky union steward out of his hair, finish the job at SoMa Centre early, collect a big cash bonus.

The son of a bitch. *Stary brudny sukinsyn.* I had bad luck with *sukinsyni* and one-night stands. I resolved to be more…discerning? Sure. More discerning I would be, in the future.

The SoMa Centre security guard radioed for the site superintendent. The super was furious, but there wasn't much he could do. My walk-on paperwork was legit. He was the one who had told me I needed a warrant or a DBI pass, and there I was, at the gate, holding one. He told me to sign in and handed over a hard hat.

Work was going at a manic pace, a commotion of workers and machines, diesel and dust. I commented on it. The superintendent shrugged suspiciously. "Earthquake slowed things down. They're getting back to normal."

"This is *normal*?"

"It's a big job, a lot going on."

"Who's the union steward, if Samuel Urias isn't working here anymore?"

"They haven't said yet."

Right. Could be someone at the union was on the take, too. Jeffrey Symond and Natalie Haring still had plenty of money to spread around if they needed to, in spite of the poor-mouth routine they'd put on for me in their conference room, with all their lawyers.

The superintendent walked me up to his mobile office trailer and offered me a cup of water. I asked him if Oskar Haring was on-site somewhere.

"Who?"

"Leopold Haring's son."

"Oh, that guy. No. He doesn't come around here."

"Never?"

The superintendent pointed his head back toward the security gate. "They have instructions."

"How about Jeffrey Symond or Natalie Haring?"

"Jeff was here earlier, but he's long gone. Why?"

"Do they have a storage space here somewhere?"

"For what?"

"Haring & Symond."

"They're architects. They work in an office."

I pointed to the trailer. "Okay, how about in there, then? A drawer in a file cabinet, anything at all?"

"No."

"You know what high-alumina cement is, right?" I asked. The superintendent seemed a little put off, but said yes, he did. "Where will I find it here, on this site?"

"You won't," he said. "We wouldn't have a use for that material."

"You haven't seen it here, anywhere?"

"No. And look, I don't know what you think you're going to—"

"I'll check back with you at your office before I go. Right now there's things I have to look into."

"Dr. Teska, this really isn't a safe place for a—"

I held the DBI pass up to his nose. "I *said*, there's things I have to look into."

The superintendent turned red. "Fine," he huffed. "But you need to sign a liability release…"

"Did that already, back at the DBI."

"Fine," he said again. He went into his trailer and slammed the door.

I stood on the trailer's little dirt hill and took a couple of minutes to spiral slowly around, surveying the whole of the SoMa Centre work site.

"*Co teraz zrobić?*" I said out loud, and cocked my head just the way my *mamusia* does when she says it.

So now what? Physical evidence. There had to be physical evidence. I knew Haring had been killed someplace other than where his body was found. That backstab into his heart would've bled a lot, especially if he was lying supine, the way he was found—but I had seen no blood in the dirt under the body after we got the pipes lifted off. I also knew, from the tears in his clothes and the postmortem trauma to his lower legs, that he'd been dragged after he'd died.

I decided to start at the spot where the body was found, and work outward from there. It was hard for me to even locate the scene, though. The pipes were long gone, and the patch of dirt where Haring had lain was now under some lumber molds. It was going to be part of the building, it seemed, once the concrete got poured in there.

I sat on the molds and dug through my go bag for my phone. I could call Eva Yung. She would certainly want to hear my half-baked theory about Denis Monaghan planting the bloody screwdriver. I stopped myself before I dialed. The right thing to do was to get the detectives involved first, not the lawyers. But the detectives didn't want any half-baked theories. They wanted a murder weapon that fit the wound, and I didn't have anything like that to offer them.

I put the phone away, scratched under the hard hat, and indulged in a nice big yawn. It had been one long day, starting with that bar fight death scene in the wee hours and going ever since. I stood and stretched, then did some step-ups on the lumber molds, just to get my blood flowing.

That was when I saw the guy with the angle grinder. He was making his way slowly along a raw concrete wall. He wore heavy gloves and protective goggles. Sparks were flying. Something dropped off the wall with a clink, and the sparks stopped. He moved a few steps, lifted his tool, shifted his shoulders, and started throwing sparks again.

I looked down. In the man's wake, every couple of feet, a metal rod lay in the dust.

I picked one up. It wasn't rebar—this thing wasn't nearly as hefty, and didn't have those ridges rebar has. It was round and smooth, grayish metal, with specks of rust. I pulled out my tape measure. The piece I held in my hand was six inches long and somewhere around a quarter inch in diameter.

It sure as shit looked like a screwdriver shaft to me.

I examined the wall. The guy was cutting the metal rods flush. They were embedded in the concrete. I measured again, this time between the cut rods. Eighteen inches. The metal was shiny and fresh where he had already gone trimming. I stepped back and looked ahead. Beyond the guy throwing sparks, the rods were sticking out of the wall at eighteen-inch intervals, all the way down, for what looked like twenty yards.

"Hey!" I hollered. He didn't hear me. I had to get right up next to him and wave to catch his eye. He shut off the angle grinder and removed a Day-Glo earplug.

"Yeah?" he said.

I held up the rod. "What's this called?"

"Huh?"

"What do you call this thing?"

The man with the angle grinder squinted, and peered sideways at me. "That's a pin. A framework pin. Why?"

I held up my DBI pass. "I'm doing an inspection."

"And you never seen a concrete framework pin?"

"Humor me."

"Okay."

"Have you seen any of these that look…unusual?"

"What'd'ya mean?"

"Like, covered in something brownish red."

The man took out his other earplug and looked around, presumably searching for someone higher up the food chain who could handle my stupid questions.

"Well?" I said.

"No."

"You're sure?"

"No. I'm not sure. I cut the tails. That's what I do this week. I don't… I don't really look at them. I just cut. That's all."

"Who picks them up, and where do they go?"

"The tails?"

"The pieces you cut off."

"Tails. Ferdinand picks them up. I don't know where he brings them."

"Where can I find Ferdinand?"

"Look, lady. I don't mean to be rude, and I know you're from the DBI and all, but can you go find somebody else to ask about this? I got a schedule to keep. The pour sequence guys are on my ass. You understand?"

"No. What's a pour sequence?"

The man sighed in a way that said *they do not pay me enough for this bullshit.* "The pour sequence for the concrete. Like, when it gets poured, and where."

"Oh. So they're pouring it here, and you have to cut these things first?"

"No. This was poured last week. I just go where the pour sequence master tells me to go, trimming the tails after the pour sets. You really with DBI…?"

"Where else will I find these rods?"

"Pins."

"Pins."

"All over the place. Seriously—I'm on a tight schedule here, and I can't help you. You need to talk to the pour sequence master."

"Where do I find the pour sequence master?"

The pin tail cutter stuck his ear protection back in and turned his power tool back on, ensuring that he wouldn't have to talk to me anymore. He pointed off toward the superintendent's trailer, then set into the next pin in the sequence with a shower of sparks.

I marched past him, along the line of pins he hadn't yet cut. The wall went around another corner and ended at a jungly tangle of rebar and plywood, where, I figured, the concrete pouring crew hadn't yet visited. I started back up to the trailer to ask about the pour sequence master, but then spotted another line of framework pins sticking out of concrete, down at the bottom of a steep dirt ramp. I followed them.

The ramp ended at another wall, this one much thicker than the one I'd just walked. It looked like it was going to be part of the foundation—its top was crowned with heavy-gauge rebar. The smaller framework pins I'd followed protruded from the foundation structure's outside face at eighteen-inch intervals, but this time with a second set of pins, lower down, paralleling them. The lower line disappeared behind a chain-link gate with a hand-lettered sign, *BG17 utility vault PGE auth only*.

The gate was latched but it wasn't locked. I went through it—and almost fell headlong off the threshold. A wooden stepladder dropped four or five feet into a dank, dark little room. It smelled like a root cellar. I pulled the flashlight out of my go bag, climbed down, and crunched onto a gravel floor.

The walls and low ceiling were made of rough concrete—in the flashlight's beam I could pick out knotty patterns left behind by plywood molds. Narrow trenches stocked partway with rubble and gravel footed the side walls, left and right of the doorway, ten feet apart. The line of framework pins marched across the wall opposite me, maybe twenty feet away. I stepped across, carefully, and shined the light over them. One pin looked different than the others. It was covered in something dark and gummy. I grabbed a vial out of my go bag and took a sample.

I've seen enough blood, on enough surfaces, fresh and dried and everything in-between, to know it before I get it back to the lab.

I sealed the vial in a specimen bag, wrote the date and my initials, and shoved it in my pocket. Then I took out my go bag's magnifying glass and peered at the metal rod, a quarter inch in diameter, that stuck six inches out of the wall at the height of a man's heart. When I got the light just right, I could make out bits of cloth stuck to it. Some were dark colored, others lighter. There was something else on the metal rod, too: spiky flakes of rust. I knew that when I got the sample turned into histology slides, I'd look under the microscope and see the same mysterious brownish-red foreign bodies I had seen in the sections taken from Haring's wound track. Ted Nguyen was right on the money when he recommended I get those sections iron-stained. I aimed the flashlight's beam down and shifted the coarse gravel back and forth with my shoe, gently, until I reached it: the black patch of Leopold Haring's spilled blood.

I bent to gather some of that, too. When I did, I caught a scent I know too well. I scanned with the flashlight and followed my nose. It pointed me to the side trench under the right-hand wall. I spotted a patch of color buried under the rubble. I dug it up.

It was a sneaker.

I cleared away more rubble and found the pant leg, then followed it to the other end and uncovered a head of hair—brown, short but thick, with curls. I brushed the gravel off his face. The dead man wore a red goatee and had freckles. He had a ragged bullet exit wound beside his nose.

Redbeard, Samuel Urias's alibi witness. I gave the leg a tug. It was cold to the touch but not stiff—so rigor mortis had passed. Based on the smell and the early marbling on the skin of his cheeks, I guessed, given how cool it was down there, that he might have been dead a couple of days. Couldn't be more—it was Thursday evening, and I had spoken to the man myself on Monday, if this really was him. It looked like the man I'd seen in the courtroom gallery the day I'd testified at Samuel Urias's preliminary hearing, but you can't always trust your eyes when it comes to the faces of the dead. I didn't want to disturb the crime scene any worse than I already had, so I left Redbeard alone and climbed out of the rubbly trench.

As I rose, my flashlight caught another pop of color, a dull yellow. It belonged to a big glob of rock that abutted the bottom of the trench, where it met the back wall. It looked like it didn't belong there—like an afterthought. I whacked at it with the end of the flashlight and broke off a sliver. It was a mix of pebbles and yellow cement with tiny silvery hairs mixed in, lightweight, for its size.

I knew then why Denis Monaghan hadn't been worried about anyone finding the real murder weapon when he planted the fake one in Samuel Urias's truck.

I went into the go bag and felt around for my cell phone. Before I could find it, the gate I'd come through clanked and a light blinded me.

"Hey! Can you not read? Authorized…"

Denis Monaghan was standing at the top of the rough wooden stairs.

I kept rummaging in the go bag, and got my hand around the phone. But I didn't pull it out. Redbeard was dead at my feet, a bullet hole in his head. Monaghan had shot him. If I tried to call 911, he would shoot me.

"Get that light down, Denis. You're blinding me."

"Jessie? I don't… What are you…?"

He pointed the light at my feet. I still had my own flashlight in my other hand. I pointed it at his eyes, but otherwise didn't move.

"I'm here on a DBI pass. Hold up your other hand, would you...?"

"Turnabout's fair play, love, but what—"

"I need to make sure I can see both your hands, please."

"Why's that?"

"Please, Denis."

He lifted his right hand from his side and held it up to shield his eyes.

"Thank you," I said, laboring to keep my voice calm and professional. "Now, let's both go outside and I'll tell you why I'm here."

"We can talk here."

"Outside. I'll follow you."

"We can talk here. It's quieter. Besides, that's an active work site out there, dangerous if you don't know what you're doing. Which you don't, love. Do you."

He hadn't budged from his position in front of the cellar doorway.

"Where's the gun, Denis?"

"Gun?"

"The one you used on Samuel Urias's alibi. I don't know why you shot that man, but you did."

"What are you talking about?"

"Leopold Haring, though—I think I know why you killed him."

"Sam Urias killed Haring. Why would you—"

"That big clot of specialty concrete over there. The yellow stuff, what's it called, hyper aluminum something."

"That's a high-alumina cement aggregate footing. What of it?"

"You tell me. Something about it alarmed Leopold Haring

265

so much that he was down here gathering a sample. I'm going to guess that you are the pour sequence master on this job?"

That got his attention. "Jessie, won't you please take that bloody light off my eyes."

I did.

He nodded thanks and dropped his hand back to his side. I didn't take my attention off it.

"Since you're asking, no, I'm not the pour sequence master. I'm contracted for the duct bank and conduit trench masonry."

"Sounds like a big job."

"Big enough."

"Down here in this vault, something went wrong with your masonry. In the foundation, right? Some serious problem—but I guess every problem with the foundation is serious. You decided to patch it with that special quick-set concrete, hoping, I guess, that no one would ever come down here and discover your mistake. But Leopold Haring did. He was going to blow the whistle on you. You found him down here—or maybe you brought him, I wouldn't put it past you—and you shoved him up against the framework pin behind me, stabbing him right through the back. Then you pulled him down. He bled into the dirt right there."

I pointed to the spot but didn't take my eyes off Monaghan. "Once the night shift had closed up and the site was empty, you dragged his body up that slope, left it underneath a trailer loaded with pipes, and cut the strap holding them. The pipes did a number on Leopold Haring. You probably figured everyone would think he was tugging on the trailer's straps or something, snooping around again—and died in an accident of his own making."

Monaghan's empty hand turned up imploringly. "Jessie. Will you only listen to yourself? You cannot really believe such a mad story. You cannot, surely."

"Why's it matter?"

"That you would believe I'm capable of such a terrible thing? I'm not, love. I'm no murderer."

He looked genuinely hurt—but, then again, he hadn't moved. He was still standing at the top of the stepladder, in the entry-way to the vault, between me and the outside.

"Let's hear your story, then."

"Will you believe me?"

I didn't answer.

"Look," Denis said, and shifted on his feet. "I can prove it. Hang on..."

He pointed his light at the trench opposite the one where I'd found Redbeard buried, went down the stepladder, and crunched through the gravel toward it. When he did, I saw daylight through the gateway, and heard the rumble of heavy equipment and distant voices. Denis bent down into the trench and moved aside some rubble. His back was to me. There was nothing between me and the doorway.

I made a dash for it. Two seconds—that was all I had been working for, all I needed to cross the distance. But just when my foot hit the bottom step, Denis Monaghan cried out, "Jes-sie, wait—! Look!"

Kurwa. I couldn't help myself. I turned and shined my flash-light at him.

Denis had a terribly pained expression. In his hands was a bundle of rags. "Look..." he said again.

And he unwrapped a gun.

He pointed it at me, and the pained expression vanished. "Go back over where you were, now."

I didn't. Outside, in the corner of my eye, I could see a pair of jeans and work boots—but they were far off, and there was a lot of construction noise. Before I could dash out or yell for help, Denis took a step closer.

"Can't miss from here, Doctor, you know that better than anyone. I didn't miss Javier, and I got him with a head shot."

267

I raised my hands in the air. "Denis…"

"Back you go, now," he said, and waved the gun barrel toward the rear of the vault. I did what he said.

"Toss over your light." I did.

He lifted his own. "Now sit down like a good lass." He pointed the beam toward the trench where the dead man lay.

"How come? You want to make it easier on yourself to shallow-grave me next to Javier there?"

"Just do it."

"No. And who is Javier, anyway? I can understand why you'd murder Haring, but why—"

Denis's pale eyes went narrow with fury. "I did not murder Leopold Haring."

"Bullshit."

"Shut your mouth or I'll shut it for you."

"I still call bullshit, Denis. I autopsied the man, remember."

He shook his head impatiently. "Killing and murder aren't the same thing."

Sweet talk or stall, those were my only options, till I came up with another. Stall first, then sweet talk, I decided.

"You killed him because he was going to expose your cutting corners on the foundation for a sixty-story building. A sixty-story building in the most valuable real estate on this continent. The Leaning Tower of Pine Street, you've heard of that mess? You were doing the same damage here. Or worse. Foundations are important. When they fail, people die."

"I didn't murder that gaffer. It was self-defense."

"Really."

"It *was*! He…" Monaghan's shoulders slouched a little. "You're not far wrong about the HAC footing, all right? There was a miscalculation in some of the conduit work. I needed a temporary fix, fast and alone, just till I can get the proper slab poured in here—and then no one will know or care. But old Leopold? Leopold wouldn't stand for anything shy of perfect."

"He came down here after work hours, when he thought you wouldn't be here. But you were."

"I always bloody am! This job is my life!"

"You were behind schedule and facing a fine. The time penalties, written into the contract."

"Stupid fucken thing. Like it's my fault that no one will let a man take the time to do a decent job."

"What happened when you found Haring down here?"

"Ach," Monaghan said, and waved the gun around. "He wouldn't listen."

"So you pinned him up against the wall like a boy with a bug."

"Jessie, would you ever just hear yourself? Use your head, woman. Where did this gun come from, do you figure?"

For the first time, I took a close look at the weapon. It was a long-barreled revolver. It looked, I suddenly realized, not like one of the guns we'll see at a crime scene or in the police ballistics lab, but like one you would see in an old movie. It was a period piece.

"That's Haring's antique revolver."

"It is. At least I assume so. I took it off him."

That made no sense. "So why didn't you shoot him with it?"

"Because, I'm telling you, I didn't mean to kill the man at all! You're right that I walked in on him down here. I tried to talk to him, hear out his concerns about my work, like—but he wasn't having it. He was bloody *furious* about that HAC concrete footing. He called it an off-the-books quick fix and kept going on and on that he wasn't going to let the likes of me ruin that precious reputation of his. Then he tried to get past me, and all I done is I put a hand on his chest, like…"

I thought of Oskar Haring, Leopold's son, and his reaction in the conference room when a schmuck lawyer laid a hand on him, and suddenly I knew how Leopold Haring had died.

"It was a fight. You pushed him up against that pin during a fight…"

"That's what I'm telling you! Self-defense!"

"It was an accident."

"All I did was to put a hand on his chest, and he wound back and clocked me square in the jaw, the old git. I punched back—I swear I didn't put me heart into it—and then he pulled out this giant fucking gun! So before he could point it, I grabbed his wrist, and he grabbed my wrist, and we grappled, like…and we ended up grappling back there, toward the wall…"

The wall with the pins. *Boże mój.*

"Denis," I said softly, "it was an accident. It really was. So why did you go to all the trouble to drag him up top and drop those pipes on him, to dress it up like one? You must've known it wouldn't work. Why didn't you just call the police…?"

Monaghan laughed mordantly. "You really are a stupid cow, aren't you. They'd send me straight back. And I told you once before, no death in Ireland for this man. I can't go back. Ever."

"What do you mean, send you back—? Haring attacked you. He had a gun in his hand! No DA would charge you with anything above involuntary manslaughter, and maybe not even that. They wouldn't have a case…"

"They don't need one. I don't have the protection of the law in this great country of ours, Jessie."

It took me a minute, but then I got it.

"You're illegal."

"On paper."

"You're an illegal immigrant."

"I'm a damned hardworking and successful entrepreneur trying to mind my own business."

My head was reeling. "Haring's death was an accident. You didn't do anything wrong. But then you went and shot Javier over here, whoever he is—and that's not a story of self-defense, is it?"

"It is, sure," he said, calm as can be. "That little gobshite was blackmailing me."

"How so?"

"You recall that day we met on the courtroom steps? You were just after testifying, and I was on my way to do the same."

"You said it was something about a lawsuit."

"Ah, now. That was a fib. I was going to testify in the same case as you had done, the people of San Francisco versus Sam Urias. But, you see, I fibbed there, too, on the stand. Had to, I'm afraid, nothing to do about it. But *that* weasel bastard—" and he pointed the flashlight into Javier's dead eyes "—tracked me down after, and called me out. He said he was going to expose me as a liar and a perjurer, young Javier was."

He kept the light on the dead man's face and contemplated it for a minute. "I don't even know his last name. He works the roach coach up top. Good enough food, though it's dearer than it should be."

"He knew you framed Urias?"

Denis said nothing—though his hard-man act fell off for just a startled second before he could pull it back on.

"Denis, I know what you did with the screwdriver. I still don't understand what it has to do with this man."

"Not a thing. He'd watched me, on the stand, you see. I testified that Sam Urias had said to me that somebody ought to get Haring out of our hair—for good. That made an impression on the court. But the truth is, Jessie, I've never had more than ten words with that dose Urias on any day we crossed paths, not if I could help it. Javier knew that. He came to me, here, while I was trying to work, and said that if I didn't go up and tell the judge the truth—that I'd been perjuring, that Urias never said any such thing to me—well, if I didn't do that, then he'd expose me, would young Javier. So I had to shut him up. Come this time tomorrow, no one will ever lay eyes on him again. Nor the gun, neither."

What did he mean by that, I wondered. Wondered, and worried. It was time to try the sweet talk.

"Denis," I said, and shook my head gently, "you're only telling me all this to stall."

"Am I, now?"

"You can't shoot me."

"Can't I, now?"

"You're cute. No, you can't. Not now and not later. You keep talking, trying to convince yourself that you'll work up the nerve to do it, but you can't shoot me. Haring was an accident. Javier was…well, okay, he was threatening you, I can see that. But me…? We had fun together, remember? You asked me if we did, and we did, Denis. You can't shoot me."

Monaghan smiled and said nothing.

I took a step toward him. He didn't order me back. I kept my voice soft. "I can help you. Let me help you out of this mess, before it gets worse."

"Oh, darling. You are so right, and so wrong. You're right that I'm stalling. But you're wrong that I won't shoot you. I will. I have to do. I'm just marking time until the masonry crew's shift change. That's when the cement mixer is due to arrive, to prep for the first slab pour, you see." He gestured toward the trenches on either side of us. "The vault's floor. Eventually all of this will be under a full meter and a half of concrete, right up flush to that top step. That's what the specs call for."

My heart was pounding. I struggled to stay still, not let him see me tremble. "You can't shoot me, Denis."

"I will, Jessie. When that cement truck pulls up—? It makes one hell of a racket. No one will hear the gunshot. Or shots, if my aim is poor."

I abandoned the cool facade—or, truth be told, I lost it. "Are you *crazy*? The supervisor escorted me onto the site! I'm carrying a DBI day pass. I signed into the clipboard in front, for Christ's sake!"

He nodded along in a patronizing way. "Finished?"

"People know I'm here, Denis!"

"Doctor, do you remember that night after the earthquake, when I drove you from the morgue to your car, where you'd left it parked? That's a lovely car you have, that BMW 235. You've the key fob in your pocket right now, haven't you. I'll find the car easy enough, drive it off to an airport lot, one of the cheap ones, short on cameras, and leave it. Or, hell, I'll just park it in front of your house. I don't know where that is, but the address will be on your license. Something. I'll come up with something. I mean, who's going to connect us? The bartender at Trad'r Sam?"

I said nothing. I tried to calm my breathing, slow my racing pulse. As I did, I noticed that outside, beyond the stepladder, the light had changed. It had gone flat and white—the night shift's work lights. I noticed something else, too. The quiet. The diesel engines seemed to have ceased, and the only voices I heard were far away, and talking, not shouting and barking orders anymore. I thought I could hear the soft tramp of work boots on dirt.

Monaghan wasn't bluffing. He had no reason to. He really was going to shoot me and lay me out with Javier in that trench, or maybe bury me in the other one, and then wrap the gun back up in the rag and ditch it again. If he was the man in charge of the cement pour, he was the man who made sure only authorized personnel came down here. He was the man who would make sure we were buried, turned into permanent structural elements in the SoMa Centre's cellar. He was going to wait for the cement mixer to arrive and cover the noise, and then I was dead meat.

He wasn't bluffing. He was waiting out the shift change—which was happening at that moment. It was so quiet. As quiet as it was ever going to be.

What happens if I make a run at you right now, Denis?

Could be he read my mind, because in the reflected glow of

his flashlight, I saw him draw up a smile that said, *I'll take my chances, darling.*

What the hell.

I threw my hard hat at Denis and sprang, nails out, screaming for help at the top of my lungs.

It almost worked. The hard hat put him off balance and I got so close, so fast, that he had to yank the unwieldy old revolver up before I could grab it. I slashed a hand sideways across his face, caught him good on the cheek, and didn't break my stride. I was still screaming. I reached the ladder and got a foot on the bottom step.

But out of the corner of my eye I saw Monaghan's bent arm, and the revolver's butt whipping down, and, once again, for the second time in under a month, I saw shooting stars and my skull exploded in pain and…

CHAPTER 16

I woke to the alarm clock beeping. It was wicked irritating. I didn't dwell on it, though—because as soon as I was conscious, I was conscious once again of a jolt of pain across the inside of my skull. I wanted to go back to sleep. I tried to.

Wait. The beeping wasn't an alarm clock. I knew what it was—I'd heard it before, I was sure—but I couldn't remember exactly. It hurt to think, but I kept at it until I could place the sound: the warning signal of a reversing vehicle. And under the beeping was a mechanical roar. That sound belonged to an engine, a big one, and close. I opened my eyes and caught my breath. Everything was a smothering gray blur.

My mouth was stuck closed. I tried to move, but my arms and legs wouldn't budge. I shook my head, rattling pebbles and a cascade of dust. Gravel—the gray blur was gravel. Monaghan must have bound me up, gagged me, and buried me in the trench opposite Redbeard. Javier, so he called him.

I swiveled my head as much as I could, trying not to choke.

My right eye didn't want to open all the way. I blinked out the crusted blood and peered through the rubble. A white lamp was shining into the utility vault. It seemed to be mounted on something. I gave my eyes time to focus.

It was a truck's rear bumper, flanked by tires and mud flaps, just beyond the vault's doorway. The cement mixer had arrived.

I started to wiggle into a position to sit up—but then froze. The engine still roared but the reverse warning had stopped. A shadow fell across the vault. A man in a hard hat was standing in the doorway, peering in.

"That's grand just there, amigo. Not a budge more."

I played possum. Denis Monaghan looked back over his shoulder, then pulled the flashlight off his belt and aimed its beam right at me—or right at my pile of rubble. He only needed a glance to assure himself, then he turned back toward the truck and started hauling at something.

I heard the truck's cab door slam. A different man shouted over the mixer's noise, "You want a hand?"

"No, thanks, amigo, tight space here, two's a crowd. Just be ready to pour, right?"

"Okay."

Denis wrestled something through the vault's doorway and it hung there in midair, pointed at the gravel floor: a bowed metal chute, caked in old cement. He tugged at a handle to adjust its angle, and then bent down with a grunt and hauled the wooden stepladder out of the vault.

As soon as he was out of sight, I shifted my shoulders in the rubble until I was able to sit up. He'd bound me with plastic zip ties at the wrists and ankles and duct tape over my mouth. It wrapped all the way around, and I couldn't pull it off. I tried raking my feet across the sharper pieces of rubble, but quickly figured that was no use either—the zip ties were heavy gauge. Same type that Yarina uses in the autopsy suite to close up the biohazard bag full of cut organs before it's sewn back into the eviscerated body. It occurred to me that my death would be a medical examiner case, a homicide by asphyxiation; specifically, suffocation in semiliquid concrete—possibly with blunt force injury to the head as a contributing factor, depending on how bad my brain looked once it was out of my skull. My own organ bag would get the same treatment.

Except, it further occurred to me, you can't do an autopsy if you don't have a corpse, and a corpse buried in concrete stays buried for good.

I twisted over, planted an elbow for leverage, and started to lift my body out of the makeshift grave. I got the hip and knee on that side working into the gravel, too, and had nearly made it onto the floor of the vault when the roar from the cement truck got louder. The metal chute rattled, and a stream of gray slurry poured out and splashed down. It flowed into the side trenches first, moving fast, seeping into the gaps in the rubble where I'd just lain and where Javier lay still.

I couldn't yell for help and I couldn't run. So I flipped sideways and rolled until I reached the rear of the vault, the spot where Leopold Haring had bled out his last. And there, at the head of the trench, I spotted the rag bundle. I scooted till I could stretch to get it into my bound hands, and worked my fingers in. I could feel the gun barrel. I tried to rotate it, find the grip, find the trigger—

And the bundle unraveled, tumbling away from me. I lurched after it, into the concrete slurry, and got my hands on the rags again. The cold, thick gobs spread and rose where I sat, seeping into my clothes, and I fumbled to unwrap Grandpa Haring's revolver.

How many rounds did the antique hold? Five, I guessed. How many had Monaghan discharged? One, at least, into the back of poor Javier's head. Four cartridges left, if Oskar kept all the cylinders loaded, and if Leopold hadn't unloaded any, or shot the gun off himself for some reason…

What does it matter, Jessie? You only need one shot, if you're lucky.
You only have one way out.

I could get a decent enough grip to steady the butt and lay my finger alongside the trigger guard, but the sludge had covered my waist and was creeping higher. I sloshed backward to try to push myself upright against the wall, and bumped up against something chunky and hard. It was Denis Monaghan's lump of HAC concrete. I got an elbow down and hoisted myself onto it, as high as I could.

I raised the gun. I didn't know if the antique revolver was single or double action, so I cocked the hammer just in case.

My head was pounding. I fought to calm my breathing, and scanned back and forth from the gun muzzle to the vault's entrance. The cement truck filled the doorway. The chute was directly in my line of fire, but I could still draw a bead on the mud flap behind it. The mud flap, and the truck's right rear tire.

I held my breath and pulled the trigger.

Sparks flashed off the bumper. No one came running. The sound of the gun's report was not nearly as loud as I had been hoping it would be—the concrete sludge must've muffled it, and the noise of the mixer itself was deafening.

I cocked the hammer again. The slurry was bubbling up, swamping everything, rising on me.

I locked my arms, aimed, and fired.

Nothing. No sparks, no bullet impact that I could see or hear. The concrete pushed against my belly with each breath.

I didn't cock the hammer. I didn't squint to aim. I bent my elbows up one time, lowered the gun back down, let it come to rest on its target, and squeezed the trigger.

The hammer pulled and snapped, and the gun went off.

The cement truck's tire burst with a huge hiss, and the whole rig groaned—then listed sideways.

The engine noise dropped from roar to idle, and its giant rotating drum stopped moving. So did the flow of slurry in the chute. I braced my legs against the HAC concrete under me, and wedged myself a little higher out of the muck. I heard the cab door again, and the engine shut down altogether. The bumper's work light went out with it. I was in the dark.

I tried to shout, but the duct tape held fast. No one heard me—but I could hear them. The mixer operator was saying they would have to stop work.

"No, it's fine, amigo, it's fine, keep it coming," Denis replied.

The man moved over to the tire. I could only see him from the knees up. I turned my head to the clods of yellow cement that had been the cause of Leopold Haring's murder and rubbed my cheek on them, trying to wear through the duct tape. But Monaghan had wrapped it tight, and all I was doing was tearing up my skin.

"I can't work the mixer if it's not level."

"Sure you can! Fire it up and carry on, will you. We've got to get it in there all at once, you know that."

"I can't keep on this pour."

"It's just a flat tire."

"Yeah, but now the mixer's not level. We'll fuck up the equipment if we—"

"What are you so worried about?" Monaghan was still relying on charm, not turning to threats just yet. "You got someplace else you need to be? Let's finish up, amigo!"

"I'm telling you…"

"Look, if we don't get all of it in there right now, the whole utility vault will be ruined. You want to explain that to the people at Pacific Gas and Electric? I do not."

"Denis, the mixer is leaning! It's a hazard as it is, sitting here. Who knows what happens if I turn the agitator back on."

"You saw the specs and you know the sequence. We can't leave this pour halfway done—and if we stop now, we'll have to shovel all that shite out. We'll have to jackhammer it out, if it sets! How long is that going to put us back?" Monaghan's tone hardened. "Turn it back on."

"I'm gonna go find the superintendent."

"Turn it back on, I said," growled Monaghan.

It was a bad approach.

"I got ninety minutes before it sticks to my drum," the mixer operator said with a cold finality. "I'll ask the super what to do." I heard his footsteps crunch away.

Denis cursed. His boots stayed still, their heels toward me. Then they ground around in the dirt, and I saw the toes stepping nearer. The boots reached the threshold, and Denis Monaghan came over it. He lowered himself down, backward, and splashed into the heavy concrete slurry. He grabbed something behind him, and turned. He had a shovel.

But I had a gun.

Monaghan flicked on his flashlight. He pointed it first to the trench where I was supposed to be buried, but soon enough found me, wedged in the back of the vault where Leopold Haring had bled to death, pointing that fat-caliber revolver's muzzle right at him.

Denis faltered. If he tried to wade through the slurry to brain me with that shovel, I would shoot him. If he tried to leave, I still might shoot him. If he stayed where he was till the cement mixer man came back with the superintendent in tow, he was screwed.

We both heard their voices at the same time. That site superintendent, God bless him, was one loudmouthed man.

Monaghan looked over his shoulder toward the truck, then back at me. He made his decision. He pushed a foot through the slurry, and lifted the shovel.

I cocked the hammer on Grandpa Haring's revolver.

Monaghan stopped. He didn't move. How could he?

"You wouldn't shoot me, love," he whispered.

I didn't respond. I mean, I wanted to, sure—but, duct tape.

I think—no, in retrospect, I know—that Denis understood my intentions just fine, because he didn't budge, and the fear in his eyes spread to take over his whole face, then his whole form. I could feel it radiate across the vault.

The superintendent and the mixer operator took their sweet time crossing the distance between my living and dying, but they made it eventually. Denis, rooted by fear, couldn't do a damn thing to stop them making that journey. They came up behind him in the vault entrance.

"You gonna dig it out on your own?" the superintendent joked, of the shovel. Denis remembered, too late, that in his other hand was a flashlight. It was illuminating a woman half-submerged in viscous concrete, duct tape across her mouth—a bloody clot in her hair, probably—and, in her zip-tied hands, pointed awkwardly right at the three of them, a great big gun.

"Oh, shit!" yelped the mixer operator.

I turned the revolver sideways, away from them, and thumbed the hammer back down. I started my muffled yelling again.

Denis Monaghan dropped the shovel and flashlight and spun around. He put his hands on the threshold of the utility vault above him, gave himself a mighty push of a lift out of the sludge, shouldered past the mixer operator and the site superintendent, and ran away.

The other two men stood staring at me, stunned.

I dropped the gun into the slurry.

The mixer operator finally snapped out of it, jumped into the vault, and waded over in a hurry. The superintendent glanced back, confused, in the direction Denis had disappeared, and then joined the other man in helping to free me. When he got close enough, he recognized me and said my name. I nodded furiously.

The mixer operator found the end of the duct tape gag and started to unwind the thing, but he was being delicate about it. Duct tape hurts when you peel it off skin, and the mixer operator was a decent man who didn't want to hurt me. I gibbered at him as best I could to hurry up.

Yeah, it hurt—but that was the least of my worries.

"Call the police!" I screamed, the second my lips were free. "Denis Monaghan murdered the architect Leopold Haring and a food services guy named Javier! Call the police!" I waved my chin to my right, where the body was submerged in the slurry. "Then shovel Javier out of there before he's gone for good. But first the cops! First cops, then shovel. Cops, shovel, in that order! *Now!*"

The superintendent fumbled with his phone. The kindhearted mixer operator worried over my bleeding head. He had his utility knife in hand and was just about to cut the zip tie off my wrists when I barked, "And the gun! Jesus, fish around and find that thing before it sinks any more. I'm going to need it for ballistics…"

The superintendent got through to 911 dispatch, and started babbling out the whole story. The mixer operator cut my arms loose. I locked them around his neck, and I let him drag me out of the mire.

CHAPTER 17

They put me in the same damn bed in the General's emergency room where they'd put me after the quake. This time the walls were festooned with cornucopias and fake foliage sprays and goofball turkeys in buckle hats. A string of letters across the top of a window commanded BE THANKFUL!

I was thankful there was no mass-casualty event out there waiting for me this time. I was also thankful that the nurse—Nurse Elissa, the same as last time—wasn't wearing her vampire costume anymore.

"Are we going to be seeing you for monthly head injuries, *Doctor*?" she'd asked, after I'd had my CT and the results were in, and she'd decided I was stable enough for taunting. The test results were mixed. I had a nondisplaced right posterior parietal fracture, a hairline break in my skull where Denis Monaghan had pistol-whipped me. Under it was a thin subdural bleed. I wouldn't need surgery, but I would need an inpatient stay for a couple of days of observation and neuro checks. This time, I had absolutely no intention of leaving before they told me to.

Inspectors Jones and Ramirez came to interview me before my transfer out of the ER and up to the neurology ward. Monaghan was in custody, they assured me right off the bat. He'd been arrested without incident, and was denied bail as a flight risk, but they didn't want to give me any more detail than that.

I told them the whole story about the utility-vault crime scene, and we worked out a chain-of-custody transfer for the plastic bags with the samples I'd gathered and stuck in my pockets—the blood from the framework pin and from the stain on the vault's floor. The latter was especially important, since that floor was now covered in half a pour of solid concrete. They assured me that the construction crew had, with the help of the responding officers from Southern Station, found Javier Aguinaldo's body and dredged it out of the wet cement before it set. They recovered the gun, too.

"Why did he truss her up and leave her there, do you figure?" Jones mused to his partner. "He coulda just shot her."

I gave him the stink eye. "You say the sweetest things, Keith."

"Well…?"

"He was worried about someone hearing the gunshot, remember," Ramirez said. "He was waiting for the cement truck before he could get rid of her. But when she made a break for it and he knocked her out, I guess he figured it was safer to tie and gag her, and stash her under the rocks down there. Let the cement do the work."

Jones grunted. "Okay, then why didn't he strangle her once she was out? That's nice and quiet."

"Usually."

"Boys," I said. "I'm moved by your concern. Maybe Monaghan didn't want to take a chance with the gunshot while people were just outside, and maybe he wasn't quite cold-blooded enough to put his hands around my neck and squeeze, but he didn't really mind leaving me to drown in sludge. How do I know? In my experience, people who resort to murder as a problem-solving technique aren't planning three moves ahead."

The detectives agreed with that opinion. As a general principle, anyway.

———

I spent all day Friday lolling on an inpatient bed, watching TV and nursing my wicked headache. Some of the people from the office came by and others sent flowers. My brother Tommy snuck me a burger and fries, and a big malted chocolate frappe that did more to improve my condition than anything else.

Anup Banerjee sent a small bouquet of carnations and daisies through an 800-number florist. It bore a printed card expressing his cordial get-well wishes.

On Saturday I had a surprise visitor. It was the public defender Eva Yung, Samuel Urias's lawyer. I was thrilled to see her, and eager to hear what was going on with her client, now that I had pieced together the case that would exonerate him.

"He's gone," she said. "I don't know where."

Jason Bevner had called Eva on Friday morning to tell her about the charges against Monaghan for the same crime her client was charged with. She immediately demanded they release Urias. Bevner agreed. It took the rest of the day to get the paperwork done, and to process Samuel Urias out of the jail. He stepped through the San Francisco County Hall of Justice door at Bryant and Seventh a free man, just before the end of business that day.

United States Immigration and Customs Enforcement officers were waiting for him there.

"Wait...what?" I said. "Why ICE? What'd he do?"

"Nothing," said Eva Yung.

"He has a green card, right?"

"Yes. Sam has a green card. And he'd been arrested on a felony. So ICE can detain him, and they can deport him."

"What—?"

The lawyer looked out the window and watched the traffic on the 101 freeway.

"That's the way it is."

"He didn't do anything! He was set up—by the guy who did the murder!"

"Jessie, don't excite yourself, all right? You have a head injury."

The only reason I didn't tell Eva Yung to stick her concern where the sun don't shine was because Eva was, herself, so very subdued. I recognized the look on her face as she studied the passing cars. It was the look I've seen in a hundred grieving mothers, the ones who have had a couple of weeks to come to terms with the loss of a child, and who were, by then, in the throes of a deep, lasting depression.

We sat in silence until she went on. She explained, or tried to, that, as far as she could tell, several disparate agencies saw Sam Urias's deportation as a win-win. For ICE, they get to connect crime and immigration. Never mind that the immigrant in question hadn't been convicted of any crime—he'd been arrested and charged in one, a serious one, and under the federal rules in place for their agency, that was enough for them to take action. As a bonus, grabbing Urias off the street the second he left jail provided the ICE guys with an opportunity to poke a sanctuary city in the eye. As for the San Francisco district attorney, they could denounce ICE and claim they'd had nothing to do with them, then proceed with a clean slate against Denis Monaghan for the murder of Leopold Haring. This time they were sure to get a conviction.

"Or, more likely, a plea. I don't see Mr. Monaghan going to trial," Eva concluded.

"But…he framed Urias. He set him up to take the blame for

the crime the DA is trying him for! Shouldn't they want to… I don't know, *explore* that aspect of the crime?"

"No. It's a distraction. You gave them the murder weapon—the real one—and the scene of the crime. Then you gave them another body, Javier Aguinaldo's, to pin on Mr. Monaghan. They don't even want to talk about that whole messy thing with the screwdriver and the two old corpses."

"Monaghan's defense attorney can raise it, then! Shit, the DA would open the door to an insurmountable pile of reasonable doubt that way… Wouldn't they?"

Eva Yung smiled—again, in the mirthless way I've seen on the faces of people who have lost loved ones—and said, "I'll bet they get the screwdriver evidence excluded. With Samuel Urias out of the picture, they can ignore him. They can pretend they never charged him. And, like I said, this isn't going to trial. No way. Did you know that Denis Monaghan is undocumented?"

I nodded. "So what?"

"So he doesn't want to be sitting in a courtroom listening to the prosecutor tell the jury he's an illegal alien murderer for days and days, that's what. They will do that. *His* immigration status won't get excluded, believe me. If Mr. Monaghan goes to trial, he'll lose, and he'll go down for life. With a plea deal instead, he might get a twenty-year term, out in fifteen, and then shipped straight back to Ireland. The DA will be eager to offer a deal like that, and his attorneys would urge him to take it."

"Fifteen years for two murders, and an attempt to kill me, too?"

"Haring's death isn't a murder, remember. It was self-defense, manslaughter, tops—and desecration of a corpse, I guess. As for you? Well, if I were the DA, I'd look to add some assault and battery and unlawful detention, but I couldn't be certain I'd make attempted murder stick, so I probably wouldn't try too hard with that. Use it to persuade the other side they don't want to even go to trial. And they wouldn't want to."

"Monaghan's immigration status is his motive for killing Javier! He was afraid of getting deported—"

"Yeah, well, the DA doesn't care much about motive if they've got all this other evidence against him. Besides, they know Mr. Monaghan is going to get deported after his stint, for sure and for good."

No death in Ireland, Denis Monaghan had said—because, without papers, he couldn't travel back there and then return to the life he'd built in San Francisco. But now he was going to get it, if he survived his last years in America, in prison.

Eva stood. "I've got to get going. Busy weekend. Get better, okay?"

"Wait,—" I said, "what about Samuel?"

"What do you mean?"

"You said you don't know where he is."

"I don't. And ICE doesn't have to tell me. They don't have to tell anybody. As far as the Feds are concerned, Samuel Urias is a guest in this country. Or was."

"But he's…not illegal. Which means he's *legal*…"

"He's not a US citizen. ICE might be holding him in detention, or they might already have sent him back to Mexico. I don't know. I won't know, not until he's free to call me, if he chooses to. If he does, I'll try to advise him about his options for gaining reentry—but I'm not an immigration attorney."

She turned her back and went to the door.

"Eva," I said, "he has a family here."

Eva Yung looked over her shoulder. She was trying to hide her pain and rage. She was doing a pretty decent job of it.

"Tomorrow is another day, Jessie. Heal up, okay?"

Heal up. I'll try, Eva.

I pulled out my cell. I wanted to call Anup, ask him what

Eva could do about Samuel Urias, ask him who he knew that worked in immigration law, who he knew that could strategize a demand for ICE to produce Urias. Demand the rule of law.

I didn't dial. I put the phone away, and laid my head back on the papery hospital pillow.

I fell asleep until a ward nurse woke me for another neuro check. He shined the penlight on my pupils and asked me how I was doing, made me stick out my tongue, squeeze his hands, raise each arm, wiggle my fingers. I passed, apparently. My headache was almost gone and I was hitting all my marks. They were going to release me in the morning. That would be Sunday morning.

"Can I go back to work on Monday?"

The nurse was a tall, slender man. He looked down at me dubiously. "You're that eager?"

"We're short-staffed."

The nurse just handed me a sheet of instructions and precautions in the care of head injury, and left.

The neurology department left me alone with my injured head for a while, until a doctor in a white coat came to bother it. I was getting a little tired of their routine.

"Hello," she said brightly.

"Hey, Doctor, I don't mean to be rude, but I just did the tests. Maybe you mixed up rooms?"

"No, no. I'm here to see you. Teska, correct? Czesława?"

She pronounced my given name perfectly. That's what made me sit up and take notice. No one ever gets Czesława right. No one who isn't Polish, anyhow—and this doctor didn't look Polish. She was an older woman, with skin the color of scorched driftwood and shining, silver-threaded black hair. She had enormous brown eyes and enviable lashes that I could tell were the real deal, no mascara. Something about those eyes was familiar to me.

"I hope you're feeling well," she said, and smiled a little nervously. She had a faint, lilting accent.

Shit, that smile. I definitely knew that smile. My eyes went automatically to the blue embroidery on the lapel of her white coat.

D. Banerjee, MD.

"Dr. Banerjee?" I said.

"Yes. Denise Banerjee, here at the hospital. Though at home I am Dakshina."

Dakshina was Anup's mother's name.

"I...can sympathize, Dr. Banerjee," I said.

"Yes, Jessie. I know you can."

I held out my hand. She took it gingerly.

"It's a real pleasure to meet you Dr. Banerjee," I said, and offered her a smile.

The nervousness evaporated from her own. "Likewise. It is."

"You aren't here on a consult."

"Well. In a sense, I am. How is your head?" she asked.

"Mending."

"That's good."

We just contemplated each other for a bit. Then I said, "How is your son?"

"Oh, you know. He pretends nothing's wrong."

"Yes. He would. Does he know you're here?"

"No...! I do rounds at the General once a week, and had a patient on this floor. I happened to spot your name on the board. It's an unusual name."

I couldn't help laugh at that. Anup's mom went on. "I asked around the nursing station. They had quite a story for me."

"It's all true, I'm afraid."

"I..."

Whatever thought she'd had, she couldn't finish it. She started giggling and didn't stop.

"What is it?"

"I just hope Anup isn't right about you. How could I face him?"

That took me off balance. "What do you mean?"

"He…oh, that boy. He's not a boy, of course, but he is, always, to me. I know when he's lying, even when he's lying to himself. He told us, me and his father, that it's over between you."

I didn't see how that was funny. It wasn't funny to me. What was wrong with this woman?

"But the lie he told," Anup's mother went on, "was in answer to my immediate next question, which was, of course, *why*? We'd been waiting so long to meet you, yet he kept putting it off. Then, out of the blue, he announces that you were gone from his life, and when I asked him why, he said he had broken it off because you worked too hard, and he didn't like that."

A flame came to Dr. Dakshina Banerjee's eyes, a flame I recognized along with her eyelashes and her smile. "Well! I let him have it, as they say. I was shocked by that, truly! We didn't raise Anup that way, to expect that a woman should wrap herself around his life, beholden to him, and I told him so. Quite sharply, I'm afraid."

I realized why she'd suffered that case of the giggles. "And then I go out and get myself nearly killed on the job, just to prove his point. That's what you mean?"

She nodded. "It struck me as hilarious, in an absurd way, and I apologize. I realize that's not the reason my son broke off his relationship with you. As I said, I know when Anup is lying to me."

Again we watched each other. I fought to maintain a poker face. She had ambushed me, after all. She seemed genuinely caring and concerned—but, still, I didn't want to let my guard down. She wanted me to tell her the real reason for the breakup. I didn't feel comfortable doing that. She didn't press me. Finally I felt obliged to correct one thing she'd said.

"He didn't break it off. It was mutual."

"I see. I…hope you will reconsider that decision. You see, I fear that Anup is…ill-equipped, sometimes, to make the right choices when it comes to…romance and such. It is our fault, really—mine and his father's. We simply don't talk about romances, about…love relationships, at home. We never have done. Now, I fear, that flaw in our parenting has led our son to make a terrible mistake."

The poor woman. She was so wrong. I didn't feel it was my place to tell her so, but Anup is a grown man, and is entitled to own his mistakes. She went on:

"I fear, you see, that Anup has manufactured in his own mind a terrible misapprehension of the duties he owes us as our son. I fear he thinks we would disapprove of his relationship with you, because you aren't…because you haven't been raised in our community. That is a nonsensical assumption. We have, I hope, never given him such an impression."

Well, lady, it's too late now, I wanted to say. Maybe Anup had invented his fear of his parents' disapproval, or maybe they had seeded it and were blind to that—or in denial of it. Not my circus. Not anymore.

I shifted in the bed to signal that this particular family therapy session was drawing to a close. Dr. Banerjee leaned away from me a small distance. Message received.

"Thank you for coming to see me, Dr. Banerjee," I said.

"Please call me Denise, won't you, dear?" She loosed another of her nervous giggles. "Or Dakshina, of course."

God, this woman was making it hard for me to dislike her. I had worked it out in my own head that she was the villain here, that she and her husband had harried Anup into the old "we know what's best for you" mindset, and that he was too weak to break free of it. Speaking to her in the flesh made me suspect that I was wrong. Anup had made the choice to exclude me from his family life quite on his own. It was a shame. It was a tragedy.

"It was kind of you to visit, and it really was a pleasure to meet you," I said.

And that was that. Dakshina nodded sadly and held out her hand to shake goodbye. I took it, and she asked if she might kiss me. I said yes, and she leaned in and planted warm lips on the edge of my chin, avoiding the cheek that was still raw from the duct tape. She held her grip on my hand for too long. I was the one who finally had to loosen it, and even then she didn't want to release me.

But she did. And then she left without another word.

CHAPTER 18

Thanksgiving was mostly a family affair, and I was grateful to be included in it. My dried-fruit stuffing was a huge hit, as was the corn pudding with sauerkraut—my mother's decades-old invention for the holiday, one of those family recipes that sounds impossibly weird to outsiders but which, as with many nontraditional side dishes, goes great with turkey. And that's all that matters, on Thanksgiving, around the family table.

Candied yams, collard greens, scalloped potatoes. And, of course, it wouldn't be a San Francisco Thanksgiving without garlic Dungeness crab.

"Pass another of them crabs over here, will you, Jessie?" said Baby Mike. I swear he had eaten three of the monster things already.

"Ooh, I'll take one too," said my brother Tomasz. I swear he saw Baby Mike's capacity for massive ingestion as a personal challenge.

I had asked Sparkle to pick me up from the General when I

was discharged on Sunday. She stayed for a cup of tea at Ma-honey Brothers #45, and I was finally able to tell her about Anup and me.

Sparkle didn't have much to say about it, and didn't really offer an opinion on the big questions, the ones that had been plaguing me: Had we been wrong for each other all along? Or had it been a mistake to give up? Maybe Sparkle had seen the breakup coming before I had, and didn't want to say so if there was no point in it. After all, Anup hadn't reached out to me except with that anodyne get-well bouquet, and I wasn't cry-ing on Sparkle's shoulder about the terrible mistake I'd made in letting it all fall apart. It hadn't been a mistake. It was over between Anup and me.

Sparkle did offer me an unexpected and generous condolence, though, after she asked what I was going to do for Thanksgiv-ing dinner, now that the plans with Anup had vanished.

"Tommy doesn't have time to cook and I don't have the en-ergy, so we'll just go out. He knows of some fancy restaurant down in Mountain View that—"

Sparkle's eyes shot wide open in horror. *"You will not,"* she snapped. "Not on Thanksgiving you will not! You are coming to my mom's."

"Sparkle! You can't—"

"Yes I can and I will and I am. You are coming to my mom's and joining the rest of my family. There's already seventeen or eighteen of us. We'll make room for one more."

"But then Tommy—"

"Two more."

So there we sat, Tommy and I, thankful and drowsy.

"Michael! Do *not* feed that dog pie from the table!" Gayle, Sparkle's mother, had insisted I bring Bea along. Gayle was an animal lover, she said, and there were two other dogs in the house already. Bea couldn't have been happier about the invitation. Gayle made sure to pull me aside, too, and thank me for coming.

"I know this sounds strange, but I miss my brother—and having you here...makes me feel better. Because you took care of Curtis. That *is* strange, isn't it?"

It wasn't, at all, and I told Gayle as much. Nothing is strange when you're mourning.

"Every year, we all hoped Curtis might show up for Thanksgiving, you know. Sometimes we knew where he was at, and sometimes he didn't want to tell us, but we always set a place for him." She smiled sadly. "I miss my baby brother. I'm glad Sparkle invited you—and yours."

When the pies went around, I squeezed in next to Tommy, who had finagled his way to the kids' end of the table. He finds ordinary adult conversation burdensome; and, besides, he has an anarchical streak that resonates with children.

I'd had some wine, not a lot, but enough that I lowered my guard to ask my brother a question that had been nagging at me ever since I got out of the hospital.

"Was *Mamusia* legal when she came here?"

He looked at me in confusion. "What do you mean?"

"Did she have the right papers. Is our mother a legal immigrant, or an illegal immigrant?"

"She married Dad, remember?"

"And he's native-born, yes, fine. So she's a citizen free and clear—now. But how did she get in? Did she have a sponsor and all that, or did she come on a visa and overstay it? It couldn't have been a student visa. Was she a tourist? Were they even giving out tourist visas to the United States from Warsaw in...what, 1982?"

The questions troubled Tomasz, though he tried not to show it. He shrugged. "You'd have to ask *Mamusia*, I suppose. Good luck with that."

"She's never mentioned anybody else from the family who

was here first. It's not like they had come here and set up, and she was just the latest link in the chain..."

"Not as far as you know, maybe. Ask her. And, like I said, *powodzenia* to you."

I had indeed gone right back to work on Monday after my discharge, though the neurology attending thought that was a terrible idea. All three days up until Thanksgiving were busy ones, too; I did two suicides (one by hanging and one by handgun), three overdoses, and a motorcycle accident. Sunshine Ted groused about Dr. Howe taking me off the homicide call rotation, but then he got lucky and only caught one over the course of three days anyway. I managed to convince Howe to return me to the rotation over the holiday long weekend. He agreed, probably figuring it would be quiet.

As soon as I got out of the autopsy suite and behind my desk each of those three days, the very first thing I did was to place a call to Eva Yung. I never got through to her, but each time I left a message asking for updates on the situation with Samuel Urias.

On Wednesday, she sent me an email in reply. It read, in its entirety, Still no word from Sam.

"Hey kids," said Tommy, "want to learn the shoelace trick for hacking bar code scanners?"

I got an email from Inspector Ramirez on Wednesday, too. He wanted to let me know that Denis Monaghan had, as Eva Yung predicted he would, taken a deal with ADA Jason Bevner. Monaghan was going to prison for twenty-two years—parole-eligible, which in his case meant deportable, after thirteen. The ADA would not need to interview or depose me, unless I insisted on pressing separate charges in the assault and battery on my person. If I did so insist, then the DA would consider a new charge. So said Ramirez, anyhow.

No, they wouldn't consider any such thing, and I knew it. They got their guy, and had avoided trial doing it. They would move on.

Natalie Haring would get her double-indemnity insurance payout. Jeffrey Symond would get the money to keep the business thriving until he could hire a new creative genius. Oskar Haring might even get Grandpa's gun back, cleaned of cement—and my blood—but no worse for wear. He could still take it out target shooting.

SoMa Centre would rise above the corner of Sixth and Folsom.

"Hey," I said to Tommy, "my head's starting to hurt again. You should stay, but I'm going home."

A steel band cover of "Don't Fear the Reaper" woke me. I managed to grab my phone and whisper hello.

It was Cameron Blake. There had been a stabbing at a home on Euclid Avenue. "I'm betting it's gonna be the carving knife," he said.

"Let me get a pen," I whispered. I did, and he gave me the address. I peered at the bedside clock. It was 2:30 in the morning. Euclid is only ten or fifteen minutes away from my cable-car cottage, so I made sure to establish that the PD was on the scene, because I was sure to arrive before the morgue van. Cameron assured me that the cops were there, and that CSI was on their way, too.

"Okay," I said.

I realized I was still whispering. Why was I whispering? The dog was asleep on the floor. In the bed, I was alone.

ACKNOWLEDGMENTS

Our deepest gratitude goes to Tom Mitchell, Rita Mitchell, and Rutka Messinger; to our agent and fairy godmother, Jessica Papin of Dystel, Goderich & Bourret; and to John Glynn, Peter Joseph, Roxanne Jones, Cathy Joyce, Grace Towery, Eden Church, Sean Kapitain, Sandra Noakes, and the entire crew at Hanover Square Press and Harlequin Books, and aboard the mothership at HarperCollins. Without Catherine Ehr at the helm of PathologyExpert, none of our books would be written.

Many thanks to our invaluable early readers: Howard Baum, PhD, Mairead Devlin, Dr. Jonathan Finks, Susan Lindsay, Ewelina Mistek-Morabito, PhD, Asit Panwalla, George Reed, Sarah Lansdale Stevenson, Dr. Tom Tremoulet, and Judith Michelle Williams, PhD. The Beta Queen is Cristin Pescosolido, who answered more petty questions in the crafting of this work than anyone should ever have to, and who did so with intelligence, good cheer, and as much kindness as she could muster.

Additional thanks to Ron Santoro, CFX, Mary Lou McSolla,

Mary Roach, Karen Lynch, Sparkle Kelly, Sheila Averbuch, Ted Nguyen, Andrew Gould, Stephen Manton-Kelly, and José Quinteiro; Faith Salie and Strand Bookstore for the fabulous launch; Mary Jo Mitchell Angersbach and Stephani Finks for design advice; Paige Kaneb, Laurel Thompson, and Rebecca Young for legal lingo; Inspector Brian Delahunty and Officer Francisco Morrow for police procedure; Rhonda Roby, PhD, for DNA science; Kelly Gould for makeup and style advice; Liam Ford and Ann Weiler for parsing the stylebook; Green Apple Books and Book Passage Corte Madera for unflagging West Coast support; Liz Hopper Whitelam of Whitelam Books and the Nahant Public Library and Town Hall for heartwarming hometown support; and Amal Bisharat for our photos and also yoga.

Mary Jo, Kristen, and Michael have been patient with one of the authors for a great many years. Dina, Leah, Daniel, and Anna have put up with everything from both of them and have given in return their love and support. Without that, we couldn't do a single thing.

This book is offered in memory of T.J.'s mentor, John Richard Briley.